I0739058

APART

J. Lauryl Jennings

Copyright © 2017 by Jennifer Lauryl Jennings

All rights reserved. No part of this book may be reproduced or transmitted in any form or by any means, electronic or mechanical, including photocopying, recording, or by any information storage and retrieval system, without permission in writing from the author.

ISBN-10: 978-0-9991011-3-1
Printed in the United States of America

Dedication

No project is birthed in a vacuum. There is always a cast of supporting characters behind every project, and their contributions, large and small, made it possible for me to bring this idea into existence. I owe them a debt of gratitude, as this novel would never have happened without them.

To my family, who were my cheerleaders even when they had no idea what I was doing, and continued to even when they did.

To my early reviewers and opinion givers, whose feedback made me take my own project seriously, when it began as a lark.

To my long-suffering husband, Bobby, who endured me agonizing over fictional people and situations that didn't exist, all the while bringing me food, coffee, and rubbing my feet every night.

And finally, to Richard, whose decades long friendship and unflagging, blunt honesty pushed me to follow a dream.

Contents

Apathy 1
Surprise 5
Dissonance 14
Taste 18
Somewhere 24
Sound 25
When 31
Aware 36
Insight 40
Dreaming 48
Feel 53
Protection 61
Pledge 69
Cognition 73
Confirmation 81
Connection 88
Love 95
Refusal 103
Decision 116
Before 123
Damage 129
Reckoning 136
Mercy 148
William 154
Crucible 168
Failing 174
Remembering ... 183
Broken 190
Knowing 198
Limbo 202
Choice 215
Here 221

Part One

1
Apathy

The day was uneventful, and unremarkable. Another cycle of twenty-four hours that neither pleased nor displeased her, and left no impressions, no memories, or value. As Karyn turned the key in the lock, she laughed flatly to herself. If the calendar on her wall before her hadn't been there, she wouldn't even know what month it was, let alone what day. The passage of time escaped her notice, with all the days blending together in an endless loop of work, sleep, and apathy. Every day was the same. Every single day.

There was a moment, once, when she lived a different life. She knew enough to know that much, but couldn't remember at what point things changed.   There was a time when life felt like more, when she wasn't in this infinite loop of non-existence, but as to when or where she couldn't say. All around her, life seemed vibrant and colorful, but this grayness clung to her like a soap bubble on the side of a glass. It encompassed and tinted all she saw and felt, a diffuser lens that blurred the world outside from her view, and frosted her vision. Her apartment reflected her myopia; it was minimal, gray, and as barren as she felt.

That perception was hers alone, however. In the rest of the real world, spring had just passed into the edge of summer, and life was in full swing. Outside, the shops and cafes bustled with people, smells, and noise. The city was a hive of activity now that the weather had ceased to be chilly. The masses, entrapped by a season of snow and ice, now spilled out into the streets with a passion for the greenery of the parks and flowers that graced storefronts everywhere.

Karyn paused for a moment to imagine that life, then unceremoniously dropped her keys on the counter. Try as she might, no emotion presented itself to her. Not anger, love, or hatred moved within her; only the the trace feeling that she had forgotten something of importance, and that there was a part of her absent for so long that she no longer knew what it was that was missing. The thought that she had forgotten something was new; it came over her on the early evening walk home as she passed a tiny shop on one of the picturesque side streets she took home from work.

The shingle outside had read, "Hypnotist", in fancy gilt lettering on a background of glossy aubergine paint. The old wooden door to the shop had been painted to match, and the brass of the antique door handle exchanged glints of light with the sign's gilding as if they were having a private conversation. Something about the storefront caught her attention as she trudged the usual path home, something she saw from the corner of her eye when she passed the door, but couldn't define what had evaded her full sight. To be honest, she never noticed the shop before on any of her previous walks home. Even though she took the same route at least twice a week, Karyn had never once noticed that shop, with its royally colored eggplant door.

She wondered lightly over why she had opened the fridge, when nothing but more barrenness greeted her. Her complete lack of regard for her larder was painfully evident; there was no food to be had in there, other than the most basic of condiments, and a jar of old pickles. Perhaps the thing she had forgotten was to go food shopping, Karyn thought with a twinge of annoyance. Sustenance ranked equally with all other things in her life - she couldn't remember the last time she had a memorable meal, or when food tasted exceptional. Her palate had become as the rest of her; dull, flat, and unremarkable. Her stomach, however, objected to the neglect and growled with hunger, so Karyn shut the fridge door, picked up her keys, and walked back out into the city for something to eat.

Her feet knew the way to the closest restaurants with the cleanest kitchens. Fine food and fare in the city was abundant, and Karyn could have enjoyed her pick of Ethiopian, Egyptian, Lebanese, or Japanese food, to name but a few - if she still enjoyed eating. Her tastebuds, which had once been exceptionally refined, had lost their ability to distinguish the flavors and nuances of food; the process of dining, of savoring a meal, had faded around the same time as all her other senses. Her taste and smell had not abandoned her completely, but the limits on her palate mimicked the limits of her emotions.

Her stomach didn't care how anything tasted or smelled, and increased its complaining. Karyn tried to remember the last time she ate, or even what she had eaten, but recalled nothing. The wafting scent of some kind of incense drifted by her as she turned down Castor street, just grazing her nostrils delicately and catching her attention. It seemed unusually strong, or maybe it just seemed strong because her gut was empty, but as she rounded the corner she found herself looking again at the hypnotist's shop.

Had she come home on Castor instead of Briarly street? She double-checked her path home from work in her mind but found no evidence as to why this shop was in front of her now. What should be there also evaded her memory, but Karyn knew it wasn't **this** store. It was another shop, and certainly not one with such a distinctive door and fancy sign, of that much she was sure. There was no mistaking that this was the place she had passed only hours before, but on a different street. As she studied the store's facade more closely, little details began to emerge; the faint light from behind the large front window that wasn't quite enough to actually see within, but enough to hint at the contents, the heavy curtains draping the edge of the window frame, and a feeling of familiarity…although there was no reason for it.

Karyn shook her head and dismissed her confusion. This was obviously just another dysfunction to add to her ongoing list of dis-associative symptoms; she'd make an appointment with her doctor in the morning and have him run another batch of whatever tests he deemed necessary and her insurance would pay for. In all likelihood, he'd just look down his nose at her again and cluck lightly that "there's nothing wrong with you that a good anti-depressant wouldn't fix." He was the third physician, in fact, to chalk everything up to depression, mental illness, or hypochondria. Karyn almost agreed with them, save for the fact that a small voice in her head said there was another reason. That voice was becoming fainter over time, smaller, and harder to hear, but she could still hear it.

Her growling stomach interrupted the unease in her head. As she turned to continue down Castor, she caught a fleeting glimpse from the corner of her eye that made her stop short.

There was a man watching her from the window, and she **knew** him.

By the time she turned fully around, he was gone. There was nothing there but the streetlight's reflection against the glass and the silence around her. Silence that was out of place in a city awash with people in the early summer. It suddenly struck Karyn that she hadn't seen another person on her walk. Castor was normally a busy thruway for pedestrians moving around Restaurant Row, and the sounds of music and traffic from nearby streets was omnipresent; yet, not a single soul had passed her and Castor was deserted at this moment, except for her.

A chill moved over her skin and she pushed herself to turn and move on. With only a few steps taken towards her dinner, Karyn heard the tinkling sound of a door bell as the shop's door opened behind her, and footsteps on the concrete announced a presence.

2
Surprise

"Can I help you?" asked a low female voice.

Karyn stopped short in her steps, and turned slowly towards the voice. She was still mentally focused on the man she glimpsed in the window. His face was familiar to her. Something about it tugged at the back of her mind and she couldn't recall exactly what it was about it that bothered her. What little she did see triggered a reaction in her gut, and she was wrestling with her confusion when the voice spoke out again.

"Can I help you?" The woman's voice had a slight edge of concern now. "Are you lost, dear?" Karyn turned towards the voice and was greeted by the kindly face of an older woman holding a set of keys in her hand, presumably belonging to the aubergine door behind her. She was probably in her late sixties, although it was hard for Karyn to tell from where she was standing. The streetlight gave a golden glow to her skin that was unnatural; it almost seemed like she was glowing from within, not from without. When she took another step down towards her, Karyn snapped out of her trance state.

"I'm sorry," she stammered. "I was passing by when I saw your shop and…" she trailed off.

"What, dear?"

"And I thought I saw someone…in your window," she finished, feeling stupid the second she finished her sentence. *I must look like a lost mental patient to this woman*, she thought, but the woman didn't seem surprised by her statement.

"You saw someone?" she repeated, and began to finger the keys on her keyring without taking her eyes off Karyn.

There was a softness in them that Karyn hadn't noticed before, a kind of sympathetic concern that made her feel safe for no reason. "Perhaps you should come inside, dear. If you saw someone, then you're supposed to be here. That's the way it works," she stated in a matter-of-fact manner. She turned around to the purple door, grasped the large brass doorknob, and pushed the antique slab of wood inward. With a sideways look over her shoulder, she waved to Karyn to come inside after her.

Karyn found herself falling in line behind the woman, without hesitation or question, as she moved into the darkened shop. Pausing for a moment to turn on a small table lamp, she gestured to Karyn to have a seat at a bistro table in the corner next to the large glass window. "I'll put the kettle on, dear, and you can tell me all about it," she said, shuffling behind a heavy curtained doorway. The sound of a gas range catching fire and clinking china cups set Karyn more at ease with her unexpected situation, and her eyes wandered around darkness while the tea water boiled.

There wasn't much to see with the limited light available. The wallpaper was an ornate paisley print in dark, muted tones, and the furniture reminded her of an Edwardian drawing room. A crushed velvet chaise with heavy braid binding along the wood frame edge sat across from her, with its single chair sibling next to it. Large antique bookcases lined the one wall. Karyn couldn't make out the titles; the leather bindings made it difficult to read anything that might have been engraved on them, and most of the books had nothing on their spines at all. That struck her as odd, the obvious high quality of the bound books juxtaposed with a complete lack of titles. Curious, she stood up and walked over to investigate.

The scent of musty leather greeted her nose with increasing strength as she crossed the room. Although her eyes had adjusted to the dim lighting, the books looked the same as they had when she was sitting at the table many feet away. The bound volumes lining the shelves seemed ancient, as if they held the knowledge of civilizations past within them. Karyn brushed the spines horizontally with her fingers, noting the arid feel of the crumbling leather. A fine layer of dust sat upon the top page edges of all the books; she guessed that none of them had been disturbed in years, maybe even decades. She pulled a single book out and idly flipped it open to see the contents.

It was blank.

The paper was aged and tea-colored, but there was no writing to be seen. Karyn thumbed through the entire book to be sure, but every page was empty. She placed the book back on the shelf, confused, and pulled a different tome. The binding made an audible crack as she parted the covers.

It was also blank.

Something in her stomach tightened, and Karyn began moving down the bookcases, randomly grabbing a book every so often, only to find more empty pages. With each vacant page, her desperation increased as she tried to find a volume with any evidence of print, but every book was an empty soldier, no matter how furiously she leafed through the pages. All had antique paper that was totally blank and devoid of any mark, any writing, any single word. She stood motionless with the last book open in her hand, trying to reconcile what was happening at that moment when the clinking of china cups jolted her back to attention.

"Tea's ready, my dear," said the woman, as she placed a silver service tray down on the bistro table. Karyn spun around on her heels and closed the book at sound of her voice. "I hope you like this blend. It's one of my favorites." She looked over at Karyn's bewildered face, book still in hand. "Are you alright, child?" she asked her.

"I'm…fine," Karyn stammered, "but…why are all these books blank?"

That same concerned look Karyn had seen earlier crossed the woman's face, and the middle of her eyebrows moved upwards slightly. "Whatever do you mean, dear?" she said.

"The books…there's nothing in them," Karyn said in a half-whisper. She cleared her throat and stated more firmly, "They're all blank."

The woman walked over to the shelves with her hands clasped together and her eyes searching Karyn's face for something. "I'm not sure if I understand what you mean, dear," she said quietly as she glided up next to Karyn's left side. "These books are certainly not blank, I assure you. I've accumulated them over the years from antiquarian dealers, and I've read every single one at least once. If they were blank, I would certainly be aware of that." She laughed lightly as she lovingly touched the books on the shelf. "I may be old, dear, but I'm not senile just yet!" she chuckled. To prove her point, she removed a book from the shelf next to them and opened it up midway through.

The pages were covered in antique typed print. The woman smiled as she turned the pages. "I have so many memories attached to these books," she said wistfully, thinking back to an earlier time in her life. "This one I 'borrowed' from a lovely young man in Frankfurt, a mathematics student…he was beautiful and brilliant…I was terribly infatuated with him, you know. I thought it would give me an excuse to see him again if I kept one of his schoolbooks," she confided in Karyn. "It worked," she said with a twinkle in her eye as she closed the book. The cover read "The Absolute Differential Calculus" by Gregorio Ricci-Curbastro.

Karyn blinked her eyes hard. The book had transformed between the time the woman first opened it and the moment she closed the cover. The leather was fresh with no traces of dry rot, the paper edges were clean and dust free, and the title emblazoned clearly on the binding. As she placed it back on the shelf with a sigh, Karyn's mind raced to recall when the transformation happened and how she had missed it. That's when she noticed the smell. The smell of old musty paper was gone from her nose. She turned to look at the shelves behind her.

All the books had changed. Every single book, bound manuscript, and thin volume was rejuvenated. Their spines all proclaimed their contents and authors, and stood proudly shoulder to shoulder down the line.

Karyn's stomach tightened a little more as she looked down into her hands at the last book she had pulled. The comfortable burgundy leather cover was well-worn, but in excellent shape. The gilding on the pages still intact, the paper crisp and not crumbling. She was holding a 1912 first edition of Carl Jung's "Psychology of the Unconscious." Her head swam and she felt she might faint at that moment.

The woman noticed her pallor and quickly took the book from her hand. "Oh my! Dear, you look simply drained right now. Let's get you over to the table and I'll pour you that cup of tea." She guided Karyn by the arm to her seat, and returned to the tea service to begin pouring. Karyn wrestled with the last few moments while vaguely studying the woman's face through the steam rising from the tea. She was definitely close to seventy, but something about her look belied her age; she felt both young and ancient at the same time, both timeless and familiar. The low lighting softened the years on her face, giving some insight as to how she must have looked when she was younger. Karyn found herself mentally removing the wrinkles, the age spots, tightening her jawline and darkening her hair. The resulting image in her mind was that of a truly stunning woman in her prime, the kind that men would forget what they were saying when they saw her. The kind of face they might even die for.

As clear as that image was to Karyn, however, she couldn't fathom why this woman seemed so nondescript earlier. In fact, she couldn't recall what the woman really looked like until just now. Considering what had transpired by the bookshelves, Karyn assumed she couldn't trust anything about her memory, her judgment, or her mental state. Was she hallucinating even now? The little voice was still there, urging her on, supporting her, but was desperately faint at times like this.

With the tea poured, the old woman rose and disappeared behind the curtain again, only to return with a 3-tiered ceramic server of treats. The vision of scones, biscuits, and attractive but unidentifiable nibbles immediately drew a grumble from Karyn's stomach. She had forgotten all about dinner until they were set before her. "I thought you might be hungry," the woman smiled, "and you can't very well have tea without biscuits now, can you?" Karyn nodded silently in agreement as she selected a scone from the bottom tier. "Oh, you'll love those," the woman crooned. "They're my personal

recipe - lemon balm and mugwort scones. Everyone asks me
for the recipe, but I'll take it to my grave," she boasted.

Karyn bit into the scone tentatively, expecting the usual
disappointment from her tastebuds. She was pleasantly proven
wrong. The buttery crumb dissolved across her tongue,
followed by the salty sweetness of lemon, honey, and a spice
she could not name. Her mouth felt like it had been aroused
from a deep slumber, the dryness washed away by a wave of
flavor that rolled through her salivary glands. The effect was
immediate, and Karyn was transfixed by what she was tasting.
As she swallowed that first bite, she looked at the woman and
asked her, "What did you say was in these?"

"Oh, no, no, no…I didn't tell Marie Antoinette, and I
shan't tell you," she clucked, and pushed Karyn's tea towards
her. Karyn was still entranced with the taste of the scone when
she brought the cup to her lips, savoring the new scent of the
steam under her nose. It complimented the scone, but was
completely different; hints of citrus, mint and rosemary wafted
up from the cup and filled her sinuses. The smile on the
woman's face was genuine through the steam, and Karyn felt a
slow warmth infusing her insides. Her hunger pangs had left
her, and her mind quieted. At that moment, she felt completely
at ease - something she could never remember feeling before.

Suddenly she recalled the reason why she was there in
the first place, also realizing that she was a complete stranger
to this woman who had treated her so kindly. "I never asked
your name," Karyn apologized, as she nibbled more of the
scone. She felt like this woman was more of an archetype than
an actual person, and probably didn't have a name at all. She
was wrong, of course.

"I never asked yours, either," the old woman replied
with a soft smile. "My name is Kalea. And yours?"

"Karyn…Kiplinger." Their eyes met for just long
enough for Karyn to get a good look at her eyes. They were
gray, green, and slightly violet, although such a combination of
colors was impossible. They seemed to swirl like cream
poured into the tea she was drinking, the colors rising forward
and falling back against the darkness of her pupils.

Kalea sat back in her chair and sipped her tea. Her every move was graceful and fluid, down to the way she set her cup ever so gently on the saucer without a clink. "Well, Karyn, now that we have some comfort in your belly, what can I do for you?" she asked, before helping herself to a cream biscuit.

Karyn blinked after breaking her gaze and said rather sheepishly, "I'm not sure, really…I really wasn't expecting to be here in the first place. I was going to dinner." She took another bite of the scone and got lost in the taste for a moment, but quickly added, "But this scone is better than anything I think I could have eaten tonight in a restaurant." Kalea smiled sweetly at the compliment, said nothing, and sipped her tea again. "I was headed that way when I noticed your shop, but…I thought I remembered it on another street," Karyn continued, "and I was thinking about that when I saw the man in your window."

"What did he look like?" Kalea asked in a soft tone.

Karyn bit her lip trying to remember. "I don't know. I just know I knew him somehow." She looked at Kalea for judgment, but there was none. "That must sound silly," she said, slightly embarrassed.

"Not at all, darling. Many times we rely on our gut instinct or the little voice in our heads instead of our rational mind. Those helpers have been with us for a million years of evolution," Kalea said. "Can you describe what he looked like?"

Karyn took another sip of tea, and it seemed to help her focus the memory. There was a feeling associated with the man that was unclear, but made her stomach flutter for a moment. "He was tall…broad shouldered…with wavy brown hair - but I only saw him for a second," she sighed.

Kalea shook her head, and said,"I'm the only one here, dear. I'm the only one who has ever been here." When she saw the disappointment in Karyn's face, she added quickly, "Perhaps this man represents something to you. The mind often does that, you know." She reached out across the table and touched her hand in a consoling manner, as though her next words would be "there, there, darling…everything will be alright," but instead she said nothing, and let her last sentence sink into Karyn's mind. Karyn continued to try to pull a clearer picture of the man in the window, ignoring Kalea's statement about being alone. Although that vision was fleeting, it **felt** very real, almost tangible, to her. The disconcerting part was that she might be mentally unstable to the point of hallucination, but even the seriousness of such a concern was nominal to her right now. She was becoming overly focused on the shadowy window figure; she needed to know who he was.

Kalea removed her hand from Karyn's, leaving a warm, tingly feeling behind in its place. The mildly electric sensation lingered as if her hand was still present and soothing. "I don't know…" Karyn began, debating whether or not to confess her all to this stranger, her lack of memory, of sensation, of the gray flannel wrapping that cloaked her everyday life and made her doubt her own sanity. Her life seemed like a monotone song on endless repeat. *How do you explain something like that*, she thought. *What do I say?* "I don't know…how my life got like this," she finally said, her voice fading away like her ability to focus.

"My dear," Kalea said quietly, "these things are often a gradual process; a culmination of little things that have a bigger effect over time. When did you first notice something was wrong, Karyn?"

She shifted in her seat and poked at the crumbs on her plate. *When did things change? Has it always been like this?* "I'm not sure…I can't really remember," she admitted. Karyn searched back in time for the moment when all her problems began; all she found was an expansive field of fog, with no distinct beginning or ending. "I feel like it's **always** been like this…but, not." *I surely look like a head case to her now*, she thought to herself. But Kalea merely smiled sympathetically and began clearing the table.

"Sometimes our minds try to protect us by suppressing or hiding things that the subconscious deems dangerous or painful, dear." Kalea continued to tidy up at a crisp clip, stacking the saucers and plates without a sound, without a clink from the British china set. Her skin seemed to glow a bit more as she spoke. "If you're meant to remember, your subconscious will determine when, and how. However, you can help it along by being an active participant."

"What exactly do you mean?" Karyn asked. Something was bobbing around in the back of her head now, making a faint splashing sound in her mind.

"I mean," she paused, before picking up the service tray, "if you really want those answers, you have to be willing to accept everything that is connected to them, and convince your subconscious that what it's protecting you from is not dangerous or a threat." Kalea picked up the tray and looked at Karyn lovingly. "The mind is a powerful thing; it's capable of shifting the very nature of reality itself, dear."

Karyn thought she saw the color of Kalea's eyes change, and then everything went black.

3
Dissonance

Karyn awoke in her bed, tangled in her nightgown and sheets, and unsure of how she got there. Her last memory was of the hypnotist's shop and her conversation with Kalea; that much was crystal clear in her mind, but everything after that was foggy and amorphous. A smell lingered in her nose, something that was reminiscent of an unidentified spice, but there was more to it than just that. There was a distinctly human feeling associated with it, as if it was the scent trail of someone she knew. It nudged her mind a little, but the more she tried to coax out the connection, the more it slipped away.

She propped her body up against the pillows and rubbed her temples. The very lightest sensations of a headache were coming on. *Probably an allergic reaction to that scone*, she thought, but quickly dismissed it; the taste of Kalea's baking was not something she wanted to forget, and Karyn would gladly hazard a full-blown migraine for another bite. She had never eaten **anything** as amazing as that scone, and the tea was exceptional as well. *The last time I ate anything that good was...* She stopped mid-thought. Had she ever eaten anything that good before? Surely she must have; it was only a scone, but no previous meals came to mind. None at all. Karyn immediately tried to remember what she had for breakfast yesterday, before work, but also drew a blank. Then, she tried to remember the last meal she had out, the last time she had dinner with friends, the last time she ate; each time, the space that should have contained a memory was empty.

What is going on with my memory? Why can't I remember something as simple as what I had for breakfast?

Try as she might, the only memory of food that Karyn could remember experiencing was Kalea's tea and scone. Even now, the thought of the butter-crumb of the scone and the citrus mist that wafted from the tea made her mouth water as if they were set on a plate before her…yet, nothing else existed in that space. Nothing. She mentally walked through the series of last night's events, reviewing each moment, when it suddenly struck her that the entire visit with that woman had been unusually…sensory. The smell of the books, the leather, the paper, the dust. The first hint of incense, in the street, that made her turn her head to notice the hypnotist's shop. The scents and tastes Karyn experienced there were more vibrant than the rest of her life. In fact, the Kalea's shop had been the **only** moment she could recollect where those senses had been heightened, where they were more present than before.

She rubbed her temples some more; the threat of headache had passed, but was now replaced with a more pressing concern for her sanity. All the things she thought she saw yesterday were circling around now; the man in the shop window, the shop being on a different street, the transformation of the books on the shelves, Kalea's swirling eyes…there was no way she could reconcile any of it in a way that would make sense. Her deep unease with this realization sank her stomach further, and Karyn resolved to call her doctor before her reality became any more inconsistent. But first, a shower was absolutely in order; she needed to revitalize herself and clear her head before facing the day.

The water was a welcome respite from the confusion. Karyn tossed her nightgown across the sink and mirror and stepped into the steaming stream, surrendering her thoughts for a blissful moment, and allowed herself to lean against the shower wall. As the water trickled over her head, through her hair and down her back, it pulled the tiredness from her body, washing it down the drain along with her angst. She felt the moist heat rise up into her nose like the tea from last night; just the thought of that calmed her more than anything. To be steamed with those luscious spices and herbs wafting through her whole body was a decadent thought, one that Karyn reveled in. Kalea's words drifted through her mind, carried deeper by the steam.

"The mind is a powerful thing; it's capable of shifting the very nature of reality itself..."

She mulled over that sentence repeatedly, the comforting softness of Kalea's voice looping the statement over and over in her ears. The words had a significance that initially slipped her notice, as if there was a subtext to Kalea's comments. The warm rivulets traced a path over the bridge of Karyn's nose and down her cheeks, making moist trails over her face like tears.

She was crying.

Karyn only just realized they were her tears, mingled amongst the water droplets from the shower head. The telltale heat from her eyes and the taste of salt in her mouth a mere second before had warned her, but it didn't register. She wasn't feeling anything that would inspire her to begin weeping; for the first time in a while, she felt calm. *Oh god, **why** am I **crying**?* she thought. *What is **wrong** with me?*

Turning the shower off with a sigh, Karyn reached for her towel and shook her head in disgust. Were her emotions so detached now that she could shed tears without knowing why, and without feeling anything? The small voice inside contradicted her assumptions, quietly assuring her that there was a reason for everything that was happening, urging her on to move forward and get dressed. Sliding the towel from around her waist to her shoulders, she tossed her hair forward and wrapped its length in a single, smooth motion; on the return trip up, Karyn raised her head for a cursory glance in the mirror, but instead found herself facing a blank wall. Her surprise at the white drywall made her spin around, thinking she got disoriented when she toweled up her hair...but there was still no mirror. The mirror was gone.

There was no mirror in the bathroom, and it looked as if there never had been. No steam stains, paint fading, wall anchors or screw holes existed above the sink. The sink still held Karyn's discarded nightgown, however, which looked as if it was completely undisturbed. But no mirror was there above the sink, and Karyn felt a surge of panic wash over her. Her moment of peace had abruptly ended.

Calling her physician was the only thing on her mind now, a mind that seemed to be quickly slipping beyond her grasp moment by moment. She ran out into the apartment, still dripping, and began digging in her purse for her appointment book. *I must find that number…I know I wrote it down the last time I was there…* Karyn felt the back of her fingers brush against the synthetic leather spine and viciously ripped it out of the purse. Flipping past the pages to last month, she frantically scanned the individual dates for her last office visit. There were none written. She searched further back through the pages, with her panic increasing by the second, but more blank pages were all she saw. The date planner looked as if it had never been used.

Her heart was racing. "Not this, please, not this…I can't handle this…" she muttered in a stilted breath as she dug through her purse again for her phone, "I **know** I have his number, I **have** his number…" Her shaking hands brought out the phone, and thumbed across the multiple screens for her contacts list. Catching sight of the familiar icon, Karyn pressed it with both hands while silently praying for an end to her anxiety. The screen flashed briefly as if the battery was failing, and then shone brightly in Karyn's face.

"You have no contacts" was in bold print next to search bar at the top of the screen, and every letter heading was empty of names, numbers, or addresses. Karyn's eyes rolled back in her head and she let out a whimper, letting the phone slowly slip from her grasp as she slumped to the floor like a broken doll.

Her whole body was numb, and her heartbeat was now ploddingly slow compared to its earlier rhythm of panic. Karyn couldn't feel anything; the roughness of the floor against her naked body and the chill spreading across her skin made no impact on her nervous system. She was in shock, and as her blood pressure continued to drop and the room began to spin, the little voice pleaded with her to hang on.

4

Taste

Again, Karyn awoke in bed. Her body was achy, miserable and somewhat hungover, as if she had been partying it up the night before; the throbbing in her head was on either side, just above her ears and deep inside her skull. Her brain felt like a walnut that had just barely escaped its shell being cracked in a vise. The memory of what made her head ache so much was not lost on her, however, and she dragged herself out of bed and made her way to the bathroom. Her need to check on her mental state was a primary priority, despite her desire to curl up and go back to sleep until the pain left her head. *Am I crazy? Have I finally lost touch with reality, or is this just all a bad dream?* she thought through the thumping pain.

Leaning against the door frame, she surveyed the bathroom. It was completely intact, with nothing missing, and nothing changed from how it had always looked before. The mirror was in its rightful place above the vanity sink, and Karyn used the opportunity to take a good, hard look at herself. Her hair was still damp, her skin clean, and her eyes slightly bloodshot. She was back in her nightgown as well. *I don't look crazy*, she thought, *but then, what do crazy people really look like, anyway?* She searched her face for any sign of imbalance, of unraveling, but the girl in the mirror told her nothing.

Karyn painfully trod into the living room, and found her purse on the couch with all its contents accounted for. Her phone was off, her date planner right next to it. She opened neither, having resigned herself to the fact that what happened last night had all been imagined. Karyn collapsed on the couch, exhausted, and threw her head back on the cushion.

The blank, sanitary white of the ceiling made her eyes unfocused, and she closed them to minimize the impact of vision on her headache. *What could cause me to imagine it all?* She retraced the moments leading to the questionable events, searching for clues to the truth, however unpleasant it might be.

Left here and went out to eat. Purple door of the hypnotist's shop...the man in the window. Kalea...the tea and scones...the books...how I got back here...

Karyn ran the scenario over and over. Each time she did, the more she felt an unease in her gut, as if there was something malicious going on of which she was unaware. She kept going back to the moment when she ate the scone, and the unusual reaction she had to it and the tea. The flavor of it all was so vibrant, so unlike her everyday experiences with food, that Karyn came to an unsettling conclusion; she had been dosed with some kind of hallucinogen when she was at the hypnotist's shop.

There seemed to be no other explanation for all the phenomena that she had experienced lately. The hallucinations in the shop, the incredible flavor of the scones and tea, the disappearance of the mirror...it all made sense to her now. That old woman spiked her food and drink with some chemical, some poison that was to blame for the suffering she had endured. The thought of being toyed with for someone's amusement stoked her anger.

Except for the books, the little voice interjected. *The books changed before you ate anything.*

Karyn dismissed the voice with her own. "There could have been something in the air in there. I **did** smell incense before I walked in," she grumbled, and began getting dressed in haste. There was purpose in her manner now, and a rising heat in her body. Her fury was growing. "How **dare** she do such a thing to me!" she growled while grinding her heels into her boots with a stamp. Grabbing her purse and keys, Karyn strode out the apartment door with only one focus and one thought; she was going right to Castor Street to confront Kalea and give her a piece of her mind.

Her stride increased with her pace as she neared Castor, and Karyn was so mad at this point she wanted to run. Her body was tired, though, and she gradually wound down her canter as she neared Castor. A hundred questions welled up in her throat, if she could manage to actually talk to the old woman before throttling her outright. But throttling her sounded like a much more satisfying choice to Karyn.

Choking a senior citizen was not to be on the menu that day, for as Karyn rounded the corner of Castor, she did not smell incense, and did not see the hypnotist's shop. Instead, the drifting scents of roasted meats, char-grilling, and woodsmoke tickled her nose. The scent was so heady, so delicious, that Karyn almost failed to notice that the hypnotist's shop was no longer there. The aubergine door was now more of an indigo-purple, but its elaborate hardware was intact, as was the big bay shop window next to it, and the hanging shop sign that read, in gilded lettering, "Blue Lotus Cafe."

Karyn's legs felt a twinge of weakness, partially from the speedwalking she had done to get there, but mostly from this latest shock. She was definitely on Castor Street, of that there was no doubt - she was standing almost right under the street sign - but this was not Kalea's shop. She surveyed the now cafe facade in minute detail; the interior was dimly lit throughout, and there were people moving amongst the tables. It was obvious to her the cafe was in full operation, not empty and dark like the hypnotist's shop was; the people sitting at tables near the bay window looked very real and lively. The delicious, vaporous scented air continued to caress her face, distracting her from the huge disconnect going on in her mind as to why nothing here was the same. She trembled in her knees, and found her feet moving forward, almost against her will, up the steps to the cafe door.

A tall, lithe young man opened the aubergine door for her, from inside. "Welcome, miss, to the Blue Lotus Cafe," he said cordially, as he bid her inside with a hand extended behind him, "Table for one, Ms. Kiplinger?"

"Y-yes," Karyn answered, not quite sure why she didn't say more, or ask any questions instead of following the graceful youth as he walked her past multiple groups of people drinking, eating, and laughing. There was nothing even vaguely reminiscent of the hypnotist's shop around her; no books, no bookcases, no dust, and no sign of Kalea. Art glass lamps hung from single wires above each table, their light reflecting off the embossed tin ceiling above her. The space had a radiant warmth and feel, as if the whole room was enclosed in a soft velvet blanket. Music filtered down from somewhere in the ceiling, a light, dreamy instrumental that gently rocked to and fro in rhythm like a lullaby sung by the ocean. The underlying thump felt like a sleeping heartbeat…or was that her own heart beating? Karyn's critical thinking skills diminished, step by step, until the young man pulled out a chair to a small table in a very private back corner in the cafe. She took the seat in a daze, as the youth that seated her glided off to serve another table.

From her seat, she had full view of the cafe floor. The place was quietly abuzz with diners noshing from small plates, engaged in conversation, smiling and enjoying their wine. The air tinkled with the light clinking of glasses and silverware. Although there was much chatter from the other tables around her, Karyn couldn't clearly make out any one conversation; try as she might, she couldn't eavesdrop on what anyone was saying. All their words blended into a single landscape of sound that followed the flow of the music, and the room seemed to pulse slightly in time. The atmosphere around her was subtly intoxicating. Swirling around her like delicious trails of exotic smoke, the spices and aromas blended in with the conversation and the music; the harder she tried to focus, the more vague she felt, as if she were drifting off into an opium den haze. The cafe was seducing her, and she began to relent to its advances.

The patrons around her moved in and out of focus, and someone brought her a glass of wine. Karyn lifted the glass to her lips without a second thought and drank. The vintage played over her tongue like a warm wave on a tropical beach, and she closed her eyes as the taste of apples, pears, clove and honey bathed her tastebuds all too briefly on its way down her throat. She allowed herself the pleasure of languishing in the moment, finally unwinding from the stress of the last few days. Karyn felt safe, ensconced in her corner, with no desire to investigate or question anything. She savored the wine, her eyes becoming heavier with each sip; when she slowly opened her lids again, her eyes were drawn across the room.

Seated at another table like hers was a man who looked vaguely like the vision in the hypnotist's window. The art glass lamp above was positioned a little too forward to adequately light his features; they hid in the shadows above his shirt collar, but she could discern the barest glimpse of his jawline below the lamplight. His forearms were solid, half exposed by the turned back cuffs of his white button-down shirt. They were well-tanned, and fringed with a bleached mantle of fine hair. He wore a silver and jade ring on his right hand, and the glinting light from its shine caught her eye like a magpie. He was clearer than the other patrons, devoid of the dreamy diffuser lens that filtered everyone else, and suddenly Karyn had the urge to get up and walk over to him, to talk to him, but her legs would not comply. She was weighted down by the will of the cafe.

Suddenly her view was cut off by the presence of the server, who stood before her with a plate resplendent with tapas, spreads, cheeses, and fruit. Smiling but saying nothing, he set the dish down in front of Karyn and then swiftly disappeared again into the cafe's background. Her eyes were locked on the plate, taking in all the offerings, both savory and sweet. Never before had food been so appealing or looked so good to her. Her mouth watered at the prospect of eating, of tasting; this was the first time she could remember wanting to eat, looking forward to eating, since her strange journey began. Kalea's scone had primed her palate in its brevity, but now she was facing a banquet. Randomly picking a slice of cheese, Karyn laid it on her tongue like a communion wafer and let it melt. Her mouth responded almost immediately, sending a flood of moisture cascading over her tongue, infusing the flavors of the cheese into her saliva; her eyes rolled back and closed in the light ecstasy of tasting, actually **tasting** something for the first time in forever.

She chose a slice of pear next. The crispness of the flesh against her teeth put up just enough resistance, and her lips closed down to meet the tart sweetness; an explosion of flavor rocked her, and the sensations flushed through her skin, leaving a shivering trail of pleasure down Karyn's back. Working her way around the plate, Karyn reveled in every mouthful, every bite, opening her eyes just long enough to choose the next morsel to indulge herself in. She eventually noticed that the man across the cafe was gone now; the regret of not meeting him was washed away as she closed her eyes again, draining the last swallow of wine from her glass. The taste of the wine paved the way for other flavor memories, washing over her in between the pulsing, hypnotic heartbeat of the cafe.

The taste of wine on her lips…the sugary icing of birthday cake…the tangy bite of lemons…butter melting on her tongue…blackberry juice…warm, sea-salted skin…blood…the taste of blood…in her mouth…

5

Somewhere

She could feel a moist heat, and the scent of lilacs. Torpor weighted her body, and there was a salty, iron taste in her mouth. Her ears felt wet. Her eyes were open, but she couldn't see anything in the dark, and part of her didn't care to look at anything, or think of anything, or feel anything. The womb-like space she occupied was enough for her.

The weightiness pulled Karyn along; a thick river current like molasses moved her through the isolating inkiness to a point where there was light gravity. She gently drifted down. The nothingness around her brightened and a field of wildflowers, and sounds passed through the air above her. Butterflies, bees and birds moved among the flower heads, unaware of her presence as Karyn floated past them. The wide screen view of the landscape, gently sloping down to a small stream, filled her field of vision. A blanket laid out nearby, and two people lying together in an embrace. The tannins of red wine haunted her tongue.

As she drifted past the lovers, the scene faded and opened again, revealing small children playing on the beach. Karyn watched dispassionately as the children ran in and out of the waves, chasing, and being chased by them. The cries of seagulls abounded, gradually declining as the whirring of helicopter blades became dominant; her perspective moved higher aloft and shifted the scene to one of city rooftops, the faces of serious young men and women in uniforms, and the hushed whispers of people around her. Dogs barked in the distance, and the sounds became indistinct. The heaviness returned to envelop her body, and Karyn sank back down into the dark.

6
Sound

*"**I** refuse to believe that nothing can be done. Surely there's some kind of intervention, some kind of treatment that can minimize the swelling."*

Karyn looked up from her book with a start, and cast a glance behind her for the owner of the voice. Although the coffee shop patio was filled with the quiet murmurings of patrons, sipping from their lattes and espressos, that voice stood out above the rest, and her heart beat a little faster. She was celebrating the return of her sense of taste with a sweet, creamy amaretto steamer, and catching up on her favorite author's latest book. She felt upbeat and relaxed despite the fact that, once again, she found herself home this morning and no memory of how she got there after dining at the Blue Lotus Cafe. Karyn knew she was a cheap date when it came to wine, but apparently she had a good sense of direction even when drunk. That would also explain the small headache she woke up with, the odd dreams, and the fact that she slept in her clothes. *A small price to pay for a meal like that,* she thought wistfully, remembering the gourmet banquet of flavors and textures.

"We have to wait and see, Will. There's a lot of damage, and I'm afraid we don't know the half of it right now."

A different voice now than the first. The first voice had sounded familiar in tone, but Karyn couldn't place where she knew it from. This second voice had a tired quality to it, like the man had been up all night working and just finished his shift. She saw no one she recognized from her furtive glance, and went back to drinking her steamer.

*"I'm telling you - I **know** she's in there somewhere. Please, Rick, I'm begging you - don't give up just yet."*

Karyn's eyes stopped following the words on the page and closed to hear the conversation better. She had definitely heard that voice before somewhere. It had a warm timbre and an indefinite accent, from someplace between Maryland and Pennsylvania; something about it hung in her ears, although she couldn't put her finger on exactly what it was that gave her pause. The noises of the coffee shop quickly covered up the men's discussion, and the clatter of espresso grounds being banged out jolted her from her nosy curiosity; she quickly lost interest and focused on her novel again.

The book was good, but Karyn eventually found herself daydreaming, listening to the sounds of summer around her instead. The light breeze blew the chirping of birds, the rhythmic clicking of heels, and traffic past her ears. She closed her book softly and closed her eyes once again, trying to imagine what the people around her looked like based on the sound and pitch of their voices. She imagined a pinched-faced spinster to her left, the whining shrillness revealing decades of unhappiness and blame; to her right, a man with a subtle Midwest accent that sounded endearing, but insincere, as if he was planning to leave no forwarding address to the woman he was chatting up. The light squeal of a young girl in response to a compliment on her hair. A twenty-something's complaint about his parents' nagging. Gradually, the mingled voices became better defined and individualized; picking them out became easier and easier, like hearing single instruments stand out from within an entire orchestra.

At some point, the voices were no longer interesting to Karyn. Almost as if answering her wish for something different, the breeze blew a tune past her ear. It was a delicate string of notes carried from down the street, plucked out on a guitar and carried solo on the wind. Karyn turned her head towards the music and listened harder, but could not bring the song into better focus. Only one phrase was clear, rising above the street and coffee shop noise, teasing her, enticing her to investigate. After several rounds of the song, Karyn could no longer resist. She finished off her steamer, gathered her things, and began to trek towards the source of the music.

The city became more vibrant with each street she crossed in search of the source. Cars appeared a bit more colorful, street signs stood out more against the background concrete, people looked more pleasant. Not radically so, but her progression downtown seemed to rouse her surroundings from a grayness; even the flowers looked more lively in the breeze. Karyn felt the flow of air and sound was tied together, because only her path following the enchanting little ditty was affected. Nothing looked different beyond a radius of twenty feet on either side; it remained rather bland and sedate in comparison to the breezeway of sound. She doubted that anyone else noticed besides her. So far, only she had ever noticed these oddities in her reality, so Karyn didn't expect a change in the status quo today. Visual hallucinations were becoming the norm with her, and gradually she was learning to accept them as part of her new normal.

The music pulled her along a small side street into a tiny park. Surrounded on three sides by tall concrete walls and completely hidden from outside view, everything about the space was lush, green, and filled with birdsong. The calls of wrens, mockingbirds, finches, chickadees and juncos flew back and forth through the air above her head. *Why are there juncos here now, in summer*, was her fleeting thought, but the symphony of song and the visual beauty of the space distracted her. Wood benches accented the splashes of color painted on the rose bushes, and the scent of lilacs wafted by her. All manner of flowers graced the beds along the edges, and the sanctity of the space made her feel warm throughout, as if she were relaxing in a sunbeam. Then birdsong quieted just enough for her to hear the notes, gently plucked from guitar strings beside her.

Startled to hear them so close to her, Karyn stepped back to see the guitarist, bent over his instrument. His face was obscured by his dark brown hair, blown across his cheek by the wind while he played, but Karyn recognized the jade ring below the moving fingers; it was the mystery man in the window from before, and in the Blue Lotus Cafe last night.

He continued his sweet sonata, unaware of her presence, and Karyn felt it rude to disturb the performance. Instead, she marveled at how deftly his fingers caressed the strings, moving to where each note was sleeping on the fret, gently rousing it just enough to sing its part in the sonata and then tucking them back into slumber until its next turn. Each string of notes was lifted by the breeze and wrapped around her, surrounding Karyn in a web of music that had texture and meaning. It blanketed her shoulders like the arm of a friend. The song was familiar; it had a place in her memory and became more familiar the more she heard.

"You know she can't hear you," came the voice of the tired shift worker, the one she heard before at the coffee shop patio.

Karyn spun around to find nobody there, and immediately turned back to the guitarist. He continued to play, undeterred by the phantom comment. His jaw flexed slightly. His music increased in depth and feeling, his hands pleading with the strings for more emotion, more resonance. The song had a tactile quality to it, draping her in musical phrase with every bar he played. A taste crept into her mouth. The taste of wine.

Amazed, but not afraid, Karyn moved a little closer and knelt down before him. He played as if he were blind to her being, strumming gently but insistently the song over and over. The sonata was so physical now that she was covered in musical filaments, as soft and delicate as silk, and strongly bound to the man with the jade ring. His head had dropped lower in defeat, the hair further obscuring his face.

*"She cannot **hear** you, Will."*

Karyn didn't turn at this last comment. She no longer cared to see where it came from, or who owned the voice. She watched the guitarist, completely captivated by his artistry, and so she saw the first droplet hit the fretboard. It splattered across the strings, followed by another, and then another. Karyn moved her eyes from his hands to his hidden face with its recognizable jawline, now stained by a trail of tears. Still, he continued to play for an unknown woman that couldn't hear him, according to the disembodied voice.

Her heart contracted at the pain he must be feeling. This man was pouring his soul out for all to hear, yet the one he played for could not hear him. *He must love her to feel so strongly, to play with so much emotion…how sad to not be heard by the one you love…* she thought. She moved closer still, and without disturbing his concert, looked up at him and said with true compassion, "**I** can hear you."

His reaction was unexpected. His hands froze, and his head snapped up, the hair falling back from his face to reveal smoky hazel eyes that were ablaze with hope and fear. They were wild and vacant, searching the space around him for the source of his disturbance; they looked right through Karyn as if she was invisible. She thought perhaps he was blind and she had frightened him with her speech, and said again, gently, "I can hear you, and you play beautifully."

More tears welled up beneath the thick lashes and poured from the corners of his eyes, and down his tanned face. Karyn was struck by his beauty, by how familiar he was, and how her heart beat a little faster just looking at him. He turned his head back and forth in his desperate search, still unable to see her only a few feet away. "Where are you?" he whispered hoarsely. "Where are you, Karyn!"

Karyn fell backwards off her knees, tipping over into the grass but never taking her eyes off him. *He said my name. Why did he say **my** name?*

No sooner had her name sprung from his lips, the musical webbing that connected them together began to fade. She could feel the song filaments melting away like spun sugar, releasing her from the lovely spell he had woven around her. Karyn stared at him, still wild-eyed and teary, taking in his entire person. She recorded everything about him in seconds, feeding it into her database of people and places, hoping to find a clue as to why he would say such a thing. Did he know her? The sounds of the city were fading, and all the birds had flown. The landscape around them began to break down and dissolve away. The bushes and the flower beds were becoming indistinct and fuzzy, the colors draining away, and soon only the two of them were left in the void of the black background. Karyn brought her focus back to the man before her, still searching the space between them, and saw her reflection in his eyes. A sharp pain shot through her head above her ears, bringing with it a poignant realization, a truth revealed that had been lost to her. Reaching out to touch him as he, too, began to dissolve away into the darkness, her hands passed through his fading form as she said breathlessly, "William."

7

When

"**W**ill! I need a tire in bay four!" the geezer yelled into the back of the garage. His voice was as raspy as it was demanding.

Karyn stood by uselessly, staring at the remnants of tire wrapped around her front wheel rim; it looked like a piece of black licorice candy that had been mauled by a toddler, with shreds of steel belt poking out at odd angles. Fortunately, she had felt the pull in the steering wheel before she heard the flapping of the tire, and managed to slow down before any real damage was done to the rim, performing a controlled coast into this grease pit. She leaned against the concrete wall, holding her forehead in her one hand. A new tire definitely wasn't in her budget right now, and this was an unexpected event she really didn't need.

"William! Where the hell are you, boy? I need-"

"I heard you, Kenny!" boomed the voice from the garage depths. "Give me a fuckin' moment to finish this other car, will ya?"

Kenny the Geezer looked over at Karyn apologetically, and said, "He'll be with you in a minute," before scurrying off into the filthy back office. Karyn smiled half-heartedly, and continued to lean against the only clean spot on the block wall. The smell of gasoline, oil, and vulcanized rubber filled her nose beyond full. *Man, how do people work in this stink?* she thought. *It has to be bad for you.* But her thoughts quickly moved from health to her empty wallet, and how she was going to pay for a new tire.

This was just one of a hundred things that had been going poorly for her. A job that she hated, a car she couldn't afford, mounting debt, a life that was going nowhere, and now this. She chewed on the side of her finger in angst about it all. Her eyes got watery the more she thought about it, and she was almost in tears when the young man with the booming voice walked out front.

"Christ, Kenny, you really oughta hire more guys. I can't do-" he stopped short when he saw Karyn, eyes brimming, instead of the leathery garage owner. "Oh jeeze, miss," he said, embarrassed at his tone and immediately apologizing while wiping the grease from his hands. "I didn't realize you were here." She just looked at him with big, sad eyes, and he thought she might cry at any moment. He glanced at what was left of the frayed Firestone, clucked his tongue and shook his head. "Wow…you were very lucky. A front tire fail like that, well…you could have lost control when that blew." He stooped down to make a note of the type and size of the tire.

"I don't feel very lucky," Karyn mumbled under her breath. She struggled with the unhappiness rising in her chest. A tear slid from the corner of her eye and hit the dirt next to his foot; he noticed immediately and ignored the tire.

"Are you okay?" he asked gently. Yanking out a dirty folding chair from the bay and laying a clean shop towel on the seat for her, he said, "How about you sit down here and take it easy for a bit while I go find you a new tire?" He patted the seat and flashed her a smile.

Karyn felt the emotions well up inside and more tears came down. She hung her head in defeat. "I can't afford a new one," she sniffed. "I'm broke, and I don't get paid until next week." She looked up into his hazel eyes. They were soft, and framed at the corners with creases caused by an understanding smile.

"Don't you worry about a thing, miss…"

"Karyn."

"…Miss Karyn; we'll get you fixed up somehow." He flashed her a sideways smile and handed her another clean shop towel to dry her eyes. "You just relax and let me handle everything." He lightly touched her shoulder and walked off into the garage office to yell at Kenny. "Christ almighty,

Kenny - don't you have any sense of customer service? Or manners? Couldn't you have at least given that poor girl a chair…" His voice died off in a trail of lightly offensive swear words.

Karyn sat on the chair drying her eyes and pondering her dilemma. The greasy young man's kindness touched her. Her week had been so miserable, so depressing, and he made her feel like she mattered, like she wasn't a pathetic failure. Someone had finally been nice and understanding to her, just when she needed it most.

He returned with tools in one hand and a tire in the other. Bouncing it on the ground with a look of satisfaction, he knelt down next to her and said through straight, white teeth, "You won't believe what just happened! I just finished yelling, er, talking, with Kenny when I almost fell over this sorta-new tire, and it **just** happened to be the right size for your car." He rolled it over to the vehicle and grabbed a jack lift from the bay. Karyn was confused and didn't know what to say; she had no money to pay for this tire or the cost of installation, and she had made that perfectly clear to the greasy fella. Her anxiety started to ramp up, wondering how to re-explain her situation to him before his job performance made her a deadbeat in his eyes.

He, on the other hand, seemed to be thoroughly enjoying the process of changing her tire. Karyn found herself wondering if he always smiled this much. Whistling a delicate little melody, he began cracking the lugs on the rim; the muscles of his forearms flexed in rotation as he spun each lug loose with the tire iron, dropping each one into the pocket of his t-shirt. The weight of them pulled the shirt collar down, exposing the shadowy depression above his collarbone; a few fine chest hairs stood out against his tanned skin, and the glistening sheen of sweat on his neck. Sliding the jack under the frame, he pumped the handle effortlessly a half-dozen times to lift the car, pulled the rim free and disappeared in the back to mount the tire.

Karyn forgot herself watching him work. She focused on his features instead of her anxiety, first noting the thick mop of wavy hair he occasionally pushed back from his face, and the lush lashes that fringed his eyelids. He had a confident air and a slight swagger that set him apart. She guessed that he was a few years older than her, but she could have easily been wrong; his strength and size were deceiving.

Ten minutes later, Karyn had a sorta-new tire on her car, and no payment in return. The young man with the hazel eyes had interrupted her before she managed to say anything and said, with a face full of compassion, "Everyone needs a break when things get tough. Just pay it forward to someone else when you can." She was dumbfounded, but his face was telling the truth.

"Really?" she asked with disbelief.

"Really," he said, firmly.

Karyn watched him walk halfway back to the garage and pause for a moment as if he'd forgotten something. Pulling a notepad from his pocket, he scribbled on the paper, turned back and handed it to her. "That's a used tire on there, so in case you have any problems, miss-"

"You can just call me Karyn," she said, a bit too earnestly.

"Karyn," he repeated, grinning now. She felt herself becoming over-warm. "In case you feel any wobble in that tire, just bring it back here and I'll re-balance it for you, okay?" She nodded silently, at a loss of words and slightly shocked at her good fortune. "Or," he said slowly, "you could call me for no reason at all."

Karyn examined the slip of paper he gave her; his name and a phone number were written down in heavy print. "William Thalheim," she mouthed the name, looking up from the paper at him.

"Yes?" He was all smiles now, looking down at her with a twinkle in his eye.

Karyn hesitated, and pushed her discomfort down. "I…um…I want to…" she began quietly, lowering her eyes and biting her lower lip.

William bent down closer to hear what she was having so much trouble saying. Karyn was amazingly awkward, searching for the right words to say, and he was truly enjoying watching her squirm a little. It was blatantly apparent that she wasn't comfortable with people being nice to her. "Yeeessss?" he asked again, and leaned in a little closer.

She continued to struggle with her words, and began with, "I…I wanted to-" before lifting herself up to meet his unsuspecting lips. He balked slightly from surprise, but instantly fell into her advance as she pressed against him.

He smelled like a day in the sun, and the edge of his top lip had the barest hint of salt from his sweat. He wrapped her up in his arms, drawing her close, the scent of him cascaded over her, and the heat from his body melted her reserve. His lips were as soft as peaches. Karyn lingered as long as she dared, then slid back down, keeping her eyes to the ground.

"-to kiss you," she finished her sentence with a sigh, dropping back down on her heels again. She raised her eyes to meet his, concerned about what her impulsive behavior had just earned her.

William gave her a quizzical look, leaned down, and turned one ear towards her. "I'm sorry, Karyn," he began, and her stomach tightened up with the fear that she had offended him. "Could you repeat all that? I'm not quite sure I heard you right," he finished with another wink.

Karyn smiled and thought, *I could get used to repeating myself.*

8

Aware

Karyn found herself back in her apartment again, standing in the exact same position she was in the park, reaching out to William before everything was erased. This time, however, she was aware of what happened. There was no break in her consciousness, and no excuse she could use that fit the circumstances. She was awake, sober, and wearing the same clothes. The book she was reading was still inside her purse. For once, Karyn didn't feel like her mind was playing tricks on her; she knew from deep inside that something was happening outside of her head, and she wanted to know what.

She dropped onto the couch to rewind the events, and the memory that came flooding into her. It was a single snapshot glimpse into who the man was, and how she knew him, but not much more had been forthcoming. It was an isolated memory, as if it were just one scene from an entire movie. Karyn was hesitant to try and extrapolate more from the small part that had been revealed to her; there wasn't enough information, and she was genuinely afraid of drawing any conclusions without more facts. *If all I can remember is the moment I first met him, that doesn't tell me anything about now*, she thought. Given the surreal nature of the event in the park, Karyn thought she should be more upset, but that wasn't what she felt. Instead, she was filled with questions as to how those visions, real or unreal, had manifested. Why hadn't she recognized William immediately, and why did she only remember that sliver of memory containing him? How much of it was real, and how much was imagined? *Why did he call my name?*

The movie scene clip of her and William's past was very real; Karyn **knew** that event had occurred, and she walked through their introduction again and again, hoping to glean some new insight. The taste and smell of him lingered with her, fanning an ember in her soul's memory. All the feelings, emotions, scents…all her senses were at full capacity in that moment. Whether it was real or not almost didn't matter; for once, in longer than she could remember, she felt alive, aware.

It was that awareness that drove away the fear, fear she should have felt when all of the scenery in the park dissolved into black and only she and William were left. It was the reason she was intensely curious now, instead of terrified out of her wits. It was the realization that part of her **was** missing, and that she might be able to regain it somehow. The intuitive knowledge was there, out of reach, beyond the opaque curtain in her mind.

She focused again on the flashback, resting her head on the back of the sofa cushion and closing her eyes. Karyn carefully fast-forwarded the memory to the point where he was changing her tire. She held that vision of him in one part of her mind while pulling up the William in the park. In comparison, side by side, the William in the park was at least fifteen years older than his counterpart in the flashback; he seemed broader in the chest, and the shadow of his beard was heavier and more pronounced. If her guess about his age was right, then the older William was around the same age as she was now. He also called her name, which meant he knows her in the present time, and she should know **him** now…but she didn't. *How much of my memory have I lost?* Karyn's eyebrows knotted in concern. *Why would I forget him?*

She could still hear his sonata in her ears. It was hauntingly beautiful, but not a classical piece by a known composer. Karyn knew her Haydn, Mozart, and Bach, and this sonata was none of theirs. It had too many minor chords, the kind that speak of sadness, or loss, and she noted an underlying hint of Spanish styling; it had to be more modern than those masters, and definitely wasn't classic European. Something about the sonata tugged at her, the way it made her feel, and she felt like she had heard it before, but if she didn't remember the William who was playing it, that was probably her imagination playing with her.

All the crawling around in her head was giving her a headache, ironically, in the exact same spot where she felt the sharp pain when the flashback of William was revealed to her. *This can't be good*, she thought. *I've got to figure this out. I've got to know what's really going on. I know I'm not crazy. I was there. He was there*... She paused and fast-forwarded the flashback again, past the tire change, to their kiss and embrace. The smell of his skin immediately came back to her in full, and she could almost feel him pressed against her if she tried hard enough to relive the memory. The pure pleasure of it distracted her from thought for one blissful moment; she lost herself in the feeling, until it faded again like his vision in the park. It left her with an unsatisfied desire to see him again, to fit in that space between his arms, and ignore the present forever.

Karyn thought back to the moment he cried out to her. He was striking, but worn, a bit haggard, and those gray hazel eyes of his looked haunted. The desperation and sadness in his face was so far removed from the William of the past; that man was lighthearted, whistling without a care in the world. She tried to imagine what could have happened to him to change him so, to make him cry the way he did before he faded away. She found herself wanting to console him, wipe away his tears and assure him that things would be fine; maybe then he could tell her his story.

No other information was forthcoming, at least not from the venue of her couch, and the apartment felt a bit oppressive; Karyn decided to retrace her steps from the coffee cafe and see where that led her.

She barely paid attention to where her feet were taking her; part of her was still lingering on the memory of William, another part asking endless questions, and yet another still playing connect the dots with the bits and pieces scattered about. More than anything, Karyn wanted one good lead as to how, why, or if all the bizarre happenings lately were synchronicity, or truly related. She refused to believe that there was no connection at all; the little voice continued to push her along with a single whispered word. *Search*, it said, and Karyn trusted that what she sought would appear soon, and it did.

Before her was the hypnotist's shop.

As if plunked from out of the aether and dropped right in her path, on a different street, in a different part of the city, there it stood, aubergine door and all. The gilded sign swung gently. The concrete steps were three feet from her toes. Any closer and the building would have landed on her like the Wicked Witch of the East.

Karyn was jolted out of her daze by the surprise manifestation. She stared at the door incredulously, trying to process the impossibility of it all, but there was nothing, nothing that accounted for this. *This goes against everything I know to be real. This is not possible. This is not reality. This is not real.* She repeated the sentences a few times, never taking her eyes off the shop, but the vision was sincerely solid and not fading. She walked closer to the steps and tapped her foot against the concrete. Solid. Stepping back, Karyn took a deep breath and did a personal assessment; she was not tired, sleeping, or dreaming. She was a bit freaked out, but her heart wasn't racing. She definitely was not afraid, and she could suddenly hear Kalea's words in her head.

"If you saw someone, then you're supposed to be here. That's the way it works."

Any rationale was better than none right now, she thought, and gave up thinking; this journey had brought her here for some reason, so why fight it? Squaring her shoulders and walking up the steps, she made the statement out loud with her hand on the doorknob: "I saw someone, I'm supposed to be here, and I want answers."

With a decisive push, Karyn opened the door and moved forward.

9
Insight

Karyn pushed her way past the heavy wood and tinkling bell, and stepped inside. The hypnotist's shop looked no different than the last time she was there. The tidy row of bookshelves against the one wall were present, as well as all the books; she immediately strode over and grabbed a bound volume to check her current level of reality. It looked intact, clean, dust-free and well-kept. She was mentally fact checking when she heard a voice from the corner.

"Has it changed?"

Karyn looked over to the source of the question. It was Kalea, sitting at the bistro table and drinking tea from the same china service, complete with the three-tiered server. A second service setting was across from her, as if she was waiting for a guest who was yet to arrive. She smiled knowingly at Karyn in between sips, and asked again.

"The book - has it changed?"

Karyn shook her head slowly and placed the book back on the shelf without looking, running her hand across the spines of the others in a blind check of the leather.

"Go ahead," Kalea encouraged, "inspect a few more, dear. Look until you're satisfied."

Karyn declined, and said with an edge, "I don't need to."

"And why is that?"

"Because I know," Karyn answered quietly. "I know because I can **feel** it."

Kalea's eyebrow raised slightly at her reply. She broke off a piece of biscuit and held it inches from her lips. "What else do you know?" she asked, popping the tidbit in her mouth.

She was subtly purposeful in her questions, divulging nothing on her part, and exploring the breadth of Karyn's knowledge base. Karyn had the distinct feeling that she was being tested, that her answers would determine and influence what she would be told. She hoped saying less and being vague would work to her advantage.

"I know I am supposed to be here," she stated with solidity. Her eyes were steely and serious.

Kalea broke into a broad smile, and clasped her hands together in approval. "That's an excellent start, Karyn." She gestured at the seat opposite her, inviting Karyn to join her. She hesitated, but slid into the chair with tacit compliance. Kalea poured her a cup of tea, and pushed the server of pastries close to her. When Karyn balked, she raised an eyebrow again; there was a twinkle in her eye that Karyn couldn't pin down, and it irritated her.

"Help yourself, dear," she said, breaking off another piece of biscuit. "I just baked these today, and they've never tasted better. My best batch ever, I think." Karyn was unconvinced, and it was blatantly obvious on her face. She made no effort to hide the fact that she held those tasty, crumbly snacks, and the woman who made them, responsible for her near nervous breakdown in the apartment.

"No thank you," Karyn said flatly.

The lack of polite inflection was not lost on Kalea. Her soft demeanor shifted and her gaze sharpened slightly, like a cat aware of a mouse in the next room. She cast her eyes down into her tea and chewed the last of her biscuit. "Were they not to your liking? Did they disagree with you in some way?" Her manner confirmed that she knew more, and she was fishing for a particular reply.

"You could say that," replied Karyn, slightly less monotone this time. *She's fucking with me,* she thought. Her ire was being stoked by Kalea's casual leading questions, as if she had no idea what she had done, and no contrition for doing it. The woman only continued to sip her tea in her graceful, feline manner.

Lifting her eyes up to meet Karyn's, with sympathy tinting her expression, Kalea asked gently, "Did something happen, child?"

That was more than Karyn could stand; she had had enough of being toyed with, and pushed back in her chair. "You **know** something happened!" she hissed. "I damn near lost my mind that night from whatever you put in those scones, woman!"

Kalea said nothing, looking at her with compassion as if she were an overtired child throwing a tantrum at bedtime. She was gauging Karyn's reaction, considering what to say next. At first, Karyn thought it was a look of condescension she saw on her face, but she quickly realized her error; there were only those beautiful, mottled, soft eyes looking deep into her soul, and her fury died down. Kalea moved her chair closer to Karyn until they were almost knee-to-knee, and sat back down facing her. Karyn found herself wondering why the anger had drained out of her so quickly, when she had been one step away from flipping the bistro table over onto the old woman. Soon though, she lost track of those thoughts and only focused on Kalea's face and its kaleidoscope irises. Her countenance became softer, and the dancing colors in those eyes began to swirl around slowly, like an eddy in the side of a stream. They drew her in like a whirlpool, and pulled her into a quiet place in her mind.

Kalea leaned forward slowly and, speaking in a slightly musical tone, addressed Karyn. "I wonder…if you can remember anything unusual…from before you ate the scone…anything at all…that comes to mind."

Karyn spoke without thinking; the little voice stepped up and vocalized in her stead. "The books…the books changed…became new…before we ate." Her own voice sounded to foreign to her, and she heard every word Kalea said from very far away.

"Does that seem…strange to you…like maybe…just maybe…something is missing…something you've forgotten…someone…you've forgotten…"

"Yes," Karyn's voice said.

"Where are you, Karyn?"

Her eyebrows knit together, and it was apparent that she was struggling with the question. Kalea quickly relieved her of the responsibility of answering by touching her on the shoulder lightly and confiding to her, "When you are ready to know, you will know…" She sat back and closed her own eyes, breaking Karyn's gaze and bringing her back to the moment with a clink of her china cup against the saucer. By the time Kalea had poured another cup of tea, Karyn had returned fully and was processing what just happened. She looked embarrassed and a bit ashamed, staying silent for a few minutes before speaking again.

"I'm sorry for accusing you of such a thing…I just…I couldn't think of anything else that might explain all the hallucinations." She looked away, avoiding the old woman's sympathetic face. "I'm… afraid." Karyn confessed.

"Whatever of, dear?" Kalea asked, genuinely concerned. Karyn shifted in her seat uncomfortably, unwilling to share her fears; admitting that she might be losing her grip on reality was not something she cared to put into words. Kalea, however, waved off her fear before it was spoken. "Oh, I know," she laughed disarmingly, "we're all so afraid of losing our faculties, aren't we? After all, our rational minds are what make us human, and so **superior** to other creatures." Karyn noted the slight sarcastic emphasis in her voice. "Perhaps if you looked at it as a matter of perspective, you might see things differently."

"Perspective?"

"Yes, perspective," Kalea repeated, selecting another crumbly shortbread-type something from the server. Karyn wanted one now that she had no fear of them being doped, but she restrained herself from eating. "Aside from my world-class scones," she smirked, waving at the tray, "what else do you remember eating?"

Karyn shook her head, and looked down. "Nothing. Nothing before that, but…" she paused, now looking to her left, "…but I didn't remember leaving here after that, and I woke up in my apartment, but it wasn't my apartment because things were different, they had changed and-"

"Changed how?" Kalea interrupted.

"Things disappeared; things that were always there before, like my bathroom mirror, and the appointments in my date planner, my cellphone contacts…" Karyn debated sharing more, lest the old woman judge her unstable. "That's why I thought you had put something in the scones, because I was hallucinating," she finished, quietly.

"That was a while ago, Karyn," she said gently. "Why didn't you come back and tell me?"

Karyn looked up with apologetic eyes. "I had every intention of doing so. I was so mad I stormed out of the apartment to confront you and…" she trailed off.

"And?"

"The shop wasn't here." Karyn didn't want to say more. *I know she thinks me nutters, now.*

"What **was** here, instead?"

She winced slightly at the question. "The Blue Lotus Cafe."

Kalea reached out and touched her hand reassuringly. "What did you do then?" she asked.

Karyn was at an impasse, and was considering the pros and cons of laying all her cards on the table before Kalea. The little voice said *share*, but she wasn't fully convinced she should. *If you want answers, you **must** share,* it said. Trusting the voice, Karyn described all the events that had happened from the time she entered the Blue Lotus, to the present moment, in excruciating detail. Nothing was left out, even the intimate memory of the garage. Divulging her private experiences was exhausting, but cathartic; it felt good to dump out the confusion, the fear, and the emotion onto her mysterious impromptu therapist, and Karyn immediately noticed her thought processes seemed clearer and less muddled. Finished revealing all she knew, she leaned back in her chair, and sighed heavily.

Kalea's face held all the compassion of the Buddha. "Feel better now?"

"Yes," Karyn nodded weakly. "But what does any of it **mean**?" she asked, absentmindedly reaching for a shortbread and biting it in half. She instantly stiffened when the flavors

hit her tongue; realizing what she had done, she looked at
directly at Kalea, who was smiling with amusement.

"Really, child…I thought we were past all that now,"
teasing her for her moment of paranoia. "If you keep this up,
you're going to give me a complex about my baking skills,"
she chuckled. "Are they **that** bad?"

Karyn felt the redness rising in her face, and chewed
with a mingling of embarrassment and pleasure. "Quite the
opposite," she mumbled through a final chew and swallow,
"These are exceptional as well. I can taste something flowery
in them."

"Lavender and lemon balm. My 'fairy shortbread'
recipe," she confirmed with satisfaction. Kalea leaned in and
said thoughtfully, "May I ask you something, Karyn?"
Nodding her approval, she continued, "Why do you think the
tea, scones, and the food you had at the Blue Lotus tasted so
good, and yet you have no memory of anything else you've
eaten before then, or ever?"

Karyn shrugged and looked disappointed in herself.
"Honestly, what I told you the first time I was here pretty much
summed it up. I have no idea why I can't remember, and I
don't recall when it all started. It feels like I was just dropped
into this life, and every day was the same as every other day. It
wasn't until the hallucinations began that I started to…**feel**
things more strongly. But I don't have a clue as to why that is.
I hoped **you** had an answer for me."

Kalea poured more tea for them both, then took Karyn's
one hand in her own. "If this hand were numb, and felt
nothing, how would it affect you?" she asked in a speculative
manner.

Karyn gave her question some serious consideration
before answering, and looked at her hand, imagining what that
would feel like. "I wouldn't feel any pain, which might be
nice, I guess, if I slammed it in a car door or something…but it
would also be bad, because I wouldn't know if I had cut myself
and was bleeding, or if it was badly infected; at least not unless
I could see the problem with my eyes, since I wouldn't be able
to feel those things."

"Would your hand function normally, like your other hand that could feel?" She watched her reaction to the question.

"I wouldn't think so. I mean, things are usually harder to use when they're numb - like when you get Novocaine at the dentist and your lips go numb, and you can't speak clearly until it wears off. I'd probably drop things a lot, or I doubt I could write."

"And would your numb hand look any different than your normal hand?"

Karyn shook her head and said, "Unless I damaged it from not being able to feel it, no."

Kalea released her hand into her lap and leaned back. "So, you wouldn't be able to feel a stab with a knife…but you also wouldn't feel the softness of a kitten's fur," she mused while sipping her tea. "You wouldn't feel a burn from the stove, nor the coolness of a mountain stream…"

Karyn thought she knew where Kalea was going with her comparisons, and was genuinely intrigued. "So you're saying I wouldn't feel the bad or the good; I would just feel nothing."

"Exactly, and you'd have to rely on your other senses to fill in the void of information." Kalea nodded, and sharpened her look. "Now replace your hand with your mind."

Karyn's eyes narrowed as she made the transition she had suggested. Her metaphor made sense when applied to her situation, and would explain the lack of feeling, the gray flannel covering that draped her life, but the causation was missing; the reason why her mind was, in effect, numb. She reviewed all the facts and added their variables to the theoretical equation, beginning to shed some light on the darker areas in question, but it was by no means clearly defined yet. Not only did she have to solve for 'X', the cause of her disconnected emotions and life, but she also had other factors that didn't fit the theorem; things like disappearing mirrors, dissolving guitarists, and buildings the appeared out of thin air.

"So what would could possibly cause my mind to go numb?" she asked, hoping for an easy answer that would magically reveal a solution.

"I don't have those answers, child; only you do."
Karyn suddenly remembered what Kalea had said from their
first meeting; "*Sometimes our minds try to protect us by
suppressing or hiding things that the subconscious deems
dangerous or painful.*"

"That doesn't tell me how to **fix** this," she said with
frustration, and clenched her hand into a fist. Kalea's eyebrow
moved north slightly.

"Have you not fixed some of this already?" she asked,
after a sip from her cup. When Karyn appeared confused, she
pointed to the shortbreads and scones on the tray. "Can you
still taste them?" Karyn nodded. "And does your nose still
work?" Another nod. "And I assume you can still hear me,"
Kalea spoke into her cup, "so I guess you've been relying on
your senses after all." There was no condescension in her
voice, just simply stated facts. She placed the cup down
noiselessly on the saucer and moved the set aside.

"But, I have no idea where to start. Can't you help
me?" Karyn implored. Kalea was sympathetic, but unmoved.

"Use your senses. Use your senses to live and connect
and feel as best you can. Not all of you is lost; there are some
senses that have come back because your mind felt it was safe
to do so. Use them to **live**, Karyn, and they will take you
where you need to go."

10
Dreaming

The atmosphere was cooler and fresher when she stepped out of the hypnotist's shop, and Karyn felt like there was forward movement in her odd journey, although she couldn't say if it was helpful. Her anxiety level was barely registering, and the little voice was murmuring in approval. She felt better than before, and that was good enough for right now. By the time she unlocked her apartment door, she was ready for a nap; Karyn was almost asleep before she laid down on the bed, but her mind stayed active.

Wine on her lips...a blanket beneath her...the sweet meadow grass smell...Karyn could see the white clouds lazily drifting across the blue sky. Lying on her back, she could hear the chirping of the birds, and the low thrum of frogs at the water's edge. She was sure a more perfect day had never existed, and surely not with more perfect company.

Rolling over on her side and curling up underneath his arm, she studied him closely. The soft scruff on his face, the thick eyelashes, the most nibble-worthy earlobes...but she dared not wake him now. His breathing was slow and steady, a sign that the huge picnic lunch and sangria had done their job, and he was safely off to dreamland. William had been working non-stop for the last three weeks and deserved some rest; between the endless car repairs at the garage and his gigging at night, he'd barely had any time for sleep or her - yet he always chose her over sleep. The breeze ruffled his hair gently, and she wondered what she had done to deserve such a man.

It was almost two years to the day since they first met over a blown tire in Kenny's filthy garage, and her whole life had taken a major turn for the better as a result. He convinced her to quit her miserable job, and she found another shortly after that was both satisfying and paid better. The money was good, she was able to go back to college without having to live in poverty, and even secured an internship at the museum. Karyn was steadily moving towards her dream of graduate school; something she never thought was attainable prior to meeting William. She'd never met anyone like him before; his presence added color and depth, a dimensionality, to every experience. His was the love she'd always wanted, and never thought she could have. He made everything easier, more relaxed, more positive; her life was immensely richer with him in it.

She sighed contentedly and closed her eyes, letting the breeze bring her the clean and green scents of late spring. The delicate smell of wildflowers mixed with water soaked into her lungs, removing the stale air and infusing her body from the inside out with peace. The scent of Will's skin was overlaid upon it, reminding her of their lovemaking this morning. He had crawled in at an ungodly hour after several sets at the club, leaving a trail of clothes on his way to bed, only to delay his precious sleep time for the carnal satisfaction of sliding slowly between Karyn's legs and waking her in the best way. She trembled slightly from the memory of it, snuggling closer into his side. A pre-dawn wakeup call like that was lovely, but she was concerned he was burning the candle at both ends too brightly; at some point she feared he may fall asleep at the wheel driving home from one of these gigs.

Karyn was Will's second love. His first love was music, and she swore she would never interfere with anything that gave him that much joy. As fine and attentive a lover as Will was, he was an even more exquisite guitarist. He had fully devoted himself to the study of classical and modern guitar, deconstructing the techniques of master guitarists in every genre. Thousands of hours of his life were dedicated to studying Andres Segovia, Richard Thompson, Robert Johnson, and Chet Atkins, to name but a few. When he played, Will didn't just strum the strings - he made love to the guitar, bringing the finest out of the instrument, acoustic or electric. With each performance he was one step closer to getting noticed by the right people and going professional, and Karyn wholeheartedly supported him in his dreams.

She thought he was dreaming now. The slight twitch in his hand or foot was a sure sign, but she peeked to see if his eyes were moving under those beautiful lashes. Without moving her head, she started her vision at the soft edge of his lips and moved east to the rounded tip of his nose, across its strong bridge, and rested on his gray-green eyes, which were looking directly at her. She scowled, and he smiled.

"You're supposed to be catching up on your sleep, William Richard," she said in her best disapproving mother tone.

He rolled over on his side and brushed the hair out of her eyes, cupping her cheek with his hand. "How can any man bother with something as unimportant as sleep, when a woman as beautiful as you is lying by his side?" He pressed his lips against her own with a delicate insistence, his tongue gently stealing a taste of sangria from her mouth. She melted, powerless against his argument, even if it was a lie; Karyn was neither a plain jane nor a stunning beauty, but she felt like the only woman on earth when she was with him. Each and every kiss was like their first, still.

"Babe, you've got to rest more. You can't keep this pace up forever. Something's got to give at some point, and I don't want it to be you," she said, resting her head on his arm.

"I'll have plenty of time to rest when I'm doing studio work," he chided her. "Gotta make hay while the sun shines, honey. The contacts and networking from my nights will pay off...I just can't say when."

"What happens then?"

*He cocked an eyebrow and looked at her sideways, knowing exactly what she was getting at. "Seriously, Karyn...baby, you know neither of us know the future, and I don't make promises I can't keep." He kissed her again, deeply. "What I **do** know," he said as he grazed his lips* *against hers, "is that I love you more than life; that will never change."*

The sky clouded over, gray for a moment, as Karyn contemplated their potential future. She knew somehow they would be separated at some point, even if it was temporary, and the thought of being without him was beyond painful. A tear formed in the corner of her eye, and William caught it with his thumb. The breeze became chilly, and she shivered with the change in temperature. The birds were suddenly quiet, and the frogs had ceased thrumming.

"We will always be together, Karyn...as long as our hearts and minds are connected and remember each other," he whispered in her ear, "I will find you...just like I'm trying to find you now."

William's words were ringing in her ears when she opened her eyes. Although no longer surrounded by wildflowers and nature, Karyn could still smell his scent all over her; she inhaled deeply before he vanished from her nose. Her body was flushed, responding to the experience of being so close to him, seeing him, touching him, and the lost knowledge of their history. She laid in the bed, reveling in the vividness of the dream. *Is this the way I can get back my memories? By dreaming them?*

She knew the importance of dreaming in other cultures from her history and anthropology studies, but never thought of applying them outside of their cultural context. She had no idea how to go about directing her dreams to get the results she desired; a shaman was what she really needed to gain control of her dreamtime, and without one, she was forced to stumble through the process and hope for the best. It wasn't an impossible task; she had accidentally gotten a glimpse of the lucid dreaming door just before the dream ended. Will never said those last words the day they were in the meadow, and she knew something was odd when the weather changed and the natural soundscape became silent. She had been too taken by the memory's moment with him to remove herself enough to seize control of the dream.

It struck her as odd that she would even know that was what she needed to do, save for some fuzzy recollections from her college years. Those hazy memories of her hallucinogen-fueled lucid dreaming experiments at Cornell were just clear enough to guide her the next time she was asleep. Provided that her subconscious mind didn't object to her information request, and that Kalea's statement about the mind was correct, Karyn assumed that her subconscious may volunteer bits of history, as long as it didn't pose any kind of threat to her. At least, that's what she hoped.

She couldn't spend her days in bed dreaming, however; Kalea had made it clear that more effort was required of Karyn if she was to accomplish her goal, and that was only one piece of the puzzle, perhaps. Her job now was to use her senses to get answers, even if she had no clue how to do so.

11
Feel

Considering it was summer, it should have been warmer. The day felt less oppressive than was normal, and Karyn noted the breezy coolness as she wandered around the park. Cricket season was more than two months away, yet she could hear the buzzing of the cicadas mingled with the occasional cricket chirp. The juncos she saw in the hidden park had also been out of their natural season as well, and she could smell the slight hint of brownness in the air, despite the abundance of summer green. None of these things would have commanded her attention until recently, but the spontaneous visit to the hypnotist's shop left a strong, lingering impression on her; it sharpened her focus, tuning her in to the reality around her. With this new, extremely daunting, quest that she had no map, nor guidebook for - aside from Kalea's instructions - throwing herself into outside world seemed to be the best course of action, and she hoped the constant external stimuli would shake something loose in her head.

The grassy earth gave gently under her feet while she walked, and she was reminded of the stolen moments alone with Will in her dream. More than anything, Karyn wanted to see him again. There were so many things she needed to ask him, and only he had those answers. The dream in the meadow unlocked and cracked open an emotional window that she never knew existed before; one where she could see more of her lost self than ever, but not enough to satisfy all her questions, or quell the distant longing that was beneath the surface.

The largest oak tree in the center of the park beckoned to her, its broad expanse of shade casting a dappled shadow under its canopy, and Karyn found a mossy spot to plant herself and lean against the trunk's rough bark. Screening out the visual distractions of Frisbee throwers and picnickers by closing her eyelids, the sounds of the park became vibrant, almost colorful in their audio detail. Like the coffee cafe, the voices and noises of the park told a story; as she listened in more closely, the conversations became clearer, almost as if she was standing behind the speakers. *My awareness gets better the more I practice*, she realized, and increased the intensity of her focus.

Karyn's skin woke from its slumber, tingling with each puff of breeze, each pressure wave of air from passersby. The hair on her arms stood at attention, relaxed, and then rolled with the next breath of wind. She felt the coolness of the earth beneath her and smelled the water vapor floating over from the fountains, crawling with laughing, splashing children. *Life...all around me*, she thought...*this is what I've forgotten...I've forgotten how to feel.*

She looked over to the kids, kicking water at each other in the fountain pools. She envied them, their vibrancy, the glow they had about them as if life had poured pure sunshine into their bodies. So innocent and so alive, without the burden of the regrets that come with adulthood and responsibility. They were fully in the moment of living, experiencing life without expectation or fear, and charging ahead boldly It occurred to Karyn that there were lessons to learn by watching them. Their fearlessness and optimism expanded their world, giving them new experiences and opportunities for growth; *children are dynamic and changing by nature*, she commented silently, *and yet I'm mired in stagnancy.*

The contrast between them made her wonder what she was so afraid of, or more to the point, what her subconscious was so afraid of that it needed to erase her memory. Karyn couldn't conceive of what would create such a schism in anyone, especially not someone with as boring a life as her own. "If I **am** hiding something, why am I hiding it from myself?" she wondered out loud, not caring if anyone could hear her.

Pain, said the little voice.

Karyn hadn't expected that answer, and instead of indulging her urge to be dismissive, she considered the information the little voice offered, combining it with the questions Kalea had asked her. *"You wouldn't be able to feel a stab with a knife…but you also wouldn't feel the softness of a kitten's fur,"* she had said. Karyn's hibernating senses had only **just** come back, and not without confusion and emotional turmoil; she could only assume that if there was pain, it had to be substantial for her own mind to go to such lengths to protect her.

As she sat beneath the grand oak working through scenarios, she heard the sonata again. Faint, but within the edge of her hearing. Someone was whistling that tune, and they weren't very far away.

Karyn kept her ears pinned forward to track the source of the melody, moving through groups of people with singleminded purpose, always following the sound of the whistling. Stepping out of the park's boundaries and into the city proper, she picked up her pacing, but the sonata seemed no louder. It led her down several side streets, eventually terminating in an alcove with two tatty lawn chairs, one of which was occupied by a homeless man in dark sunglasses; he was the one whistling William's sonata. A small sign, handwritten on a piece of cardboard, read "whistled tunes - $1". A large coffee can sat beside the sign.

"Excuse me," she said approaching the man with some hesitation, "where did you hear that song? Does it have a name?"

He lifted his head in the direction of her voice, and smiled a smile full of missing teeth. "You like that one, eh?" He scratched the side of his sandy beard with a grimy hand while he pondered her question. "I don't rightly know where I first heard it…but it might come to me sooner with the right inspiration," nudging the can towards her with his foot. Karen fished around in her pocket and dropped a five dollar bill in the can. His eyebrows peeked out over the edge of the sunglasses. "You're mighty generous, missy," he said appreciatively, and removed his glasses to get a better look at her.

His eyes were completely opaque, with irises almost as snowy as the sclera. Although obviously blind, his china-white eyes tracked her movements as she shifted uncomfortably from one foot to the other, and Karyn imagined the man possessed some kind of superpower, the type only granted as compensation for his disability.

"I'm beginning to remember better now, but you'll have to answer a few questions first." He reached in the can and pulled out her money, fingering it gently like a page of braille. "What's your name, girl?"

"Karyn." *I'm not giving this derelict any more personal info than that,* she thought to herself. "And your name is…"

"Sunträumer. Benedict Sunträumer. Ben to my friends." He stuffed the bill into his pocket and covered his ruined eyes in sunglasses again. "Of course," he drawled, "I'm not sure if we're friends or not just yet."

"We might be, if you tell me where you learned that song, Mr. Sunträumer." Karyn had an inkling of the type of personality she was dealing with now, and she knew that being accommodating would go further than demands.

"Ha!" Sunträumer chuckled, slapping his hand down on his knee, "I knew I liked you, Karyn. You've got some fire in there after all. C'mere and take a load off while I tell you what I know about that tune." He patted the chair next to him; she hoped it wouldn't collapse under her like it looked it would. She sat gingerly, waiting for the seat to give way under her and dump her ungracefully on the ground. Sunträumer waited until she got settled and began to whistle the song in its entirety.

Despite his less than attractive exterior of dirt and missing teeth, his whistling was clear, smooth, and perfectly keyed. Karyn felt her emotions stirring as he worked the sonata's phrasing, refrain, and coda with clarity and inflection worthy of a master musician. By the time he reached the final few bars, Karyn had tears in her eyes and a lump in her throat.

"Was that the song you were lookin' for?" he asked her in a quieter tone than his earlier, raucous one.

She nodded, then spoke up when she remembered he was blind. "Yes," she sniffed, "Where did you learn it?"

Sunträumer leaned his arm on one knee, speaking confidentially. "I first heard it many years ago when I was in Germany. I was stationed over there and whooping it up on leave, half-shot in the ass already from really good German beer, and it wasn't even five o'clock yet." His face lit up while reminiscing. "I had just come out of the beer garden, and it was clear as day, coming over the other side of the fence. Couldn't see who was playing it, though. It was the kind of tune that sticks with you, ya know? Anyways, I hadn't heard it since, well, until the other day. I heard it from a couple streets over…someone was playing it on a guitar." He leaned back and smiled holes. "Man, whoever they were, they sure could play."

Karyn sighed, disappointed in the amount of information Sunträumer had to offer. "Why the heavy breath, missy? Not what you were looking for?" he asked.

"Not really. I need to find the man that was playing it," she said defeatedly. "It's important that I talk to him."

He shook his head in disagreement. "What makes you think you need to talk to him? You don't need to talk to him at all." Sunträumer wagged a finger at Karyn, and his attitude seemed to shift. "Your problem is that you can see, so you **can't** see. You can't see what's really going on, little missy." Karyn was silent, but becoming more annoyed as he became more animated. *What the hell does he know about my life anyway?* He pointed to his sunglasses. "When you got eyes like this, you **really** begin to **see** things, **learn** things about people. You learn that the eyes **lie** sometimes, that we rely on them too much. They hide things, cover things up," he said emphatically, waving his hands around in the air, "until you don't know what's real and what's not!"

Karyn stood up to leave, having second thoughts about the whole conversation, believing she wasted her time with a crazy street person. Four steps away from him, Sunträumer commented to her back, "That lump in your throat and tears in your eyes were real, though, weren't they? You oughta look **inside** for an answer to **that**."

She stopped walking and looked back over her shoulder at him, ready to snap a sharp reply, but Sunträumer was already oblivious to her presence, whistling another tune, and it wasn't Will's sonata.

Two hours later, Karyn was back under the big oak tree, less annoyed, and doing forensic analysis on the blind man's diatribe. She was sifting through Sunträumer's conversation for the valuable bits of information, like a desperate goldminer panning for ore, only now she wasn't sure if she had struck gold, or a pile of pyrite. His rant was splashing around in the back of her head with other proven, valuable information, her gut didn't disagree, and the little voice was silent; whether that silence was an acknowledgment of truth or a confirmation of falsehoods, she wasn't sure, but Karyn felt there was honesty in what Sunträumer said. She just needed time to figure it all out.

Time was passing, however, and the sun was sinking slowly into the city skyline. Gathering herself up from the mossy base of the tree, she wandered towards home with a preoccupied mind. Her thoughts always came back to William, where he was, what he was doing, and what they were to each other. Her feet carried her along on their own, taking streets she wouldn't recognize had she been paying attention, and leading into a part of the city unknown to her. The noticeable absence of sound was what caught her ear. It was numbingly silent, and completely unnatural.

Now on alert, Karyn's senses kicked into high gear. The small side street she found herself on was empty. The amber streetlights were dimly glowing as they warmed up, casting small pools of light on alternate sides of the street, the end of which was almost pitch black. She squinted to see beyond the furthest light, to no avail, and decided to take another route home, but the distant cry from the darkness made her stop short and turn around.

It was a pitiful wail, like a wounded animal caught in a trap, but it was definitely human. Karyn couldn't identify the gender of the individual making the noise; it was throaty, harsh and androgynous, full of emotion in short bursts of sound. It gave her chills. *Someone's in trouble…maybe they're injured,* she thought. *I should probably see if they need help…*

Her rationalization overrode her better judgment, forcing Karyn's legs to move in the direction of the darkness. Each cry loosened her resolve to stay uninvolved, such was the suffering of the poor person at the inky end of the street. With slow, measured steps, Karyn cautiously moved closer, staying within the puddles of sodium light. She was a third of the way there when a voice, a child's voice, broke the spell.

"You don't want to go down there!"

Karyn shot a glance over her shoulder to see a girl, about ten years old, behind her. There was not a single soul on the street with her a second ago, and yet now she was not alone. The child stood adamantly, hands on her hips, with a serious look that was out of place on a face as young as hers, and her dark eyes had age to them. The girl had an unnatural air to her; her dark brown bobbed hair didn't move with the breeze. "You don't want to go down there!" she repeated.

Karyn took another step down the street. "But someone needs help, and-"

"-No! You can't!" the child shouted and ran up behind her, hooking her arms around Karyn's elbow. She was surprisingly strong for her size, and by leaning backwards she succeeded in halting Karyn from walking further. Her flawless, creamy complexion was becoming red with exertion, a small vein was raised on her forehead from the strain. Another wail came from the darkness, commanding Karyn forward; the girl tensed in anticipation of being pulled along, and dug her sneakers into the pavement.

Listen, whispered the little voice.

Keeping her eyes locked on the black end of the street and without looking back at the child, Karyn asked, "Why? Why shouldn't I help?"

The girl's body relaxed a little, and her fingers ceased their digging into her bicep. "Because…you're not ready," she said quietly. Karyn now turned to face her, debating what to do in her head. The scene had become surreal. *This is another one of those moments…like I'm dreaming. I need to take control of this dream.*

"Ready for what?" she demanded. The girl shook her head slowly with eyes cast at the asphalt. Karyn pulled her arm

free from the child's grasp and asked again, forcefully,
"Ready…for…what?"

Her big dark eyes lifted up and locked with Karyn's; her voice was emotionless when she said a single word, "Pain." As if on cue, another wail, worse and more desperate than all the other cries, erupted from the darkness, and Karyn bolted. Running full bore towards the sound, she distanced herself from the girl with all her might. The street began to stretch and distort, and the air felt like she was running into a volcano. The heat was suffocating, unbearable, and ate up all the oxygen in her lungs. Karyn could hear the child angrily shouting behind her, "I won't let you! You cannot go!" as her vision blurred into a whiteout and a deafening ringing filled her ears.

12
Protection

Her snowblindness began to fade away, and the noise in her ears dialed down to zero. The brightness lessened as the space surrounding Karyn filled in with the outlines of walls, then furniture, then objects. Thin lines ran in all directions, as if she was inside of a giant Etch-A-Sketch drawing in all the details of the room with automated precision and clarity. Color permeated the outlined objects as if painted by an invisible brush, flooding in from the center and spreading to the edges, until the entire room was fully colored and complete. When the last bit of painting finished, Karyn stood in a very familiar space - the living room of her old Haddonfield apartment.

She hadn't recognized it until the final lines had been drawn and colored; it was then that the smell of old varnished wood floors and magnolia blossoms caressed her, coming through the tilted stained glass transom windows. As her eyes made contact with each piece of furniture, each bit of artwork, their history sprung up in her memory; where she bought them, what she paid for them, and who was with her at the time was instantly restored to her. Karyn walked through the living room, touching the surfaces as she walked by. The smooth waxed wood of the table, the cool ceramic of the thrown saltware lamp made her fingers tingle with sensation. "This is amazing," she whispered incredulously. "Every detail is correct…nothing seems to be missing at all." The blown glass vase held fresh lilacs, and she twirled her fingers around the tassel on a throw pillow, a housewarming present her Mother had given her when she first moved out; the velveteen still smelled faintly of her Mother's perfume. Her eyes welled with tears; it had been years since both her parents had passed.

What I wouldn't give to see them again, even just for a moment, Karyn thought, closing her eyes to recall their faces in her mind. They had been so excited to hear that she and Will were moving in together. They adored him. *If only our professional goals hadn't pulled us apart...*

She moved to the window and checked to see if the street was the same. The giant magnolia partially blocked her view, as it always had, but Karyn could see the sidewalk littered with blossom petals; the creamy, paper-like cutouts dotted the concrete under the amber streetlight. Her old green Karman Ghia, replete with rust spots in both back fenders and a dented back bumper, was nosed in as close as she could legally be to the fire hydrant, where she always parked it. A cursory glance down the street confirmed who her neighbors were; Karyn knew everyone on the block back then, and she and Will had made fast friends with most of them, all in their twenties and trying so hard to be grown-ups. Barely apparent from the window, tucked behind another tree, was a familiar set of taillights and a Woodstock Company bumper sticker. Karyn's breath caught in her throat. *That's got to be Will's car! It has to be!*

Her rational mind began to work out what that really meant, given that she wasn't exactly sure **where** she was, or in what state. Was this a dream, a hallucination, or some kind of alternate reality? If Will's car was here, is Will? Her heart beat faster as Karyn struggled with possibilities, the slew of questions that were bombarding her; all of which were abruptly halted by the scratching sound of a key in the apartment door lock.

This is my apartment, so if it's my apartment, then who's coming in? She scrambled to hide before the door opened. It was a small apartment with little storage, and her mind raced to remember anyplace that might be big enough to stow away. Behind the high-backed, overstuffed wing chair in the corner seemed to be her best bet; there was space enough for her to squeeze in and it was dark enough to conceal her for the moment, at least until she came up with a better plan. Karyn dove for the corner, and tucked up tightly as the door

swung open and laughter erupted in the foyer. Male and
female laughter.

"Seriously, Will, you need to get new tires on that thing
before one of them blows."

Impossible! she thought. *That's MY voice - but I'm
right here!*

"What's the matter, baby? Afraid I'll meet a pretty girl
at some greasy garage when she changes my tire?"

Will's voice! What the hell is going on?

The sound of grocery bags on the counter, the thud of a
purse, and other noises of settling in came from around the
corner. Karyn strained her ears to hear more, but the moments
of silence were telling; they were intimate, flecked with the
small sighs of lovers in between kisses. The humor of her
situation was not lost on her. She was hiding in her own
apartment from her other self who was kissing the man she, or
rather, they both, loved. The fact that she had nothing to gauge
what this moment actually was kept her hidden. If this was a
dream, or even if this was real, making her presence known
may disturb something and prevent her from getting more
information, more answers she desperately needed. As badly
as she wanted to see William, Karyn resolved to stay put and
watch from her secret spot in the corner.

Footsteps moved in her direction. They were coming
into the living room, and Karyn prayed they would leave the
lights off. There was just enough streetlight for her to see in
the room without betraying her position, but she couldn't hide
from a floor lamp. If they flicked the switch, she was exposed.
She held her breath as the couple entered.

William strode in first, and walked straight to the
window, standing exactly where Karyn had been gazing
outside a moment before. It was the Will of that time, young,
beautiful, and so real that she could almost smell his scent from
across the room. The sodium vapor lamplight gave him a
golden glow, although he seemed to be glowing from the inside
out. A look of confusion flashed across his face, and he
scanned around the room as if something was out of place, but
he couldn't pinpoint what. He was rumpled and handsome,
just as she remembered him.

Lighter footfalls signaled the approach of her doppelganger, and Karyn braced for what she was going to see. As she expected, true to the time period, her earlier self trotted in and cuddled up to William's back. She nuzzled into the space between his shoulder blades, wrapping her hands around his waist. Karyn flinched, feeling a twinge of jealousy at seeing another woman touch him. *This is crazy to feel jealous of her*, she admonished herself silently, *because she's **me**, and I doubt any of this is real.* Still, her twin's face was turned away from Karyn, and all she could really see was another woman in the sacred space that she longed to be within.

"I'm pretty tired, Will - do you mind if I take a nap after I grab a shower? The groceries can wait; there's nothing frozen so we can put them away later," the younger Karyn said, stretching up to kiss him from behind. He twisted around and nodded as she kissed him, but something in his face was conflicted. Karyn could see his eyebrows knit with a slight pained look. He was struggling with something, and her twin was oblivious to it. She smiled as she vacated the room, her footsteps moving out and up the stairs, ending with the bang of the bathroom door. *That door never did close right*, she smiled, but her amusement faded when Will turned back to the window. The slight pained look was now a look of deep contemplation and sadness.

Remember, the little voice said, and Karyn instantly began comparing the last few scenes with her gradually returning memory of their time together. Although her memory was far from trustworthy, her gut knew something was wrong; some behavioral inconsistencies in the couple's interaction told her this was not a true memory. For one, Karyn never remembered napping, or even wanting to take a nap. Sleeping anything less than several hours only served to make her more groggy, so she always skipped taking a nap and opted for full sleep. The doppelganger's choice to leave the groceries was also a red flag. She hated to leave anything out on the counters because it made the kitchen feel cramped. *Does this mean I'm dreaming?* She wondered.

Stuck behind the wingback chair, Karyn contemplated what those inconsistent behaviors meant, all the while watching William from her hiding space. If this was a dream, then what was the harm in revealing her position? Now that her twin was upstairs, there was no chance of meeting herself, although Karyn had no idea if that would make any difference in this situation. Perhaps if this was an alternate reality or if she had mastered time travel accidentally, that might pose a problem, a Butterfly Effect, but that seemed ridiculous to her. This was obviously a dream, but seeing Will so close, so real, dug deeply at her insides. She wanted nothing more than to talk to him, touch him, and be the Karyn nuzzled into his back.

Will stiffened, and looked again around the room as if expecting to see something. Karyn tightened her crouch silently, watching him intensely as he shook his head and rubbed his face up into his hair. "You've got real problems, buddy, torturing yourself with dreams and illusions…" he muttered, and sulked over to the couch, throwing himself down as if exhausted. He was looking older, and the years were rising up through his skin. Karyn was transfixed. *What did he mean by that? Was my thinking all wrong?* That one sentence from his lips brought new confusion that she wasn't prepared for. She debated what to do next, leaning to one side to get a better view of him and bumping the chair with her knee.

It barely moved an inch, but it was a noisy inch. The feet of the wingback scraped against the varnish, and Will's head snapped around to see what made the noise. His entire posture became defensive, and he edged off the couch, never taking his eyes off the chair. Slowly standing, he moved sideways towards the window, where they always kept an Easton baseball bat, just in case of intruders. "I'm really not liking this dream now," he mumbled quietly while he reached behind the curtain. "It's starting to get weird…"

Karyn considered her options, which had quickly dwindled down to only two: risk getting beaten in her dream with her own baseball bat in her own apartment by her own boyfriend, or come out and deal with the dream reality before her. She chose the latter, and cleared her throat as she peeked around the side of the chair. She kept her eyes on Will, and slowly rose from behind the furniture.

William's eyes widened for a moment, then readjusted to what he was seeing. Karyn thought he'd be shocked, but his reaction was completely unlike her expectation. He just stood there, shaking his head from one side to the other slowly, with an odd look of relief, surprise, and confusion all rolled into one. "This is, by far, the oddest dream I've had yet," he said, dropping the bat back into its place.

Karyn decided to play along with his notion, since she herself wasn't sure which one of them was dreaming, or was the dream. She stepped forward into the center of the room so he could see her better, and she, him. He looked her over carefully, small changes in his face signaling that he was unsure of what her presence meant, or what he was supposed to do now that she was here. "What's so odd about it?" she asked tentatively, hoping he would proffer some information she could use to determine where she was and what was really happening.

He smiled a crooked smile. "Oh, I don't know, Karyn…you just walked upstairs to take a shower and a nap. A you that is considerably younger, in an apartment that we haven't lived in since…" He shifted his stance and waved an arm around the room. "…since college, right? And **this** you was hiding behind a chair. Doesn't that seem a bit odd to you?" She could see behind his smooth exterior that Will was trying to reconcile the weirdness as well.

"Anything can happen in dreams, Will." She was three feet from him, and he smelled like she remembered. All she wanted to do was touch him, crush herself against his chest and tell him she missed him. It was maddening, but she feared breaking the spell they shared with any rash moves.

"True," he agreed, moving back to the couch and taking a seat, "but I'm not sure this is a dream. Well, I'm not sure **all** of this is a dream just yet." Karyn moved over and sat down across from him. She could feel the coolness of the leather through her clothes, and visions of them making love there flashed before her eyes. Her face flushed with the memory of their passion, wondering if he remembered as well. She forced herself to concentrate on this moment and not lose herself to remembrance.

"What part of this do you think is a dream, then?" *Please tell me what you know, Will…because I'm not sure myself.*

He sank back into the couch, but kept his eyes on her. *He looks relaxed, but he's really uneasy,* she thought. She had seen this mannerism once before, when they were almost mugged in the city; Will used that deception to catch the mugger off guard and coldcock him when he dropped his guard. "Not sure. I probably shouldn't be questioning it; I mean, I just spent the last hour reliving my youth with the woman I **loved**, and now I'm sitting with the woman I **love**," he said as he patted the sofa, "on the couch we made love on." Karyn felt herself flushing again, and Will's eyes narrowed imperceptibly; her reaction had caught his attention for some reason, and his focus intensified. "I know the earlier bit was a dream - I've had it before - but this…this is different. This **feels** different." *Which one of us is the dreamer? Am I the dream after all?* She could feel his gaze burning through her now. He leaned forward and asked her pointedly, "Are you real, Karyn?"

His question disturbed her inside, and she shifted uncomfortably on the cushion. "I'm not sure…and I'm not sure what's real either. I don't know which one of us is the dream, and which is the dreamer." Her eyes started to fill. Will immediately reached for her, but she retreated with a yell. "NO! Don't!"

"Why not?" he demanded, his face showing a mix of desperation and hope. "Why can't I touch you? Tell me!"

"I don't know!" she yelled back, crying. The emotions were rising too fast for her to keep down. "I'm afraid! I'm afraid that you'll disappear and I won't find you again!" she sobbed into her hands.

William's eyes widened slowly as he pieced things together, and he softened his tone with her. Respecting her wishes, he did not touch her, but leaned in and spoke quietly. "Baby, I know the woman upstairs is a dream. I can touch her, kiss her, make love to her, and it **feels** real, but she's **not** real. She's a dream." He pursed his lips and pressed them together, carefully measuring his words. "If I can touch you, then you're probably a dream, too, but if I can't…" he paused as he extended his hand to her face, "…then I know you're just lost, Karyn."

She lifted her face almost in time to ask what he meant by "lost", but Will's hand had already moved to caress her cheek; the passage of his hand through her felt like a hot breeze, but met no resistance. She was incorporeal, and the look on Will's face confirmed it. She clutched at his hands, unable to connect, and panicked as the room began its slow dissolution, just like the park had. William was still solid, but beginning to fade. His face radiated love and happiness, despite the tears falling from his eyes, and the words he spoke were clear and calm.

"I love you, Karyn. Find your way back to me, baby. I'll wait for you."

13
Pledge

"*William! Stop joking around and hand me that hammer, dammit!*"

He held the tool just out of her reach and made her jump for it. He enjoyed torquing her up occasionally, just enough to get her bouncing around in her tank top, and her eyes flash with a bit of fire.

"*Your parents didn't raise you properly. What's the magic word?*" *he said, egging her on.*

"*My parents raised me to not need a man - at least not a man like you - who is now impeding my progress to get this apartment finished before classes start!*" *she said, jumping up and snatching the hammer from his hand faster than he could move it away. She tapped the hammer head in her hand lightly and gave him an insincere stink-eye. "*I've half a mind to crack you with this, except-*"

"*I know, I know...you don't want to break the hammer,*" *he finished with a wink. His hazel eyes had the devil in them, and Karyn doubted that she'd ever get anything done as long as he was here. Given that they only had a few days left together before Europe called him away, she wondered why hanging artwork* **now** *was so important to her. Deep inside, though, she knew. She knew she was avoiding the reality of their separation, filling that gap between his presence and his impending absence with frenetic activity, in order to lessen the pain of him leaving.*

They had agreed to support one another in their professional careers and personal growth, almost from the beginning of their relationship; in fact, it was that foundation of trust and unconditional love that made their relationship unlike any other. The "freedoms" that she and Will allowed each other, which most people would consider dangerous to the stability of a relationship because they emphasized individual growth over bonding as a couple, were not freedoms - they were inalienable human rights. Rights that Karyn and Will had discussed, debated, defined and agreed upon over their time together. Rights that had expanded their life experiences and made them better people. Rights that bonded them beyond the normal connection that couples share in a relationship. Rights that would divide them physically in a few days.

As Karyn tapped the picture hook into the wall, her throat became tight, her eyes became watery, and she missed the nail head and banged a dent into the plaster. "Shit!" she grumbled, and touched her forehead to the wall in frustration; her hair hid the fact that she was crying.

Will came closer to inspect the damage and tried to allay her irritation. "Awww, don't freak, babe - I can patch that up in no time. Let me go get the spackle and-" By then, she had tilted her head back, and he could see the wet streams on her cheeks, and realized this was no frustration from a missed hammer blow. "Honey," he said gently, taking the hammer from Karyn and turning her around by the shoulders to pull her close. "Come here." She burrowed herself into his embrace and let go in a round of soft cries and sniffles, her chest heaving while he slowly ran his one hand through her hair, over and over until she calmed down.

*"I'm sorry...I really am," she said, muffled into his shirt. "I thought I could be cool with all this...and... I **know** it's the right thing for us to do...but..." Another short round of sobbing ensued, and Will led her over to the sofa to sit down. "It's just that...I don't want us to be apart, ever...but I want you to pursue your dream...and I don't wanna let you go, but that would be so selfish of me...and I...I..." The tears flowed again in a torrent again, until she was almost breathless from crying.*

Will continued to hold her close, and said nothing, allowing her space to expend the pent-up emotions she'd held in check for weeks. She'd been a staunch supporter of him leaving on tour from the moment he got the call from his agent; initially she was thrilled for him, but as the days progressed, he could see that the full impact of accepting this job was sinking in, and stoking her fears. Karyn had been careful to hide them, so she wouldn't influence his decision, but with the date of departure looming ever closer, she couldn't keep her chin up anymore.

As she settled down again, his eyes began misting over, partially from how their future separation was affecting her, but also because he was uneasy with the situation, as well. Being away from the only woman he'd ever completely been himself with, the only woman who had ever loved him without reservation or restriction, was not something he looked forward to, but it was a necessary step if he was to move forward in his music career. All the long nights, poorly paid gigs, and the struggling artist lifestyle would be a thing of the past with Europe; the opportunity to tour and play with world-class musicians was a rare chance, and if he proved his worth, they'd have a comfortable future together. She'd have her doctorate and a guaranteed position at the university, and he'd never be without work in the music industry. But, part of him was afraid that they might lose sight of each other in the process. Will knew exactly how Karyn was struggling. He was struggling as well.

He stroked her cheek with his thumb, the wetness of her tears softening the roughness of his callus, while she settled down in her breathing and her body relaxed. She curled up tighter to him and said in an almost whisper, "I'm going to lose you. I just know it." She felt William's body tense for a moment, and she lifted her head up to look at his face. The normally jovial expression he wore was tinged with poignancy, and she could see below the surface that they shared the same concern. "You feel it too, don't you?" she asked, nervously. "You're afraid the temporary separation might become permanent, that we'll lose each other permanently, right?"

Will shook his head, softly correcting her assumption. "I'm not sure what will happen, but none of knows what the future holds, baby." He slid down on the couch and pulled her up along side of him, still running his fingers over her hair.

"What I do know is this: I know I love you more than life. I know that nothing worth having comes without risk, and risk is an inherent part of life." He paused to kiss the top of her head. "I know the life of a musician is hard, and even harder on the ones you love. And I know that some paths we have to walk alone...until we don't."

"But I don't want to walk alone; I want to walk with you, Will, so you won't have to be alone...and I won't be alone, either," she said, reaching up to hold the hand in her hair. He knew she'd begin bargaining again, and delicately put a damper on it, bringing her hand to his lips to kiss her fingertips.

"We've already talked about this, Karyn," he sighed. "I've got to go. You've got to stay."

"But-"

"-But nothing. You can't do your doctoral research on the road with me, and if you leave here now you can't teach the undergrad classes that are required to maintain your graduate funding. You need to be here, at least until you've completed your PhD. You've worked too hard for this, and I won't let you throw that away for me, baby." He sounded tired and a bit sad, and Karyn regretted bringing up the discussion again.

She knew he was right. They would have to part for now, but the urge to run away with him was so seductive. They'd shared so much, become so bonded and enmeshed that division now would rip at her, leaving her wounded; for how long, she had no idea. With no definite return date, it could be forever, and that terrified her.

"What if we become lost to each other, Will?" she asked, afraid of the answer. He only hugged her closer, kissing her again, and sighed.

"A part of us will always be together, darling, but if that happens, I will find you. I promise."

14

Cognition

That quick, Will was gone, and Karyn was alone once again in the place that had become her static reset button - the apartment. All she had left from the moment they shared was the smell of him in her nose and the last look he gave her before evaporating out of her life again, but his logic was firmly entrenched within her. She stayed immobile on her couch, slowly digesting the whole of what William had said, examining each and every sentence for an answer. Somewhere, in those few bits of conversation, there was a clue, a key, to unlocking her life.

How Will determined what was real and what was a dream had her intrigued. At some point during their meeting, he had decided that she was not part of the dream and then tested that theory with physical contact, but what made him question the nature of her existence in the first place? Why would he ever think she was real if he was dreaming, and dreaming lucidly enough to recognize that he was in a dream to begin with? Karyn had tried lucid dreaming in the past with limited success; once she was able to make herself fly, another time she dispatched an ex-boyfriend with Bruce Lee-style martial arts, but accidental successes like those were a far cry from being able to control her dreams. Did Will consciously control the content of his dream? If he did, then anything he didn't specifically wish to be there would have been suspect - like her.

She had taken a different approach to divining whether the apartment scene was a real memory or not; once her younger self displayed an aberrant behavior, Karyn immediately knew something was not right. She didn't have the clear logic that William seemed to have, but she still knew it wasn't a memory. What did Will know that made this dream different, and when did he know it?

There were other issues that confounded her. Will stated that he knew he was in a dream, but if he was the dreamer, how did **she** wind up in **his** dream? What allowed her to move into his dream space and share it with him? He also seemed to sense something was amiss before she revealed herself; several times he looked around the room expectantly, but Karyn had no idea if that was because he could feel a presence other than his own, or if he was just edgy. She wished she had come forward earlier and asked him when she had the chance, instead of being so cautious. She wished that Will hadn't moved so quickly to touch her. If he had just waited, they would have had time to talk more. Why didn't he wait? Didn't he have questions as well, like why she was in his dream? *He always was impetuous*, she smiled to herself, but his timing was bad; his rush to prove his hypothesis meant she was on her own, with no support. *I'll never get a chance to ask now*, she thought. *I've got to figure this out alone.*

She lay back and rested her head on the sofa arm. The canvas felt nothing like the leather of the Haddonfield couch, she noted, and her mind wandered back to when she and Will had struggled to lift that behemoth up the stairs; she at the top, trying not to fall backward and Will holding the majority of the couch's weight below. She giggled, remembering how the veins pulsed in his neck from the strain as she fumbled with the keys to unlock the door, being patient with her clumsiness despite the crushing load threatening to bulldoze him down the stairwell. It was only after they had situated the thing in the living room, both panting and gasping, that he admitted being in severe pain the whole time. Karyn had panicked, thinking he was hurt, and he played her along, removing pieces of clothing so she could check him over until he was practically naked; christening the troublesome furniture with their lovemaking was unavoidable at that point. The heat rose to her face again, thinking about how his eyes had changed from laughing to hungry, practically devouring her like a starving man before he took her on the smooth, cool leather.

His eyes...he noticed something when we were on the couch...

Karyn ran back over their conversation on the couch, realizing that William's attention sharpened just before he asked her if she was real; the trigger had to be in that moment, in something she did or did not do. *What was I doing at the time*, she asked herself, but all she recalled was the flashback of their lovemaking and the flushing excitement rising into her face.

Is that what he saw? Was it my reaction that made him question if I was real? She thought back over the situation several times, and could come up with nothing else. If Will had experienced that dream before, then he would be expecting the dream Karyn to behave a certain way; perhaps blushing when **he** mentioned making love on the couch was the tell that she was not another dream Karyn. Becoming upset when he asked her if she was real may have been another hint, and at that point he needed to test his hypothesis by touching her. If the resulting reaction was different than what he experienced with the Karyn he **knew** to be a dream, then he could safely conclude that she was genuine. William's rationale was not scientific method by any standard, but it did clarify if she was a dream or not. The question was, if she wasn't a dream, what was she?

More review and analysis revealed little, and the shortage of information forced her to dig further back, back to when the she first saw William playing guitar in the park. She hadn't known who he was at the time, despite the years they had spent together, and that piece of knowledge only came to her with the shooting pain in her head and her futile grab at his fading form. *Did I connect with something before he disappeared...some kind of energy, perhaps?* That seemed unlikely, as he was already half gone when she tried to touch him and felt nothing when she passed through him, but when Will tried the same thing, she could feel heat and air movement. Furthermore, the scenery around them didn't begin to change until **after** he made contact with the space she occupied. It was a stretch to assume that one action triggered the other, but Karyn couldn't help but draw that conclusion, as tenuous as it was.

Although physical contact was impossible, sound obviously made it through the divide. She could hear William's music and he could hear her speaking to him, but only she could see him. Yet, she was invisible to him at the park, but not in their apartment. *There are no laws of physics that can explain this...unless...oh, god...* A quick burst of panic welled up in her chest with a possibility that Karyn had never considered, but one that could explain everything easily. As unlikely it seemed to Karyn, she couldn't rule it out. Physical laws didn't apply, and the hallucinations and bizarre happenings would fit within the context neatly, if her notion was correct. The thought made her momentarily sick, but stifling the urge to give in to her fear, she asked herself the hard question.

Am I...dead?

Almost as soon as she voiced the thought in her head, the panic dissipated and her heart stopped racing; it was only fear momentarily grabbing the reins from her rational mind, and her anxiety passed with a few deep breaths. Karyn certainly didn't feel dead (as if she would even know what that felt like), and others around her had acknowledged her existence. Unless the afterlife was radically different than what the nuns had told her in grade school, being dead seemed like a slim possibility. It did, however, pry open the door to a line of thought that never crossed Karyn's mind before, where the laws of theoretical physics might apply.

She was no physicist, but her Father was a high school physics teacher with a passion for quantum mechanics and Stephen Hawking, fascinated with the notion of multiple planes of existence, the Multiverse, and Einstein's Unified Theory. Many an evening passed with the two of them debating over dinner and dessert, whether coexisting universes were possible, if the human soul was a non-physical manifestation of matter, or if string theory was true. The conversations they had gradually percolated up to the surface of her memory, becoming permanent once they bobbed above the turbid darkness. Karyn reviewed their content, keeping in mind that she was still solving for an equation with too many unknown variables. She was open to any line of thinking, as long as there was a potential for an answer; a closed mind was not going to open any doors for her, at least not as long as she was "lost", as William had put it. *What did he know that I don't,* she wondered.

Taking inventory of what she **did** know was her first course of action. She was conscious and aware of the world around her. She could taste, smell, and feel. She could see, and had been seen, by other people. She was an active participant in her life, capable of interacting with her surroundings, and not just watching everything as a spectator. Her world seemed very real, solid, and tangible, although occasionally bizarre and unpredictable. All these things did not conflict in the least with the quantum discussions she and her Father had, but they also didn't rule out her initial fear - she **could** be dead, by quantum standards.

The night of her Aunt's funeral was what kindled that particular topic, the "physics of death." Karyn was grieving her Aunt Josie hard, crying for hours before, during, and after the funeral. Josie was her favorite Aunt, the most fun, irreverent and lively of them all, which made her death from glioblastoma that much more tragic. She and Dad sat on the couch that evening, trying to reconcile the unfairness of her passing when he mentioned that "maybe death is just another state of matter."

She sniffled, stretching to reach the kleenex. "What do you mean, Pop?" Her eyes were burning from all the tears.

"Well, kitten, look at it this way," he said, handing her the box, "Water can take three different forms: ice, vapor or steam, and liquid water. The form water chooses depends on the forces applied to it. Temperature is what determines the form water molecules will take, right?"

She nodded, wiping her nose. "Unless it's pressure causing it."

The creases around his eyes deepened with a slight smile; he had succeeded in distracting her for the moment. "Pressure is still a form of temperature, Karyn. Pressure creates heat, remember?" She looked disappointed that she overlooked such an obvious fact, but he ruffled her hair and continued. "Anyway, look at people as if they're a water molecule. In this form, we're like ice - solid; but once we die, maybe we change our form of matter to something less tangible, like spirit."

She wrinkled her brow a bit more. "What about the other two forms of matter, like plasma and Bose-Einstein Condensates? I would think those two states would be far closer to what we'd consider 'spirit', wouldn't they?"

Her question caught him off guard; Ethan hadn't counted on Karyn jumping ahead of him in the conversation, especially as physics wasn't her field of expertise. He was impressed that his daughter's analytical mind functioned even though she was emotionally devastated. She never ceased to amaze him.

"Whoa, there, little missy...where did that come from? Have you been watching Nikola Tesla documentaries again behind my back?" he teased. She smiled sheepishly as she wiped her nose, but her eyes were curious as to how he was going to work his analogy. "Those forms of matter don't lend themselves to my metaphor as well. Remember, humans are comprised of mostly water; plasma and BECs are more closely related to electricity or fusion - and don't try the old "humans are bioelectric" angle, 'cause it don't apply here, kiddo." She giggled at his defense, and their grief eased slightly. "We'll get to that in a moment. Just bear with your old man while he tries to sound smart, okay?"

"Okay," she complied. He paused to gather his thoughts.

"I want you to consider the physical nature of being human...and how it defines us. It's the only form we know. We're born with it, it carries us around...but what if our physical selves weren't the real core of being human? What if our consciousness was the real part of being human, and the body was just a wrapping, like the clothes we wear? Maybe we're just using our bodies to carry our consciousness around, like we use cars to travel. Sometimes you use a car, sometimes a plane, sometimes a train. In the end, you get out of that car, *plane or train at your destination. If your destination is the afterlife, which might be in another plane of existence, you won't need a physical body for that, right?"*

Karyn carefully considered what he was saying, but immediately countered his theory. "Then how do you account for the whole 'matter cannot be lost or destroyed' concept? If the body is left behind to decompose, then doesn't that go against the Conservation of Mass?"

*Her Father nodded, and said, "It would, if our perceptions about our physical bodies are correct," he said, hugging her close to him. "But, I don't think they are. There's far too many things we can't account for in the realm of human experience, physical or metaphysical. Perhaps that's where the other forms of matter come in. If we assume that Tesla's theories were right, that means plasma, aether, akasha - whatever you want to call it - permeates everything at a subatomic level. All the physical matter we're familiar with is solid to us, but at the atomic level there's **huge** amounts of space between the molecules...maybe even enough to serve as a superhighway for the soul. If that's the case, matter still isn't lost when the body decays because it's transformed, and it can travel in ways that only religion has documented. The Conservation of Mass still holds true. It also means the soul exists, and that science and religion aren't the polar opposites we always think them to be. We just think they are because the physical human form is all we know."*

Karyn thought hard about her Father's supposition, and didn't dismiss it. "Is this from that Lanza guy's book you were telling me about before? The guy that says death doesn't exist, that it only exists because we tie our consciousness to our physical form?"

"The very same guy."

She mulled over this new way of looking at her Aunt Jo's passing. "So that could mean that Aunt Josie really isn't dead; she's just transformed and moved on." That thought eased her loss a little, and she suppressed a small laugh. "You know, Dad, if Tesla and Lanza are right, their theories would rewrite some major religious constructs, but I think the Vatican would eat that shit right up."

*Ethan Kiplinger laughed out loud. "I think it will take a lot more than that to sway any major religion into sharing a common space with science - you can never have two gurus in the same room - and your heathen Aunt would be rolling in her grave if she thought she shared **anything** in common with organized religion. I know she'd rather join the ancestors in the aethers and laugh at us fumbling around down here."*

Based on that exchange, Karyn could very well be dead. Her consciousness could be free of her body, and she just not aware of it. But Will said she was lost, not dead, and the splashing in her mind seemed to confirm that she wasn't. She was going to assume for now that, since she was conscious, she was alive in some form or another. "So," she said out loud, sitting up, "that means the question isn't **what** am I. The question is **where** am I."

15

Confirmation

Karyn now had a lead, although it was more of a hypothesis. Once it was tested out, proved or disproved, she could move forward to the next theory. Eventually, she would narrow down exactly what was what, or where was where. She would get the answers she needed, one way or another.

That meant the next stop on her journey was to see Kalea again, provided she could intentionally find the hypnotist's shop. Previous efforts had been accidental, or seemingly accidental, but when she thought carefully back to those moments she found there was a need from her that may have triggered its appearance; first, when she was going to the restaurant, bemoaning her life, and second when she needed answers and the shop almost landed right on her. If this was the universe responding to her needs, this time she would make them loud and clear. Hitting the street with serious determination and moving towards the original site of the shop, Karyn paused before rounding the corner and said out loud, "I wish to see Kalea." Putting aside all doubt about her magical thinking, she crossed her fingers and she rounded the corner to behold the gilded sign and the purple door with its gleaming brass hardware. Her hunch had worked, and she ran excitedly to the door. Kalea opened it just as she reached the top concrete step.

"I've been waiting for you, child," she smiled lovingly, and held out her hand. She was glowing from the inside out again, and seemed younger than the last time they spoke.

Karyn returned the smile and accepted the offer, her hand filling with the tingling warmth she had felt before as she followed Kalea inside the darkened shop. "I thought you would be," she said. They sat down at the bistro table and Karyn got down to brass tacks right away. "I've learned a few things, but I want to confirm what I think I've learned to be sure."

"What makes you think I can confirm them?" Kalea said, still smiling.

"Because I **know** you can, just like I knew I could find you; I know that you are part of all this," she said with absolute certainty, and waving her arm broadly. "You aren't responsible for any of it, but you have knowledge. And I need answers."

Kalea nodded. "I'm impressed…and I understand your need for answers, Karyn, but in order for me to do so, I need to know what **you** know. There are restrictions on what I'm allowed to say."

Karyn's eyebrows raised in surprise. "Restrictions? From whom? By whom?"

"All in due time, darling. Please trust me on this." She leaned forward to listen. "Now, what have you learned?"

Karyn took a deep breath, and recounted her experiences since last they spoke. She omitted no detail too small and overlooked nothing, in the hopes that all the information she gave would earn some reciprocity with the mysterious powers that held sway over Kalea. Kalea listened attentively, the corner of her mouth upturning when Karyn mentioned almost meeting herself, and the memory of the leather couch. She didn't blush as she mentioned it; her intuition said that this woman, the one she had guessed was an archetype, was aware of everything already. Karyn was merely detailing facts without emotion.

As she wrapped up her end of the conversation, Kalea nodded again approvingly. "You've been hard at work on your conundrum, it seems," she said. "Now, what do **you** make of it all?"

She pushed the hair out of her face, and leaned on the palm of her hand. "I'm not sure, and that's why I'm here talking to you, but I have a few theories. One," she said, raising her index finger, "there could be more than one reality, and somehow I'm in a different one than I was previously.

Two, if other realities are possible, then one of those realities might be that I am no longer physically alive, but consciously alive. Three, I am in a place other than those two possibilities, but I don't know where that is."

"What makes you think you're in an alternate reality?" Kalea asked with genuine interest.

"Because I was able to speak with William in our old apartment, and we were able to hear each other in the park. When we tried to touch each other, however, it caused a change in the surroundings and everything fell apart. Now, I'm no Einstein, but I'm guessing that has something to do with some unknown law of physics that prevents alternate realities from overlapping or intersecting." She thought some more and added, "There have been other times when I am transported from one place to another, like when I tried to investigate that wailing at the end of the dark street, and after I saw William in the park. Every time I've been moved from one place to another as if teleported, and the one time may have been inside a dream - or another reality where Will was."

Kalea nodded, noting her logic. "What makes you think you might be dead?" she asked with a serious tone.

"From a theoretical, less scientific perspective…Lanza's premise that perception is a plane of existence. If our consciousness exists beyond the death of our physical body, then I could be dead now and not know it, just like the spirits of people who have died and not "moved on" to the afterlife. For all I know, I may be one of those folks, and William can hear and see me, but not touch me. That would also explain why William and I can't physically connect with each other."

"Do you believe you are dead?"

"No, but it's still a possibility."

"What makes you think you are not?"

Karyn sat back in her chair and sighed. "No real proof, except that I don't believe I am, and Will said that I was "lost".

"Did he mean you were a lost soul? A ghost?" Kalea prodded.

"I don't think he did. He said he would wait for me, and that I needed to find a way back to him. If I were dead, that wouldn't make any sense, unless…" she paused, "…unless he was dead as well. Then he'd be waiting for me in the afterlife, I guess." Karyn finished.

Kalea's countenance was intense, her kaleidoscope irises swirling slowly. "So what about that third possibility, Karyn?" Karyn leaned in with equal interest.

"I take it you're about to tell me," she said. Kalea shook her head in disagreement.

"I can **tell** you nothing, dear, but I can **ask** you some leading questions." Karyn's face darkened with disappointment.

"Why not? Why can't you tell me?" she demanded.

"I cannot give you answers, because the others haven't approved of me doing so. I am governed and bound by their decisions. They require you to make serious choices, and any answer not arrived at on your own would unduly influence you in making those decisions. I'm sorry, Karyn, but I cannot cross that line." Her face looked pained at not being able to give her the answer she wanted, and Karyn felt there was no point in asking who "the others" were; Kalea would have been otherwise forthcoming and told her. There was weight and seriousness in her voice, hinting at how very important and necessary the rules were.

"Okay," Karyn said quietly, "then…what questions did you want to ask me?"

Kalea stretched her legs and stood up, walking a few steps towards the wall of bookcases and turning around to face Karyn again. "Nothing you need worry about; I know you have all the answers already. Feel free to speak up anytime, or just listen to all I ask and think carefully on the questions. Ready?" Karyn nodded nervously, giving her the okay. "Good, let's begin then." She drew herself up and clasped her hands together.

"Do you have a job, Karyn?"

Karyn gave her a confused look. "Of course I do."

"Where?"

She opened her mouth to answer, but she had no words; her mind had gone blank. "I work at…I work…I work at…the University…I think." She stumbled trying to reply. All of a

sudden, she couldn't remember working, although she was sure
she did. Kalea ignored the look on her face, and continued.

"What do you do there?"

"I…ummm…I…" Still no memories came to her
rescue. She had nothing but a blank space where her
professional working life had been, if it had ever really been
there.

"Where do you live?" Karyn had nothing to offer.
"What's the address of the place you live?"

Still nothing came forward in her head, but there was a
pounding now in Karyn's temples, progressing to either side of
her head above her ears. Kalea strolled back and forth in front
of Karyn, firing off question after question.

"Does your cellphone ever ring? Who calls you?
When was the last time you went out with your friends? Can
you name one of your friends?…"

Kalea's questions came rapid fire, and her voice
sounded farther and farther away as the thumping in her brain
gradually overpowered it. Her heartbeat was echoing in her
skull, drowning out all else. She felt dizzy, her vision clouded
over, and she tried to hone in on Kalea's voice to get clear. An
eternity seemed to pass until there was a break of absolute
silence, when Karyn realized Kalea was sitting directly across
from her, quiet, and holding both her hands in her own. Their
warmth was comforting.

"Are you alright, dear?" she asked, reaching over to
tuck the hair from Karyn's face behind her ear, as a mother
would for her own child. Karyn looked at her with wide eyes,
speechless, silent, and stunned. She whispered to Karyn,
"Take your time processing it all. Do not rush to any
conclusions. Listen **inside** yourself, and I'll go make some
tea." She glided beyond the curtained doorway and put the
kettle on, while Karyn sat, catatonic, staring out into the shop.

While her demeanor outside was motionless and stoic,
Karyn's insides were in turmoil. All her synapses were firing
at lightning speed, shooting impulses along neurons, creating
new neural pathways, and weaving together every bit of
information she had accumulated with the revelations of
moments before. The little voice spoke the word *"truth"*

clearly, and Karyn was left to divine exactly what that truth was. Was her whole life here fake, a lie? Why did she have memories of being with Will years ago, yet nothing at all of her present life? What was the purpose of this deception, and where the hell was she?

Has none of this been real? Have I imagined all this, or is some of this real…and how can I distinguish between the two?

She struggled to reconcile the space between her experiences, sorting out the discordant information from that which she knew to be true; the fact that her cellphone never rang, she couldn't remember a single name of any friend, nor her own apartment's address. The hallucination in her apartment was now probably more a reality than not, she guessed, and everything she had believed to be real was now suspect, including her own existence.

No, I exist still, she thought. *My consciousness is proof that I exist in some capacity, some format…even if Lanza is right, as long as I am conscious and aware, there is a chance I can figure out what's going on. I exist!*

Kalea returned with the tea and the usual accompaniments, pouring Karyn a cup silently so as not to disturb her thoughts. Karyn's eyes were still wide and unblinking, but she wasn't in shock. Her brain was too absorbed with the task at hand to be bothered with visual input, and she needed every bit of mental strength she could scrape together to work through the snarl of details. Vision would be a distraction, so she ignored it while her brain worked overtime.

I know I exist. I know William exists. We may not exist in the same reality. He says I am lost, and he will wait for me. Where is he waiting? Where am I in relation to where he is? This reality is questionable, and I am capable of altering it to suit my needs if I exert my desire to do so. There are places here where I am prevented from going even if I desire to. When I push to do so, I am removed to another place. Why? Why was I not allowed to go down that dark street? What is the pain there that the child spoke of? Who decided to move me away from there?

You did, said the little voice. *You.*

Me? That makes no sense…I would **never** *choose something like this. Why would I choose* **this***?*

Safety, the voice replied. *You needed safety.*

Safety from what? Karyn asked, but the voice went silent.

Thoughts flooded her mind, settling and sinking in, slowly getting sorted. Kalea could see her eyelids begin to flutter down as Karyn processed more and more of the situation, finally closing completely. With that physical sign, Kalea knelt next to her and gently asked, "Where are you, Karyn?"

She opened her eyes and looked directly at Kalea. A fierceness of spirit underwrote her expression, a smoldering emotion that had just been breathed into flame again spread across her face, and she inhaled deeply before answering her.

"I don't know right now…but nothing will stop me from finding out. Nothing."

16
Connection

Karyn's mind was ablaze as she walked back to her apartment. Her head felt as if it was on fire, stoked by words, thoughts, and scenes that fueled her search for the truth of her situation. Fortunately, the headache that began with Kalea's interrogation was fading now, allowing her a welcome respite from the stress of the last few hours. She was calmer, focused, and more coherent than ever before. Thanks to the enlightening conversation they shared afterward, she had new insight and determination as well.

After she worked through the initial shock of Kalea's revelatory questioning, they settled in to tea, biscuits, and a discussion about the nature of reality; Karyn's reality, to be specific.

"I would think you'd be more upset at still not knowing exactly where you were; it was your sole goal, was it not?" Kalea said with a raised eyebrow. "You don't seem upset at all at not getting the answer you wanted."

Karyn sipped her tea with slow appreciation of the flavor. "I'm a little surprised myself, actually." She picked a biscuit from the tray and sniffed it; the savory aroma was delicious, but hard to pin down for ingredients. She looked at Kalea for the ingredient list, with a twinkle in her eye this time.

"Sesame, ginger, turmeric, Gruyere, and a bit of gotu kola for the ol' brain pan," she giggled, tapping her right temple. "You know by now I can't bake anything pedestrian."

"Nothing about you, or this place, is even mildly close to pedestrian," she laughed. She munched half of the cracker and rolled her eyes back with pleasure. The flavor was Asian;

warm, salty, with a touch of heat and green. "Exquisite," she mumbled through the mouthful, and politely swallowed before continuing with her thought. "Apparently, I'm very…Descartian…deep down inside. You know, 'I think, therefore, I am,' and all that. It was more important for me to believe I exist, physically or not, than where I was. That was what concerned me most, more than being dead, or being… 'lost'."

Kalea looked truly surprised. "Why?"

*"Because none of us really know what is real, if you think about it. I mean, we each have our own interpretations of reality. It's all individual perception. There are some basic commonalities in everyone's reality - things like how gravity functions and other proven laws of physics - but beyond that, people share very little when it comes to their interpretation of reality." She pointed to the cup of tea in her hand. "This tea, for example, has hints of citrus; I think it's orange, but it might be bergamot, or lemon. You might think it tangerine. The fact of what the actual tea recipe includes is one reality, but what you and I **perceive** is a different reality, our **personal** reality. And regardless of whether it's tea, the color of the sky, or whatever, everyone has a unique personal reality." She munched on a second biscuit.*

*"And what would be **your** personal reality?" she asked Karyn with a lifted brow.*

"Not this one. One where I can be with Will again."

"Why Will?"

Karyn sighed. "I just know he's an anchor of some sort. The missing piece. Wherever he is, that's where I'm supposed to be. I'm supposed to be with him."

Kalea smirked. "That sounds very unscientific, darling, but I understand. But, that's not where you are now, of course."

She got Karyn's attention immediately. "Of course…so…where am I now?" She tensed for the moment when Kalea refused to tell her, but it didn't come to pass. Instead, the archetype sat back and relaxed down into her chair, smirking.

*"Your notions about the nature of reality are more spot on than you know, Karyn. In fact, you very succinctly distilled the nature of your problem, as well. Your problem is not **if** you are, or **what** you are, but **where** you are and **how** you are."*

"By 'where I am' do you mean mentally, or physically?" she asked.

"Where the body resides is not necessarily where the mind is, or where the soul or the spirit is. Humans are very attached to their physical forms, and place a huge amount of emphasis on that part of their being, but they also have an etheric body, an astral body, and a body of consciousness. For millenia, medicine men and shamans have known that humans are beings of multiple layers; that's why astral travel to the spirit world is a reality to them, and why they can cross those planes to commune with their gods. When they do so, there is always intention and planning, and protection in place so they aren't disturbed in their journey - otherwise they risk becoming severed from their other selves, becoming lost."

The significance of that word hit Karyn. Lost. "What happens to them if they become…lost?" she asked, although she already had an idea.

"They become disconnected, destabilized, unable to become whole again. Their soul becomes fragmented." Kalea lifted her cup for a sip, giving her time to let it sink in. "Sound familiar?"

Karyn nodded slowly; she was hoping that the shamans had discovered a way to correct her problem, and that Kalea could tell her what it was. "But I'm no shaman," she said.

"True," she said, "but you still managed wind up in the same predicament. Your layers are separated."

"So my mind and my body are in different places?"

"Yes."

*She thought back to that moment in her apartment when she thought she was hallucinating; the first time she felt something was really wrong. "You do realize that **you** were responsible for all that," Kalea said, with an empathetic look. Karyn had not spoken a word, yet Kalea heard her thought. "Your mind was aware at its most primal level that there was a disconnect between here," she pointed down, "and where you* *really* are. *What you perceived as a hallucination was your consciousness trying to reconcile the difference in realities."*

*"And why didn't it? Why do I **still** not know what the hell is going on?" Karyn asked, annoyed at being mind-read.*

"Because your subconscious intervened, and just in the nick of time before you were damaged by the failed reconciliation." Karyn's face made it obvious that she didn't follow. Kalea reminded her of their first conversation. "The subconscious mind is always on alert to protect us and keep us safe, remember?"

*"I **am** safe. I **need** to get to where William is."*

"Are you? Can you honestly say you are safe, not knowing where your physical self is right now? If Lanza's theory means that your consciousness can exist apart from your body, and maybe even your soul, then anything could have happened to your corporeal self and you wouldn't know...but your subconscious knows everything. And for some reason, a very good reason, it decided to keep you away from that knowledge." She placed her cup noiselessly on the saucer. "The subconscious has gatekeepers; sub-personalities whose sole purpose is to protect an individual from information that would be damaging or threatening to the person's psychology. Your apartment hallucination was a test, a test to see what information you were ready to accept. Once your conscious mind began to buck against accepting the information, your subconcious prevented any further damage by distracting you and changing your surroundings."

*Karyn scowled. "But that's not fair - I **want** to know!"*

*Kalea shook her head. "Please try to understand...you **say** you want to know, but your subconscious always knows what you **really** want. It's on the inside looking out, and it knows when to act in your best interest, even if you consciously disagree."*

*She smacked her hand down on the bistro table, jostling the china. The ringing electrified the air. "I tell you I **want** to **know**! I came here for answers, dammit!" Karyn shouted.*

Kalea was unmoved. "What if those answers destroyed you? Would you still want them? What if acquiring that knowledge created a schism in your psyche so deep that your consciousness couldn't recover, ceased to exist? Would you still stomp your feet so adamantly?"

Karyn looked at her with doubt and some suspicion. "You're telling me that this…thing my subconscious is protecting me from is **that** *terrible, that horrific that it would kill me? If it was that awful, I'm sure I'd have remembered it already." In seconds, she instantly regretted making the statement.*

"Oh, really?" Kalea half-smiled in amusement. "You've apparently already forgotten how much you had forgotten, dear." She softened at seeing Karyn wilt in frustration, and tried a different approach. "Maybe a different scenario would help. Hmmm…like…like the married woman who suspects her husband is cheating on her." She sat up in her chair. "There are lots of little clues around that hint at his infidelity, but the wife rationalizes them all away because the truth would be too painful for her to deal with. Perfume on his clothes, late nights at the office and those weekend business trips all point to the fact that her husband is having an affair; but, if she accepted that reality, it would ruin the illusion of the reality she prefers - that of her in a happy marriage with a man that is devoted and faithful to only her. Her need to maintain that illusion might be so important that she will ignore more blatant evidence to the contrary, again, because her psyche couldn't handle the painful truth of her husband's cheating." Karyn nodded that she was following along, and Kalea continued. "One day, she comes home early from shopping and walks in to find her husband and his mistress, in flagrante delicto, on the living room floor. Now, she is confronted with a reality she cannot handle," Kalea placed her hands out to her sides, palms up, simulating a scale, "and her subconscious must make a decision on how best to keep her safe. It would remove her from that painful moment - even if that means giving her a psychotic break - rather than forcing her to accept a reality that is abhorrent to her." She dropped her one hand down into her lap, as if weighted with lead. "That lack of balance means the wife is spared from a painful reality, but she is also lost to that world in its entirety, at least until she

chooses to move through and accept the things that she cannot stomach."

Karyn carefully considered Kalea's scenario, applying it to her situation. It did make sense, although Karyn couldn't imagine anything that would cause her to break with reality. Freaking out in her apartment was one thing, but separating her mind from her body was another. Still, the concept intrigued her.

"Assuming your example is applicable to my situation," she asked, "you're saying I have experienced something so traumatic that my subconscious mind felt the only option for self-preservation was to send my conscious mind away."

"Do you doubt it possible? Does any of it seem impossible, given what you've experienced in your time here? Why do you think your subconscious has tried so hard to isolate you, to keep you here? Do you think where you really are is all sunshine and rainbows?" she chuckled. "More than likely, you were being protected from something beyond your ability to deal with right now, something so traumatic that you would sustain severe damage to your psyche if you approached it directly."

"No...it sounds entirely plausible..." Karyn said, still thinking about the scenario.

Kalea was watching her closely, measuring her response to this latest round of information. "But..." she said.

"But, that means in order to reach my physical body I must face the trauma that caused the split in the first place, and I have no idea what it was, or if my subconscious mind will let me do so." She looked down at the floor briefly. "How does one accomplish that?" she asked with a slightly defeated tone.

The ageless woman smiled warmly at her with soft, swirling eyes. "The same way you managed to get this far already. Question everything around you. Use what you know about this world to your advantage. The gatekeepers will know when you are ready, and you will find your way, child." Kalea rose from her chair, walked over to Karyn, and took her face in her hands. She placed a soft, gentle kiss on her forehead before stepping back to give her a nod of approval. "I know *you will take the right path. All the answers you seek are inside of you.”*

"All the answers are inside of me, eh?" Karyn mumbled as she entered her apartment, dragging her feet. She was exhausted from her time with Kalea, but at least now her headache was completely gone and replaced with some semblance of clarity. She yearned for the softness of her bed and deep, peaceful, undisturbed sleep. Removing her clothing as she trod into the bedroom, Karyn fell into her bed with a final drowsy thought.

I wish Will was here…

17
Love

The pressure was light. Slight. It crept over her upturned hip and traced its way past the curve of her pelvis, pausing occasionally, just long enough to evade her sleeping attention. The calloused tip of a finger pad, flat to her skin, was lazily smoothing a path along the edge of her stomach. Karyn was so deeply entrenched in her dream state that she barely noticed it; her mind was floating in the space between worlds, soft and warm in her bed.

The grazing of her inner thigh sent a weightless feeling through her lower body. The tingling ran beyond the edge of her groin, lighting up the sensory map in her brain, sending a bright flash past her closed eyelids, rousing her from the depths of slumber. The pressure on the bed distorted slightly as she slowly became more aware of her surroundings, her sleepiness falling away. There was mass and heat behind her, but there was no contact. Just the sense of a presence…and that single finger.

Scouting quietly as if to remain a secret, the fingertip continued its journey of discovery up the inside of her thigh, brushing against her ever so gracefully with the back of a knuckle; the small, pleasant shock coaxed her from slumber further, but didn't demand her to wake. The visitor treated the bump as inconsequential, and meandered around the edge of her belly, detoured north, and traced a circle around her navel. The finger then lifted from her skin, and was replaced by a strong, muscular hand that covered her stomach, headed east, and wrapped its fingers across her left waist.

It tugged her backwards slightly, and the heat behind her increased as the distance closed between her and her gentle assailant. Karyn was now pulled against his chest, and her back felt the radiating warmth from him, simmering from the back of her neck to the base of her spine. Her sleepy mind was hovering between dreamland and wakefulness, but there was no question as to who the stranger was in her bed. The feel of the chest behind her and the waves of heat from it filled her memory with images, and the closeness sparked her other senses. Her own fire had been kindled, and her body burned with desire at the thought of what he would do next, not wanting to reveal how much more she wanted from him. His hand rode the edge of her torso under her left breast, and paused. She puzzled at the wait, until she felt breath on her neck and William's whisper in her ear.

"Remember me…"

It was a request, but the strength behind the whisper demanded something. Something forgotten. Something of her spirit. Something locked away for a very long time. He punctuated the request with a firm grasp, pulling her closer to him. His fingertips brushed her nipple so delicately that she strained for more, but the hand remained just out of reach, leaving her aching, creating a pulsing between her legs and a pounding in her ears.

Another brush of fingertips, and his hand slid diagonally across her belly, back to her right hip and paused again, his palm just below the crest of her hipbone. Will's fingers gripped her again, pulling her back and down this time, landing her in the crescent of his body. She could feel him rough against her as his fingers flared outward, sliding along the edge of her groin, seeking to further their exploration. She halfheartedly tried to curl forward to cut short their access, make him earn the honor, but quickly relented; she sighed with pleasure when he pressed her hip backwards and she allowed it to fall, clearing the way to her softest self.

Scenes were playing out inside her closed lids, and her thoughts turned to the smells of summer filling her senses, and cicadas humming in the distance. Patches of gooseflesh flashed across her body as the chirping insects were joined by music now, the pulsing rhythm of the musical beats coming into sync with her own heart. There was the smell of water, a

taste of wine, and the scent of sweaty flesh and salt. The slow
motions of carefree lovers with all the time in the world came
through and passed before her eyes, intermingling with her
physical present. Her body followed the trail of pleasure,
leaving her mind to drift alone to the scenes replaying in her
memory.

Remember me...

The barest of movements sent electric shocks through
her spine, feathering out to all her extremities. His soft exhale
across her breasts stiffened her nipples further, making them
strain against their limits of skin. Karyn was amazed at the
power he had over her, such little movement causing so much
pleasure, and she craved more. She wanted to be supple, pliant,
and exposed, stripped of mind and left with nothing but this
place in her being that was his alone. Her unspoken need was
answered by his deft caresses, maddening her flesh and jolting
her body with their intensity. She fell further backwards, and
the lips that had spoken now devoured her. Spread open like a
flower, the last bit of her conscious mind let go to ride the
rising tide of ecstasy. His hardness rose up against her
hamstrings, slipping between her thighs, and rested just below
the inferno of her being. She strained down to meet him, but
he purposely stayed just out of reach, denying her the one thing
she so desperately desired. Whimpering and crouching was to
no avail; he held himself in reserve, waiting for some unknown
moment to enter.

Remember me, Karyn...

Sounds and motions, memories and feelings swamped
her; her mind kept reaching out for the forgotten thing, the
missing piece she knew was there, in the haze, just beyond the
lovers' setting. Karyn was so close now, so close to that
obscure memory...if only she could grasp it, remember it, then
all would be restored to her...but, her body was no longer her
own; possessed by William, it writhed like a cat in heat while
her untethered mind ran after the lost piece of itself. The scent
of his skin was trumped by lilacs and gasoline as she closed the
foggy distance between her and the missing knowledge, when
the clarity was suddenly torn from her, yanking her down,
down, down, and back into her tortured, lustful body. William

drove upwards into her, plunging through and breaching her center.

Remember me, Karyn, and we will never be apart...

He pushed her over the edge into the void. Her whole world collapsed inward with each massive contraction from the base of her spine, the pounding in her head deafening her with his every thrust. She was a Catherine wheel of orgasm, spinning and spouting fireworks, burning out as her mind and body swirled together and funneled down into a single self again. Into the inky blackness and silence of the deepest sleep.

The beam of daylight crossed her pillow, marking time like a sundial, until it graced the edge of her face with warmth. Karyn groaned and rolled away from the intrusive sunbeam, cracking one eye just wide enough to check the clock, then realizing there was no need to care about time anymore. "What does it matter? It's not like I have a real job, or any of this is real anyway," she grumbled and curled back up into her pillow.

Her thoughts drifted back to the lovemaking in her dream, although it hadn't been completely a dream. It was actually part dream and part a returned memory; a memory of the night before William left for Europe. She had fallen asleep, exhausted from unpacking the apartment, waiting for him to return from one last show, and he had slipped in beside her, gently teasing her body awake. Their passion was beyond anything they had shared before. She, an unrestrained volcano of emotion, and he, an unstoppable force that imprinted itself on her very soul that night, only to leave her empty and alone upon waking. By the time she woke up, Will was gone and already on the plane. All that he left her was a letter, propped against the lamp on the nightstand, explaining how he couldn't bear to see her cry, and how he knew he'd never leave if he did.

She cried for days. The emptiness and devastation was unlike anything she had ever experienced; Karyn stayed in bed for almost a week, eating little to nothing, until her graduate school obligations forced her to move forward. By then, the first letter from Will had arrived, full of further apologies and tales from the road. It didn't make up for the fact that he denied her the opportunity of saying goodbye on her own terms, but she knew he was right. As much as she hated his choice of departure, she couldn't argue against it. He was as emotionally sensitive as Karyn was; he was just more resilient and practical than she.

She could remember learning to accept the new, long-distance version of their relationship, their letters crossing the Atlantic back and forth as he gained more respect in the music world and she moved ever closer to completing her thesis. Over time, the letters became fewer and more far between…but Karyn couldn't recall why they weren't together now. The memories that followed were missing.

Why didn't we get back together? What prevented that from happening? Did he find someone else?

That last thought made her wince. It was bad enough that she had pangs of jealousy seeing her younger self in his arms; another woman with him was something she couldn't bear. After re-experiencing the bliss and the flood of history that had been absent from her archives, Karyn felt all the old emotions over again, even though they belonged to the Karyn of then. The Karyn of now had evolved beyond that girl, and her younger self would be a complete stranger to her, were it not for these bursts of returned memories every so often. With each added piece of her history, she extended her story further along. The added memory would then create a border that she couldn't pass, but fill in all the missing bits up to that point. Karyn had all the memories of her life up until she and Will lost touch, but nothing beyond.

Turning over in the bed, eyes still closed, she tried to see his face as it was now; older, a bit more weathered, with those stunning gray hazel eyes. *If I could only talk to him, he could fill me in on what happened to us after Europe…give me the key to getting out of here…to be with him.* She thought back to their moment on the couch, in the apartment; how very cautious he was at first when she surprised him in the living room, and how delicate he was in the park, becoming wild and frantic at the sound of her voice. What was his life in the time

they were apart? What had happened to William in her
absence that had him crying each time he saw her?

*Maybe another woman broke his heart…someone he
met on the road, perhaps…*

The fact was there were so many years between,
unaccounted for, where anything could have happened to either
of them. She had no knowledge of her own life's history, let
alone a man that, despite the years they had shared together,
she didn't recognize at first glance. Hazarding any guess about
Will's life would be irresponsible, even if her uneducated
guessing gave her a false sense of comfort. She already had
enough issues with reality; she didn't need any more.

She needed William, though. She needed him to
recapture the disparate parts of her spirit, and bind them to her.
Whatever mystical abilities Will had enabled him to break
through the veil separating them, so there might be a chance he
could fuse her consciousness and her body together again. He
was a key player in her situation, and the lack of rules in her
present reality meant almost anything might be possible,
although uniting Karyn's realities was probably beyond his
ken.

*He's not some kind of magical being…but there's
something about him…pulling me…*

She shivered, clenching her thighs together. The dream
was still so vivid and clear, and the emotions of their past so
fresh in her present that she couldn't isolate herself from them.
She loved Will beyond reason, beyond the returned memories
she'd so recently regained, and this last memory cut the locks
on her emotional floodgates. The depth and breadth of feeling
she had for him was overwhelming, distracting, and was
further compounded by the knowledge that he loved her, too.
Before this memory moment, she had heard him speak the
words, but didn't have the understanding behind them. The
recent download of emotional data changed all that. Will had
said, "I love you," and, "I'm sitting with the woman I **love**."
Love, present tense. Whatever had transpired before she
became 'lost' hadn't lessened the bond between them. It was
only now that Karyn was able to connect with those emotions,
now that the memory was released.

She leaned up on one arm and rubbed her eyes. Was this was the governing rule on how this reality was wired? Was a memory a single unit containing the events, smells, emotions and all things interwoven into its fabric? Could Karyn have full access to everything in the missing memory file, provided she could figure out the secret code to the memory's door? The notion seemed reasonable enough, given that her experience thus far had proved the theory true, but where to go with it?

What are my options now? How do I get to William from here? She rolled to one side and wrapped her arms around the pillow, propping her chin up. *I can influence this reality, move within it to some degree, but I've only tried it once…there's no guarantee I can do it again, or travel outside of this reality intentionally…how do I cross that space to find him? I don't even know where he is…*

A hot shower, coffee, and a few hours later improved Karyn's ability to think clearly considerably. She spent the majority of the day in meditation on the couch, deep in thought and pondering her next move. Her efforts led her to only one conclusion. With no formal education on how to manipulate time, space and planes of existence, Karyn had to try using sheer force of will alone to reach the man she loved; she had no other tools at her disposal. She assumed her subconscious didn't have any reason to see William as a threat to her safety, so it should allow her passage, but as to where that path would take her, she had no idea. All Karyn could hope for was to channel the power of her emotions for William, and pray the Gatekeepers let her reach him. She still remembered some holotropic breathing techniques from her college days that could facilitate a trance state, although this plan was a hail Mary pass; still, the plan was as good as any, and she had nothing to lose by trying.

After taking a moment to get settled and comfortable, Karyn closed her eyes and began the paced, deep breathing required to increase her blood oxygen levels and shift her perception. With each inhalation, she spoke her desired goal in her mind, picturing William clearly while holding the breath, then pushed her request out as she emptied her lungs. Keeping a steady, unwavering rhythm of air and thought, Karyn focused her entire presence of mind to be with him, hoping her subconscious would hear her plea and allow her to move beyond to where he was. Gradually, her fingers began to tingle from the increased oxygenation, and the feeling of the couch cushions beneath her disappeared. Soon, she lost track of the room, feeling warm and floaty, listening to the sound of her own heartbeat in her ears in time with her breath. Letting go of anything that might restrain her spirit, she let her consciousness drift away with one final thought: *Take me to William.*

18

Refusal

Maintaining her breathwork became more difficult the lighter her being felt; at some points, Karyn thought what little of her consciousness remained might slip entirely from her, like a silk scarf on the wind. Her physical self was going through a transformation, a disintegration process where she thought she could feel the space in between every molecule. She wasn't even sure if she was breathing anymore, but she kept her focus and went through the motions. Now that she was moving somewhere, there was no chance Karyn would stop the experiment before the results were in. She got her wish soon enough; feeling less like a vapor and more like a solid, heavier, and more substantial as the gaps closed in her structure, Karyn opened her eyes slowly, wondering what she would be facing next.

She was on the leather couch. The leather couch of memory, of lovemaking, and of her and William's last meeting. She had returned to their Haddonfield apartment.

The room was slightly different, and the season had changed outside. It was winter, and snow several feet deep covered the sidewalks. The snow fell silently, illuminated by the orange glow of the streetlights. The couch and other furniture had been moved around to make room for the Christmas tree in the corner, which had replaced the chair Karyn had hidden behind during her last visit. Boxes of Christmas ornaments were open on the floor. A bottle of wine and two glasses sat on the counter. The fresh smell of pine scented the air, and Karyn's heart ached seeing the holiday setup; it was their tradition to decorate the tree, drink the bottle, and unwrap each other on the living room floor in the glow of the tree lights. *There was so much love here…so many memories…no wonder he stays in this dream*, she thought.

She reflexively looked at the clock. It was 6pm, a good three hours before her other self would be returning from classes. There was no fear of running into herself again tonight. Besides, if William had any control over this dream like he had hinted, once he saw her here the dream Karyn probably wouldn't make an appearance. No guarantees, but one less thing to worry about tipping the delicate balance in this unstable reality.

She could hear him walking across the wide pine floorboards above her. His footsteps were distinct; a slight favoring of one leg from a high school knee injury meant his feet didn't keep exact pace, even when shuffling through the apartment or walking down the stairs, as was the case now. Karyn walked to the window so he would have a clear view of her when he came down. She didn't want to surprise him, nor wanted him confused if he thought her dream self was home early. She needed to talk to him, and there was no way she was going to risk William ruining all her efforts to see him with accidental or impulsive contact. As it was, she didn't know the metaphysical rules of engagement in the dreamspace; an interruption now might mean she would be "lost" even longer, and Karyn was depending on Will's help. Only he knew where she really was, and he was going to tell her, now.

His hand palmed the top of the newel post as his uneven gait reached the bottom step, and he rounded the turn with downcast eyes, deep in thought. He was the current, older version of himself. She hesitated at breaking his concentration with her voice, so she cleared her throat gently as a warning. He lifted his chin to see her form outlined by the streetlight, and she stepped forward towards him, her hands held up and out in warning.

"Don't try to touch me, Will. I can't risk losing this chance with you." Her face implored him to obey, and his expression showed he knew she was no part of his dream.

"How did you-"

"-I'm not sure how I did it, and I'm not sure I can do it again," Karyn stated, lowering her hands to her sides. "All I know is that I managed to get here somehow." William looked truly stunned and walked up to her, slowly studying her from head to toe. She could almost see the wheels turning in his head while he calculated her likelihood of being real. "And I assure you, I **am** real; at least as real as I can be in **this** reality."

Her comment broke him out of his examination trance, and he smiled a slightly sad smile. "Nice to know the true essence of your personality survived **this** reality," he said, and added quietly, "how I've missed you, baby…"

Karyn smiled an equally poignant smile. "I've missed you too, Will…but there's a lot more than you that I've been missing." She pointed to her head and said, "I'm missing huge amounts of my memory."

William's smile faded. "What do you mean?"

"Exactly what I said."

"No, I mean, from a specific time, or just random moments?" he asked anxiously. "How do you know you're missing parts of your memory?" Will nervously shifted his weight to his good knee. Karyn noted his concern, and his posture told her something was wrong. He was tense, edgy. She looked away from him, towards the undecorated tree.

"I've lost everything past the time you left for Europe. I can only remember a week or two past that. I have no memories at all beyond that point."

The color drained from Will's face at her statement, and he fell back into the closest chair. "Nothing? You don't remember…anything after I left?" he asked, weakly.

"No. I only recently connected to that last memory, and I don't know how I did that, either. I think that I may have wished it to happen, but things are so weird where I am…I don't know, Will…" Her lip began to tremble and the corners of her mouth turned down. William could see the tears pooling in her eyes.

"Honey…" He sprung up and pulled another chair over for her, far enough away where he couldn't accidentally touch her, but close enough to be supportive. "…maybe you should sit and tell me what things are like…where you are; it would help me understand exactly what you've been going through. Tell me everything, baby."

Karyn looked a little panicked at his request. "I don't know how long I have here, or how long this moment will last - there's no time!"

Will shook his head. "This is my dream, and I have the final say here. You take as much time as you need. Tell me where you've been. Tell me everything."

She was afraid, but the little voice spoke up and said *"talk"*. She obliged him, pouring out the tale of her journey; hesitant at first, but soon spilling over with details of the shop, Kalea, the cafe, the park, the dreams…everything he had asked for, in spades. William listened in rapt attention, elbows on his knees at times, hanging on her every word. At the end of her story, Karyn slumped in the chair, spent. Will kicked back as well, scratching his stubble thoughtfully, processing the massive amount of information she had shared. His eyes brightened, and she could almost see the questions rising in his mind before he asked them.

"Go ahead…" she sighed, leaning her head on one hand and tucking her legs up.

"Go ahead…what?"

"Start asking all those questions you've got. I don't know if I have any real answers, but I'll do my best."

He grinned. "You know, even when you're exhausted, you're beautiful. That really **is** the real you, isn't it?" She gave a tired nod and waved her hand for him to get on with it. "Okay, then…this Kalea woman…do you think she's right? That she told you the truth?"

"I do."

"Why? You said you didn't know for sure that she was real."

"Does it even matter?" she groaned. "None of it may be real, but it's where I exist now, apparently, so that's as real as it's gonna get."

"So why do you believe her?"

"Because it felt like the truth. When I accepted the reality of my…reality, things became clearer. Not much, but more than there was before."

"Do you believe she was right about the whole consciousness-separation thing?"

"I don't know, but…probably. I know I don't feel…complete, somehow." She rubbed her eyes. "I always thought it was the memories that were missing, but if not all of my consciousness, my soul, spirit, whatever, is together…then, I guess she might be right."

"And every time you had an…episode, or a dream, you would recall all of your past up to that point?" She nodded again. "And nothing beyond?" Another nod. Will stood up and walked to the window. The snow was still falling, blanketing the neighborhood with its purity. "Tell me…was the dream sex really that good?" he asked offhandedly.

Karyn sat up. "What?" She could almost hear him smirking. "Seriously, Will?" she said, getting out of the chair with a grumble. "I go to all this trouble to come from…another fucking dimension maybe, and all you can ask is how was the sex?" She scowled at him from next to the window.

He didn't take his eyes off the street; they were pensive and tired. He closed them with a sigh. "Easy, baby…this is…a lot for me to handle at once. And," he said, turning to look her right in the eyes, "I was curious, that's all."

"Really?…" she said coolly as she walked over to the Christmas tree, picking an ornament from the box. "Well…I'm curious, too." She was all attitude. "Why do you stay here, Will? Are you always in this place in your dreams?" If he wanted to play on her precious time, so be it. She hung the ornament on the tree, a small white china bell they had bought at a thrift store together.

"It's one of my favorite memories of us," Will replied, his voice tinged with sadness.

"But it isn't reality," she said lightly, pulling another bell from the ornament box.

"This is the reality I want."

"Why? What reality is going on right now that you don't want?" she said casually. *Now we're gonna get somewhere, dammit,* she thought.

He looked back out to the street. "I can't say."

"Can't say - or **won't** say?" she pressured him.

"Either."

"Why not?" she said testily. "I want to know what's happening where you are, just like you wanted to know about me. What, this is a one-way sharing fest all of a sudden?" She waved her hands around, making the bell tinkle in the air.

He winced slightly at her comment, but remained reserved. "It's not like that, Karyn. It's more…involved."

Will was measuring his words carefully, as if to sidestep some land mine that would blow up between them. Karyn couldn't guess what would keep him so closed up; their relationship had always been so open in the past, but perhaps something had changed in her missing memory time, something he didn't want to divulge to her now. When she defined the breadth of her memory loss, he appeared truly shocked, but now he was closing up. *Why is he shutting me out? What's happened to him in his world?* she wondered.

"Is there…someone else, Will?" she asked tentatively.

His face registered surprise, and then subtle amusement. "No, darling," he answered with a half smile. "I'm not involved with anyone, if that's what you're asking." For a moment, she saw a flash of the old William, before he acquired this air of sadness. She felt he was carrying some heavy burden deep inside; something terrible he wouldn't share.

"Then why won't you tell me?" she asked. "There was never anything that we couldn't talk about before, so…why keep this to yourself? It can't be that bad-"

He cut her off with a bark. "**It is**…believe me, it is." Karyn cringed at the loudness of his response, and decided to change the subject.

"Okay, okay…then…how about you help me get the rest of my memories back instead?" She finally hung the bell in her hand, carefully spacing it from the last, and plucked the next one from the box. "Tell me what happened to us after Europe," she said lightheartedly, searching for the next ornament space. "Did we get back together like a romance novel and ride off into the sunset? Did you become rich and famous? Did I finish my thesis and get tenure?" She glanced back over her shoulder for his smile, but there was none. He was struggling internally, and silent; those questions were also on the 'do not ask' list as well.

Her frustration began to get the better of her, and she lashed out at him. "So you won't tell me any of that, either? What the hell, Will?" Her voice began to elevate in pitch. "Is there **anything** you **can** tell me, or have I just been wasting my time here? Or perhaps you'd rather spend your time with your fantasy dream version of me? I bet **she** doesn't ask as many questions!"

Will crumpled at her accusation, looking like a beaten puppy, and said in a barely audible voice, "I love you, Karyn. You've got to believe me that I love you, and the reason why I can't tell you anything is a very good one." He begged her with his eyes to not push further with any more questions; they were becoming watery again, and she was shocked at how fragile he had become. She wished she hadn't spoken so rashly.

"Will, I need you to stop being cryptic and tell me everything you know about where I am," she pleaded, "I can't get out of where I am without your help."

He shook his head no and his face contracted in pain. "If you don't know, I cannot tell you. I agree with that Kalea woman, Karyn; me telling you what I know means I would be influencing you, and I love you too much to do that…no matter how badly I want you to be with me." His posture was tightly wound as he turned to face her, shifting his weight to his other leg again. Karyn recognized that behavior; it meant Will was reaching his limit on that moment, a thing that rarely occurred. Looking at the floor, he said plainly, "It's not my place to tell you, Karyn."

His refusal shocked her into dropping the china bell, shattering it into fragments on the wood floor. He had denied her. Refused her the one chance she had to escape her situation and be with him. The pain in her head was returning again.

Why? Why would he abandon me now when I need him, when he said he loved me, that he'd wait for me? I don't understand…

A flash of pain in her parietal lobes flicked a switch, and she grabbed her head with her hands as she dropped to her

knees. "Why…can't…you…tell…me!" she spit through
gritted teeth. "What am I not…allowed to know?" The sharp
pain passed as quickly as it came, and Karyn staggered back to
her feet, falling sideways into the couch. She curled up until
the throbbing ceased, while her mind was racing through the
conversations she had with Kalea, all of which were suddenly
fresh in her mind, as was the vision of Will in the park. That's
when she realized why Will was crying in the park, and crying
the last time she saw him. Gradually, Karyn moved both feet
to the floor and sat up.

"You know, **don't** you," she asked him in a low, deep
growl, with her head still down and aching. "You know where
I am." She looked at him accusingly. "You **know** where I am
- don't you!"

His hesitation in answering her confirmed his guilt, and
his face didn't lie. "Yes, I know where your physical self is,"
he admitted, running his hands through his hair, "but, please
understand-"

"I **don't** understand! You say you love me, you want
us together, but you're not helping me! That makes no sense,
Will! Tell me what you know!"

"If you don't know, I cannot tell you!" he yelled back at
her, instantly regretting raising his voice, and softened his tone
to continue. "I cannot interfere, Karyn. Your situation
is…tenuous. If I tell you anything, anything at all, I risk
tipping the balance for you."

She stood and marched over to him. "What the hell are
you talking about? What balance? I need to get out of here!"

"And just how do you think you're to accomplish that,
darling?" he snapped back. "If you could've just waltzed out
of here, you'd have already done it. A part of you has decided
it's safer to be here than where the rest of you is, and until you
change that, you'll stay lost."

"I don't want to be here! Why would I want to be
here?"

"That's what I'm trying to tell you!" He threw his
hands up in the air and paced around the floor, bits of china
crunching under his feet. He paused and rubbed his forehead
into his thick hair. "You remember what Kalea said? **You**

have to do this alone, and I cannot help you. If I told you what I know, you may make the wrong choice - for **you**, not for me - and I won't be party to that. Your life is **yours** to control, not mine to influence."

His statement did not sit well with her, and it brought up deep anger from within her. "If you really loved me, you'd tell me," she said coldly. Karyn was ashamed to play that card, but she was desperate. She had to force his hand and tell her what was going on.

"No! It's **because** I love you that I **won't**." The look on his face was full of love, but unmoved. His reserve was strengthening; she knew he wasn't going to budge now unless she came up with something fast. Their moment in the park instantly came to mind, and the reasons behind his refusal were coming into focus. With nothing else to lose, she threw it out on the floor.

"The reason you won't tell me has to do with the other voice I heard in the park, doesn't it?"

William came up short at her statement, and for one second he looked both guilty and frightened. His poker face was gone. Karyn had him, and she ruthlessly ploughed forward.

"Who was the other voice I heard that day in the park, Will? Who was it?" she demanded. The anger within her was driving her actions.

Will tilted his head down in defeat, and looked at her with eyes brimming with tears and regret that confirmed her suspicions. "Baby…please don't do this. I'm begging you…please don't ask me anything else."

Karyn didn't care. She was so close to caving him in, and she was going for it. She invaded his personal space, only inches from his face, and shouted shrilly again, "Who was the other voice? Tell me! Tell me, Will!"

William slumped forward slightly, and she thought he might fall over and crumple. Instead, he pounced on her, wrapping her in his arms and pressing his lips to hers before she could escape, trapping her in a kiss that took her breath away as he broke the enchantment on their shared moment. Karyn could taste his tears in her mouth and feel the warmth of

his body briefly, before the space between her molecules
stretched out, and she became as thin and vaporous as the air
around him.

19
Decision

The sounds Karyn heard as Will drew her body into his own were indescribable; a cacophony of pulsing, vibrations, and frequencies that were both tactile and psychic, rolling through her in waves. They carried private knowledge of him, his emotions, and his thoughts at the moment they were enmeshed. She found no answers within his mind, however. He had locked down that forbidden information before he embraced her, leaving only an imprint of intense love and sadness. Karyn knew she had overstepped her bounds and hurt him with her aggression, but she also knew Will forgave her trespass before he kissed her away. None of that mattered now, of course. Her rash actions had cost her dearly, and standing alone in her apartment again, the only tears she could taste were her own. Karyn fell into the couch, sobbing until she was out of breath and exhausted.

She lay limply on the cushions, the tears running from her eyes and puddling in her ears while she replayed her go around with William over and over again. With each replay, Karyn kicked herself a little harder, berated herself a little more. She could have had hours with him, gradually working her way through the murkiness of her memories, enjoying what precious time they could share…but no. She just had to push him too far, allowing her needs and emotions to override all else until Will had no other recourse but to send her on her way. Her anger overwhelmed her so quickly, ruining everything.

I'm such an idiot, she thought. *I never considered his feelings…not once…and now I'm back here again, alone.*

The visit hadn't been a total loss, however. She learned a very painful, but useful, lesson in those moments; that her emotions were both her strongest asset and her Achilles' heel. They were powerful enough to propel her consciousness through the space between realities to see William. If she could harness and restrain the downside of those same emotions, the ones that separated her consciousness and sent her into this realm in the first place, there was a chance that she could reunite all parts of her mind with her physical body. That is…if she truly wanted to. And now, she wasn't so sure.

Will's reactions, and the reason he gave for not telling her where she really was, were beginning to dovetail together into an answer she probably wouldn't like. He wasn't crying just because he missed her; in all likelihood, things were very bad wherever Karyn really was, and Will knew exactly how bad they were. The pain on his face was a dead giveaway to the burden he carried. The disembodied voice in the park had implied something was very wrong when it spoke out. It didn't matter that Will never divulged who the owner of the voice was; he knew who they were, and they had told him, *"She cannot **hear** you, Will."*

She cannot hear you. Will was playing in the park with tears streaming down his cheeks for a girl that couldn't hear him, and Karyn could only assume that girl was her. It made sense, when she recalled how wild-eyed he was at hearing her voice, as if it were an impossibility. That reaction confirmed that William knew she was in a bad way, and once she added in Will's evasive answers and Kalea's description of soul fracturing, there was no doubt left in her mind. *The 'she'*, Karyn thought, ***must** be me*!

Maybe things are so bad that he's afraid I won't come back if I know the truth, she guessed. Will said he agreed with Kalea's soul theory; it kept him tight-lipped, and might be the reason he looked so shocked when she told him her memories were missing. Will would have no other reason to **not** tell her where she was, unless he thought the truth was more than she could handle, which brought her back full-circle to how she got here in the first place - to some event so bad that her psyche couldn't deal with the damage any other way than to fracture, sending her away to this plane of existence.

A chill ran down her back. What could have happened to her in the other world? What broke her soul into shards? Suddenly the thought of discovering the truth was far less appealing to her. If Kalea was correct, that truth was what she had to confront in order to escape this place and get back to Will; even if she did, and it worked...would it be worth it? How hard would it be for her once she faced that reality, once she was back, if she made it back? William placed serious gravity on not influencing her decisions; if her life wasn't bad, he wouldn't have balked at telling her everything. Karyn was beginning to realize how serious her situation might really be. It was a serious question: the evil she knew, being stuck here, versus the evil she didn't - the unknown thing she must deal with in order to be whole again. It gave her pause. She considered the implications of abandoning her quest to leave, and why it might be easier just to stay where she was.

What am I like in Will's world? Maybe it would be better to live here instead...

She stood up and wandered around the room, casually assessing this level of reality. In theory, she could make this room look like anything she wanted. She could change the wall color, the furnishings, or even the couch, but of what benefit would that be? Even if she could create the perfect surroundings, the perfect world for her to stay here and exist within...was that false existence of any value? Now that she **knew** she was in the wrong place, could she stay here and avoid whatever ugly reality awaited her and be at peace knowing that a part of her was elsewhere? Could willful ignorance truly be bliss, or just be a lie she chose to live in?

The lie was seductive. Her current existence, while not exactly what she wanted, was relatively safe. Karyn even had a fair amount of security in this life and the ability to manipulate the reality to some degree. Thrusting herself into a traumatic situation, one that could potentially further damage her consciousness, paled in comparison to a peaceful life in a world of her own making. If creating a fantasy life was possible, a life where she could essentially have anything she wanted, whenever she wanted, there would be little motivation for her to return to the real world. Of course, Karyn had no idea of how much her consciousness could influence this plane, but that just meant she had to do a bit of testing. Testing that would confirm or deny her boundaries.

She began with her apartment. Karyn reasoned that if her mind could change the appearance of something here, like when it removed the mirror when she was in the shower, it might be possible to manipulate other things, so she set about a basic test, such as changing the color of the wall. Picking the wall across from where she stood, Karyn closed her eyes and envisioned one of her favorite colors, a deep terracotta, applied to the whole length of the wall. She focused intensely from behind closed eyelids for one minute, detailing the exact shade and depth of the reddish brown pigment, spreading it across the blank white canvas of the wall, and at the end of that concentrated effort, she opened her eyes.

The wall, which previously bore the snowy emptiness of flat, white paint, was now a rich, deep, earthen terracotta. Karyn's jaw slacked in surprise. She didn't really think it would work, but the gorgeous colored wall confirmed that this current reality could be manipulated. Delighted, Karyn continued to test the limits with more experiments. She boldly imagined Van Gogh's painting, "Starry Night", hanging on the newly recolored surface, as vibrant and gorgeous as it had been when she gazed at it in the Museum of Modern Art, and upon lifting her eyelids, found it placed in her apartment in its gallery setting, perfectly reproduced. She giggled at the outrageous thought of having such a famous masterpiece only feet from her, as if she plucked it from the museum and brought it home like something from the gift shop.

After such a bold attempt, Karyn tried for something closer to her heart next. She manifested an antique chaise lounger that her Grandmother owned, resplendent with gold braid, emerald tufted velvet, and hairy paw feet, so real that it even smelled like her Grandmother's house. Further emboldened by her success, Karyn then turned her focus to the couch, shut her eyes, and imagined replacing it with the leather couch from her and Will's apartment; using the same amount of focus and intent she had for everything else, she opened her eyes to find she had failed. The same old couch remained and nothing about it had changed. It was the same miserable couch that had always been in her apartment for as long as she could remember.

Why hasn't it changed? What did I do wrong? she wondered. There was obviously a flaw in her theory of manifestation, and Karyn tried to narrow down the incorrect assumption. She ran through the commonalities among the objects, looking for the formulas that resulted in success. Until this point, every object she pulled from her memory had appeared, so what was the disconnect? It wasn't her ownership or possession of an object that made it appear; most of what she had just manifested was someone else's property, so that wasn't the issue. She tried to recreate a framed photograph of her and Will from her nightstand in college, to no avail, yet the David Cassidy poster she had on her bedroom wall in sixth grade was right in front of her, as was an autographed copy of Laurie Bernstein's, "Sonia's Daughters", and her favorite teddy bear. On a whim, Karyn attempted to bring back the salt glazed lamp she had admired from the old apartment, and when nothing materialized, she had a pretty good idea of why.

The common denominator was William. Anything connected to, or associated with Will was impossible to manifest. It didn't seem to matter whether it was a picture containing his image, or an object that had a memory of him attached; once he was affiliated with it, it was off limits to Karyn's abilities. She repeatedly attempted to manifest other objects tied to Will, and all failed. She had finally defined the limits of her imaginative talent, but, her discovery created more difficult and pressing questions.

Above all else, Will was the one person she wanted to see, and Karyn could only guess that her subconscious had decided that wasn't a good idea. Her present reality was a creation of her subconscious, for the sole purpose of keeping her safe, yet it had allowed her to see William from another plane and access him in his dreams; why would it prevent her from recreating objects associated with him now? Karyn wasn't concerned as to what form she existed in if she could still talk to Will, or have some contact with him. She knew she existed, and that was all that mattered, but her subconscious seemed to be hinting that her priorities were incorrect, and for the life of her, Karyn had no idea why.

Avoidance, said the little voice clearly.

"Avoidance?" she repeated out loud. "I'm not avoiding anything."

Comfortable, it replied. *Easier*, it admonished.

Her stomach knotted up and her throat tightened. "That's not it!" she croaked.

Afraid, it said with disappointment, and retreated back into silence. Karyn could say nothing in her defense; her throat was gripped with the painful tightness that comes from pure emotion. Emotion that pained her because the voice was absolutely right. She was afraid, and she was stalling in making her decision. Some part of her subconscious, the little voice, just called her out on it, and she was ashamed to admit how afraid she was.

All this dabbling in psychological, magical trickery was merely a distraction, and her subconscious disapproved. Such fantasies allowed her to have the privilege of William without doing the real dirty work required to reunite herself. It decided Karyn would never take the steps towards unification if she was comfortable in her false reality, choosing to surround herself with props from her memories of happier days, instead of moving forward. Her passive avoidance would then be her undoing; she would float, lost like the shamans in the in-between of non-existence, until her soul shards, her body, and all that comprised her eroded away in time. There could be no avoidance anymore. Now that she knew the path to take, she had to walk it, even if the outcome was unbearable.

An hour later, and after a cup of tea and some quiet moments of contemplation, Karyn sat in the chair opposite her apartment door and called out to the voice. She knew that beyond the door would be the portal to the gauntlet she must face, if the Gatekeepers would let her through. The little voice came forward in her mind, asking, *What do you want?*

"Show me the path that leads to my true existence."

That road is hard. Uncertain.

"Life is hard and uncertain. That is the nature of life."

But you will feel pain.

"Pain, pleasure, sadness, joy...I want to feel **everything** again," Karyn asserted.

But you are safe here.

"I am **not** safe here. This is an illusion of control and safety. I choose the challenge of living over the perception of safety."

Your life is here.

"My life is **not** here. This is **not** my life. This is not **living**. I choose to face my true life, no matter what awaits me there. Now, will you grant my request?" she asked with an unwavering tone.

What makes you think you're ready to leave? asked a new voice. This one was deeper, and the tonality was resistant; Karyn could only assume it was another part of her subconscious stepping up, perhaps one of the Gatekeepers that Kalea spoke of. She thought carefully before answering.

"I can do no more here, in this reality. I need to move forward."

What have you learned in order to do so?

"I know that only by facing my past can I live fully in the present. I know that avoidance or action are my choices alone, and I take complete responsibility for my fate."

There was a significant silence, a pause that made Karyn worry if she had given the wrong answers. Then, a third voice made its presence known. It spoke with a heavy, lumbering pentameter, as if it was the voice of a mountain god. It rumbled and resonated through Karyn's head. *What gives you the right to leave here? Why should we release you as you ask?*

She spoke with absolute conviction, and her voice was clear and sharp. "I have the right to choose my path. I choose to live a real life."

Another long pause filled the quiet in her mind, as if the voices were considering her reply carefully, like a panel of judges in a courtroom. Karyn thought they had left her alone, until the little voice, the one that had always been with her, spoke up softly with the gentleness and caring of an old friend. It asked again, *What do you want?*

Karyn took a deep breath and made her last, best answer as simple and convincing as she could.

"I want to be whole again," she said.

With that, the door of her apartment opened slowly before her, and the doorway was illuminated with blue-white light so brilliant that it blocked the view of what was beyond it. The Gatekeepers had approved her request. Karyn raised herself from the chair, and gave a last glance around the apartment, the imagined place that had been both her refuge and her prison; a place that she created unknowingly and lived in ignorantly for what felt like a lifetime. The space she chose to no longer inhabit.

The light of the doorway beckoned her, and a magnetism that caught her breath in her throat and pulled on her as she walked towards it. There was a gravity to it that wrapped around her, and for a moment it felt like the sound filaments of William's sonata, weaving around her in the park. It adhered to her in diaphanous strips, each attachment removing a little weight from her steps until she was almost floating to the doorway. An almost imperceptible hum greeted her as she tilted her head back on the final step into the brilliance, resonating through her entire body as she was enveloped…and then gone.

Part Two

20

Before

The crisp, clean air was a welcome respite from the stuffiness of the office, and Karyn reveled in the painted hues of the trees as they passed by her car window. A week of warm days and cool nights were the ideal recipe for the vibrant reds and yellows of fall, and the oaks and maples lining the roadside were truly a sight to behold. The autumn was, without doubt, her favorite time of the year.

She had other reasons to be excited, however. Company was coming for the weekend, and very special company at that; someone she hadn't seen in more years than she cared to say, who held a very special place in her heart, despite the fact that almost fifteen years had passed without any contact between them. After everything that Karyn had been through, all the loss and all the moves, the last thing she expected was to be found by William Thalheim - but found her he did, and he was all she could think about now.

It began with a simple, unassuming email. A single sentence asking, "How are you?" had materialized in her inbox. How the email made it past the spam filters was a miracle, and she gasped when she saw his name.

Will said he had been actively searching for her for months, although Karyn couldn't believe she was of such importance to warrant such attention on his part. After so much time apart she doubted that he ever thought of her at all, especially not with all the success he was enjoying. All his dreams had come true, thanks to his hard work, sacrifice, and dedication to his craft, and there wasn't a music producer in music industry who didn't know his name. He rubbed elbows with the top names in the arts, not just in music, but in film and theater as well, and she doubted there was a woman alive who wouldn't want to be on his arm. But, he was still single…and he wanted to talk to her.

The years had fallen away with their first phone call, and it was as if their relationship never missed a beat. He was still the stable, amusing, whip-smart arts geek, full of stories and tales. His voice was an audible smile, and his laugh warmed her soul; a soul worn, beaten and broken by the wheel of life these last few years. Every time they spoke, the hands of time were pushed back and she was young again, full of the promises of youth and a carefree life together.

That didn't happen in the end, however. Their lives had both taken very different paths back then. She was headed to graduate school, and William was embarking on his musical career abroad. They both wanted to pursue their dreams, and made the difficult and painful decision to part company after sharing a few final weeks together. Those last weeks were the most passionate and intense of her life. Just recalling them made her grip the steering wheel tighter, and her insides quiver with weakness.

Karyn had thought about William almost every day since they separated. During bleak moments of her life he was a small, distant hope, a Christmas present filled with beautiful memories that she could reminisce about privately, alone, and in silence. Those cherished mementos kept her going; they were the only thing she allowed herself to keep, the only thing not torn from her by her own hands when she abandoned her previous life. A life that was once promising…and gradually slid into abuse.

Of course, it didn't begin that way. The beginning of that life was almost fairy tale in nature; a dashing young man crossed her path at a time when she felt most alone, and his timing couldn't have been better. By then, Karyn's deepest fear had come true. Communications with William had gradually fallen silent over the five years since he had left, with only an occasional letter every couple of months. Their tone had degraded from the romantic, upbeat, lighthearted banter that peppered their relationship together, to a faded and colorless version of conversation that she barely recognized as his. Something was seriously wrong, but with no permanent address for him on the road there was no way she could find him, intervene, and reconnect. Karyn had almost accepted the fact that they were lost to each other now, as painful as that truth was.

That pain eased when she crossed the campus quadrangle and was almost knocked flat by Bryce. Her books went flying, and she landed face first on the stranger, almost nose to nose with a mop of blond hair and crystal blue eyes. His soft southern voice asked her if she was alright as he helped her back to her feet and gathered her books, apologizing the entire time. By the time Karyn straightened out her clothing, she had already asked him to coffee at the local cafe. He accepted, and thus the fairy tale began. It was a magical time for her. Bryce erased the pain and disappointment she carried while waiting for William and replaced them with romance, wonder, and devotion. His inner beauty equaled his external beauty; his patience and gentility healed the hole in her heart, and lifted her depression. She fell deeper into love than she ever thought possible, but, like the old classic fairy tales, a darker theme began to emerge over time.

At first, Karyn didn't notice. The change in Bryce's behavior was subtle, and the gradual evolution of him from a gracious, kind and loving man to a critical and resentful beast progressed stealthily at a slow, steady pace while they were together. She chalked some of it up to the recent passing of his strong-willed, Southern belle mother, and him being her only child. Bryce took her death exceptionally hard, and he fell into a deep depression just as Karyn's professional career was taking off; small warning signs that should have alerted her to their unsavory future were ignored, and by the time Karyn got the message loud and clear, he was already unstable and becoming violent.

She hadn't planned on leaving all the things and people she loved in haste, but she had been smart enough to know that it was a possibility. The man she loved had changed beyond recognition. There was nothing she could do right, nothing she could say right anymore, and he had replaced his regular barrage of invectives with a rain of blows. The more time passed, the further her promising life moved away, along with any hopes of happiness and love, until she was isolated from everything that mattered to her and completely at Bryce's mercy.

Bryce, however, didn't know what mercy was. He had degenerated into someone unrecognizable, unsalvageable, and incapable of feeling anything other than the rage he directed out from within himself and onto Karyn. She finally left him with almost nothing but her wallet and the clothes on her back. Her savior-turned-tormentor had spent the evening criticizing, berating, and eventually beating her almost to the point of unconsciousness before leaving for an evening out; when Karyn awoke, she instinctively knew that if she didn't leave at that moment, she would never get another chance to leave him. She'd just be another domestic abuse fatality statistic, dead from her denial of a reality she couldn't accept.

When she stepped on the Greyhound bus, her heart beat a little slower, and her legs nearly gave way. She collapsed in the seat and slept despite the staring faces of the other passengers. The bruises told her story, and she slept dreamlessly until she was far, far from him.

The sun rested in the treetops, shining its golden red light across the road in dappled patches as it gradually slid below the tree line towards its evening home, and the passenger side window was down to enjoy the freshness of the early twilight air blowing across her face. Moments like this just reminded Karyn how really good life was. Everything was shifting, from the darkness of struggle to the light of success; her position at the college had been renewed for the next two years, and her students' enthusiasm made her job a joy. Watching their young minds at work, connecting the dots during research and discovery, reminded her of herself at that age. Their optimism and curiosity stoked fires of her own she thought had long died out; teaching became her lifeline during her unsure resettlement time, and with her new extended contract, Karyn considered what to research for her publishing obligation. In a 'publish or perish' world of academia, a book certainly wouldn't hurt if they offered her tenure at some point, and she loved the whole research process. The exploration of ideas, formulation of theses, and digging through piles of primary source documents were an academic's guilty pleasure. She felt her best and brightest when she was hot on the trail of a forgotten piece of information that might shed new light on an old notion. That was the beauty of history for her - deconstructing the past allowed for a better understanding of the present.

The sky was more red than gold by the time Karyn pulled into her driveway. Balancing both bags of groceries on her one arm, she unlocked her door and shouldered it open. The house felt unusually cool; Karyn wondered if she had forgotten to change the thermostat schedule now that the nights were cooler, but she could hear the heater running in the basement. She kicked the door closed with her foot while juggling her way into the kitchen.

"Scraps! Where are you, boy? I got you a new bone," she hollered as she gently slid the bags onto the counter. Normally, Scraps would be at the door the second he heard her car pull in the driveway, always ready with a wagging tail and a happy dog face to make even her worst day better. She should have been hearing his nails on the tile floor by now though, and stopped unpacking the bags to go find him.

"Probably entranced at the window by the neighbor's cat again," she groaned, walking around the kitchen island to the family room. The scruffy rescue mutt was her first and only companion since she moved to the area, protecting her against the loneliness of restarting her life from scratch, making new friends, and finding work. Many a night she had cried herself to sleep, or woken up crying from the nightmares to find solace in Scraps' big brown concerned eyes and sloppy doggy kisses. He nuzzled away the pain better than any opiate, and soothed her broken self in a way no antidepressant could. *Will's gonna love him*, she smiled. *He's so totally a dog person, he's sure to love him.*

The family room was even cooler than the kitchen, but that thought was fleeting when she saw Scraps. The dog was casually stretched out in his dog bed as if napping. His back was towards her, and as she got closer she could see the band of red that ran from his throat to his belly; his eyes were open and unblinking, his tongue hanging out of the bottom side of his mouth. The floor in front of him was soaked with blood. The dog bed was the only thing preventing his guts from spilling onto the floor.

At first, Karyn didn't know what she was witnessing. The scene didn't register in her brain as real; it was something out of a bad horror movie, and any minute Scraps would be racing up to her, begging for that bone. Seconds passed, and in those incredibly long moments it took her to absorb the reality at her feet, a chill passed over her. There was a breeze coming from somewhere in the house. A reflection on the floor next to Scraps' body caught her attention, and she realized it was broken glass from the window, above her beloved, gutted pet. The breeze blew lightly across her face again, and time ground to a halt. There was a deafness, a deadening of sound in her head that allowed only her own heartbeat to pound through. *Someone…in the house…must get out of here* was the only thought in her head now. She backed away slowly towards the kitchen, in shock and unsure what to do next. Moving automatically, she backed into something, and realized too late that the something was a someone, as their hands compressed her carotids and she blacked out.

21

Damage

A splitting headache roused Karyn from the void as her eyes gradually adjusted to the dim light in the room. Her nose was instantly assaulted with the smell of rot and animal waste, combined with the residual, cloying scent of a solvent. Her urge to vomit forced her to turn onto her stomach, but with her ankles bound and her arms tied and immobilized at her sides, the best she could manage was a caterpillar lurch on the floor. She barely made it in time to retch her guts next to her, splashing her cheek in the process. Sputtering and spitting, with her stomach relieved of its burden, she rolled back and began to assess her situation.

Her fear was increasing minute by minute. This was not her house, and she had been physically transported by someone with violent ability. Anyone who could gut her dog probably held little regard for people, although, she was still alive and unharmed at this point so Karyn clung to the hope that she could reason with her abductor. She could still see Scraps in her mind, disemboweled and bloody; it was that thought that made her more nauseas than the fetid atmosphere around her. The origin of the stench was all around her. She could see the gray outlines of piles of dog feces laying about, interspersed with bags of garbage. The rotting air was not food, however; it had a distinct quality that she couldn't place at first, but moments later she named it. Flesh. Like the aroma of a roadkilled deer drifting in your car window as you pass it on the highway, except this was much closer, and far more foul.

The smallest amount of moonlight filtered through the broken glass of the windows, shining on the peeling, water stained wallpaper. A chunk of the plaster ceiling had fallen in, exposing the lath above, and a rodent was scratching around nearby. In its putrid condition, the house had to be abandoned, which meant there was little chance of anyone finding her by accident. No doubt her kidnapper had chosen this place for that reason. Being undisturbed would be his top priority; his reasons for wanting such privacy only made her sick to her stomach again.

I've got to get out of here! she screamed in her head.

She crunched up enough to sit, and get a good look at how she was bound. Rough hemp rope, the kind you rarely saw in stores, was wound around her ankles in a figure eight and triple wrapped in between. Her wrists were as well, but tied in tandem to her waist. Wiggling around did nothing; the fibrous texture of the rope acted like Velcro against itself, but she reasoned it could be scissored away against something sharp if she could get to her feet. With another roll to her left and a push with her one shoulder got Karyn to her knees, and after two tries, she managed to rock back onto her feet and stand.

The air was considerably better once she was up. A light fall breeze pushed the miasma away and she took repeated deep breaths to clear her lungs. The room was large for a farmhouse, almost too large, and there were no furnishings to give away its original function. If she didn't know better, Karyn would have guessed it was a barn, except barns didn't have plaster ceilings and wallpaper. She hopped towards to the nearest window to look outside and pinpoint her locale, but the bags of trash blocked her way. It was still too dark to see much in the space, so she hopped and stopped every few feet to search for a sharp object with which to free herself. Karyn had almost crossed the middle of the room when she heard the scraping on the floor.

She froze in place. The sound came from behind her, from the darkest part of the room. Her heart was pounding; she was out in the open and unable to run. She prayed it was a stray dog, a rabid raccoon…anything but the human who brought her here. But it was human footsteps she heard next, walking towards her in a casual, leisurely pace, the hard soles of shoes lightly scuffing with each step. The dread rose in her throat, still tasting of vomit, as they paused in their movement and waited. Karyn knew she had to face the owner of those footsteps; a single glimpse might mean identifying her kidnapper later if she escaped, but her feet were locked in place. She was willing herself to turn at the waist when his words cut the chill night air between them.

"It's good to see you again, darling."

Her heart almost stopped beating.

I know that voice, she thought, *but that's impossible…*

Karyn couldn't stop herself from turning to face him, eyes wide with disbelief at hearing a voice she thought she had put far behind her, in a place she swore she would never revisit.

"I thought you would be more happy to see me…" he continued in a syrupy sweet tone as he sidled up behind her, "…since you forgot to kiss me goodbye when you left." His slight southern drawl was edged in ice; Karyn's blood went cold to her core, and she began to shake uncontrollably. His face lit up at her reaction, rocking back and forth on his heels while he watched her unravel. Running his hand through his short blond hair, Bryce kept his eyes locked on Karyn as he moved in front of her, feeding on her increasing fear. "You and I have some unfinished business to discuss, and we have all the time in the world to do it."

He walked back to the darkest corner and brought out the folding chair he had been sitting on. He had been watching her the entire time, like some twisted audience to Karyn's unintentional performance art. He could see the recognition of that fact on her face, and laughed. "Oh yes, Karyn…I've been here since the moment I dumped you on that filthy floor, right where you belong." His eyes were a little too wide open as he looked at her. "It was a tad boring while you napped…I probably used a bit too much chloroform…but it was downright lovely to watch you wear your own puke."

Karyn was on high alert now, and her mind was racing, searching for an escape route. For one moment, she thought she could talk her way out of this with Bryce, but this was not the Bryce that she had left years ago. This was a different man, one she had never experienced, and it terrified her. His whole manner reeked of instability and rage. It was as if his personality had taken a chaotic left turn for the worse; his personality was bad when she left him, but nowhere near what she'd witnessed in the short span of these few minutes. *This has to be a bad dream*, she prayed.

"Let it never be said that Bryce Rutlege is not a true southern gentleman, even to the most worthless woman." He placed the chair behind her and gestured to it. "Sit down," he said politely. She hesitated, still processing the unlikelihood of the moment being a nightmare when he exploded in a bellow at her. "**SIT!**" he yelled, pushing her backwards so that she landed sideways on the seat, almost toppling over. "Thank you," he continued in his previous polite tone, as if he had never raised his voice. He scuffed over to another garbage pile and produced a wooden crate, plunking it down across from her and alighted upon it as if it were an upholstered antique. A pale beam of moonlight passed between them, giving just enough illumination for Karyn to make out the bizarre serenity that graced his face, a classically beautiful face that betrayed the cruelty within.

Bryce pulled out a pack of cigarettes and tapped one down against the closed lid. The knot in Karyn's stomach got tighter.

"Why do you think you're here, Karyn?" he asked blithely, as he lit his smoke. The lighter flame danced as he inhaled.

She quickly considered what answer to offer against such a dangerously open-ended question. Karyn already knew anything she said would be wrong; the goal was to be the least wrong possible, and avoid torquing him up further. She still wasn't sure who she was dealing with, and until she did, Karyn was working on old, probably outdated, information. She gave him the answer she thought he wanted to hear. "Because you wanted to see me, Bryce," she said, calmly.

"You're damn right I wanted to see you," he exhaled the smoke and smiled a chilling grin, "and you made that considerably harder for me, didn't you?"

She swallowed hard. There was nothing she could say now. Anything else would be dangerous with this unstable version of Bryce.

"I had no idea where you went. I stepped out to watch the football game..."

...after beating the shit out of me...

"...and returned to find my house untidy, my stove cold, and my woman gone."

*I am **not** your woman.*

"No goodbye kiss, no note or letter..." he inhaled again, "...no explanation...do you have any idea how bad that made me look to the guys? I mean, it looked like I couldn't keep my woman in line..."

I am not your woman*, she repeated the mantra to herself again.

"...because if I could, you'd still be right where you were supposed to be. With me. Doing what I told you to do, when I told you to do it..." Bryce flicked the ash off his cigarette onto a pile of dog dung nearby, "...just like my woman should."

I AM NOT YOUR FUCKING WOMAN! Karyn screamed in her thoughts. Deep within her, a door was being unlocked; she could almost hear the key scraping against the tumblers every time he spoke. The abuse she had tried so hard to lock away and forget was percolating up and sickening her. Her thoughts were rising above her fear, driven by the years of suffering she had endured at his hands.

He sat back on the crate and wagged a finger at her. "You did a fine job of covering your tracks, girl, I'll give you that. No forwarding addresses, no social media accounts...I really had to work to find you. Even when you sold your parents' house, you had the smarts to put that money in a trust." He leaned forward and asked her with a glint in his eye, "Just how long had you been planning to leave me, honey?"

It took me forever, you bastard, she seethed in her head. *I could have killed you and been out of jail sooner.* She forced her anger down and hoped it was dark enough that Bryce didn't notice anything.

"Not that long. I was hoping things would get better between us," she lied, keeping her statement from blaming him. Don't poke the rabid dog.

"Were you really?" he mused.

No. I wasn't, she simmered inside.

"Yes," she lied again, trying to look amenable. Bryce seemed a bit more interested for a moment. He took another drag from his cigarette and moved the crate close enough to bump their knees together when he sat back down. Draped in the silvery moonlight and entirely too close for her comfort, Karyn wondered if she could manage a hard enough kick to his balls to make him pass out.

"I almost want to believe you're telling the truth," he said, dryly, "but you've already proved what a deceitful bitch you are by leaving me in the first place. For the record, we'd still be together if you'd just unfucked yourself like I told you to. You could have had it so easy, but you chose to not listen, not follow the most simple, basic rules. They were for your own good, you stupid girl." Bryce shook his head at her in disappointment, and Karyn felt the anger bubbling in her throat.

Sanctimonious, self-important prick. How dare you...

"And it seems you haven't improved yourself in the least during our time apart," he continued. "You should see how pathetic you are, Karyn…puke on your face, and still no clue as to why you're here. You might not be, you know," he exhaled offhandedly, "if you had gotten yourself a decent watchdog." He flashed a big smile at her, owning the murder of her dog with genuine pride. "That half-breed piece of shit put up an okay fight, but you know how much I fucking **hate** mongrels, baby…"

The image of her dog came back to her on a wave of fury that boiled beyond her physical restraints. She spat on him with all the hatred she could muster as he bent down to stub out his cigarette out on the floor. He raised his face in disbelief, amazed that she would attack him from her current position of weakness, and gave her an evil grin as he sent her rocketing backwards out of the chair and onto the floor. A thin snapping sound accompanied a backhand so hard she was almost knocked unconscious. He stood over her, enjoying the look of her crumpled on the filthy wood boards.

"Maybe you have changed after all," Bryce said, wiping Karyn's spit from his face. He dragged her up by her one arm, righted the chair, and threw her back into it. After fishing around in the darkness, he produced some additional rope, and began to bind her to the chair. "You seem a bit spunkier compared to the lame, lazy doll you were before. That's good," he crooned, and pulled a folded knife from his back pocket. "It means I'll have more playtime with you before I strangle you with your own intestines, darling."

Karyn's head was just beginning to clear from the blow, and her left eye was ballooning shut. Bryce flipped the knife open, and cut a wide strip of fabric from the bottom of her shirt, which he repurposed as a gag. He deftly tied it over her mouth in one smooth motion, and kissed her on the top of her head, saying lightly, "Think on that for a while. I'll be back later, and then we'll have some real fun."

22

Reckoning

She waited until she heard him drive away, the country music blaring from his radio becoming fainter and fainter, before she allowed herself to cry. There was no way she would give Bryce the satisfaction of her misery while she was still alive; it was obvious that would only feed the beast. With only the sounds of chirping crickets and calling owls around her now, she opened the floodgates and let her pain pour from her eyes in torrents, away from his gloating, demented stare.

The darkness in the room was almost comforting now. Before, she had been afraid of what might be in the room with her; Bryce had proved to be the most frightening thing, and he was gone for the moment, giving her privacy in the dark to cry out her weakness and fear. Once that was done, she would figure out what to do next.

She was more immobile than when she first woke up. Bryce had bound each ankle to a chair leg, and run the rope through the rungs, across her lap, and around her waist to her chest with multiple loops. It made it impossible to stand up with the chair, and combined with her original bindings, the only thing Karyn might be capable of was hopping an inch at a time, but…hop to where? Until there was some daylight, she reasoned it might be safer to stay put and conserve her energy; she was exhausted, and found herself nodding off.

While her body was restrained, her mind traveled free.

"Are you looking for something in particular, miss?"
The twenty-something youth's question jarred her out of her fog, and she looked over to see him with an expectant and helpful smile. "Oh no, I'm just browsing," she replied,

and went back to absentmindedly flipping through the rows of CDs. The boy seemed genuinely disappointed that she passed up his offer to be helpful, and tried again.

"If it's jazz you like, this quartet has a fantastic repertoire," he said, reaching around her right side to the next bin over and handing her the jewel case. The cover art was a Picasso-style portrait of the musicians, the group being a disorganized and abstract series of colored lines. The kid didn't stop there, however. "I saw that you were also looking at the Counting Crows latest, so you might like this as well. Oh, and this group is really fresh. They just finished their first tour; I saw them live before they were picked up by a big label." The boy handed her two more CDs before his manager called him back to unload the latest music shipment.

"Thank you," Karyn said softly, much too late for the kid to hear her words. He was already at the back of the store, and she was left staring at a handful of music.

She was tired. Bryce was supposed to pick her up after work, but he hadn't shown up yet, no doubt doing whatever he wanted while she waited for him to return with her car. It was one more way he kept an eye on her, kept her under his thumb, by limiting her movement. He would drop her off at work, watching to make sure she entered the building, noting who she spoke to on the way in, and berated her if she looked too happy or engaged in conversation with other people, especially men. His paranoia had reached a new high lately, and Karyn was close to snapping from the stress. She was tired, gaunt, and felt years older than her actual age. The fact that the overly-helpful young man had called her 'miss' would have amused her, if she wasn't so beaten down already.

He hadn't hit her lately, so that was a plus. Too often some innocuous slight on her part drew Bryce's wrath to her like a swarm of bees. Once that happened, there was little she could do but shield herself just enough to protect her face, and take the brunt of a blow somewhere else on her body where her clothes would cover the abuse. Karyn had become quite adept at delivering the subtle, casual lies that alleviated the concern from her co-workers' and friends' faces, allowing them to feel comfortable that they had inquired about her well being, but were relieved of the responsibility of the truth. The truth was a disallowed thing, a changing thing, a twisted, evolving thing that only came from Bryce's lips, and was forbidden to be spoken of by her. Everyone knew, but nobody dared say anything, at least not if they had already met Bryce.

The colorful Cubist style of the quartet in her hand drew her eyes downward, and she found herself reading the list of musicians out of boredom. She passed over the rows of exotic and foreign names; percussionists, saxophonists, vocalists and...guitarists. One name elevated itself from the jewel case and jarred her from her funk: William Thalheim.

*Karyn was jolted awake. Was that **her** William? A tingling ran through her body at the thought. It very well might be him. There was no face on the cover to confirm it, but studio musicians were rarely shown in the limelight. She stared at the name again, remembering his smile from such a long time ago. Before Bryce. Before everything went bad. Before he left.*

She wondered how he was, if he looked the same, how far had his career gone after Europe. "He probably wouldn't even remember me," she thought, "not with this much time between us." He was married to someone, for sure, and living a beautiful life far away. Far away from her reality.

Her reality consisted of a daily minefield of Bryce's accusations, threats, and unstable behavior. It was not a beautiful life, but it was the life she had chosen, and been swallowed up in its darkness. For a while she had tried to fix it, and when that didn't work, she tried appeasing him. She became the docile, compliant woman who did everything he wanted, but that, too, didn't work. Now, with years behind her and deeply entrenched in the quicksand of Bryce's mental illness, William's name reminded her of who she used to be, and Karyn could feel a small, bright light go on in her soul.

"I don't want this life anymore," she whispered to herself, just as Bryce pulled up and the sound of an angry, impatient horn sounded outside the store.

"Wakey, wakey, princess. Time to rise and shine!" Bryce said cheerily as he pulled her head back by her hair. He wasn't gentle in his grip by any means, but at least he hadn't roused her with a slap across the face. Karyn squinted as she tried to focus her unswollen eye to see clearly. The gag had absorbed all the moisture in her mouth, and her tongue was parched. In her mind, she was still standing in the music store, remembering that defining moment of her life.

"My, my, darling…were you dreaming? Did I disturb your beauty sleep?" he said while stepping back to view her bound in the chair. "I think you need to sleep a hundred years to fix that face, girl," he chuckled. "Lucky for you, I brought some toiletries to make you a bit more…pleasant." On the chair next to him was a gallon of water, a toothbrush, toothpaste, soap, a washcloth, and a hand towel. She tried to fathom what Bryce was up to; if he intended to kill her, those were the wrong items for the job. Karyn prayed this was a sign that she could reason with him.

While his words were snide and biting, his demeanor was not. There was a noticeable difference in him, a slight softness to the dangerous edge that she witnessed yesterday, and he looked a little drawn and tired. Her hatred of him prevented her from giving any thought to why he appeared worn out; the pounding in her swollen eye had now moved into her cheekbone, which was on fire. The snapping sound she heard when he knocked her across the room yesterday had probably been her cheekbone.

"I had some trouble sleeping last night," he began, "and I got to thinking that maybe I've been a little hard on you. I mean, maybe we got off on the wrong foot yesterday." He strolled over and gently brushed the hair out of her eyes, resting the back of his hand for a moment against her cheek, and her skin crawled with the touch. "Momma and I had a long chat, and she said I should give you another chance. She always liked you, you know. Said you were sweet as sorghum pie." Karyn's eyes welled up against her will at hearing he spent the night talking to his long-dead mother; there was no doubt that he was unhinged now, but Bryce perceived the tears as compliance. She let them flow like a great actress in a silent film, and hoped that he would buy the act.

"I see you agree with me," he nodded, and reached behind her head to loosen the gag, warning her as well. "Any misbehavior, Karyn, and that's it. Got it?" She nodded and looked downward in submission. "Good." The gag dropped around her neck, and she closed her mouth in an effort to remoisten her tongue. Bryce popped the top off the jug of water and lifted it to her lips to drink. She drank greedily, almost choking in the process. It had been at least a day since she'd had anything to drink, and the water was delicious. Her cracked lips and parched mouth welcomed the hydration, and slowly she pulled her head back from the jug to show she had enough.

Bryce sat back on his crate across from her. His face showed a subtle shift of emotions, alternately sad, then loving, then confused. It was obvious he was struggling internally with his thoughts, and she decided to wait and see what he had to say first. Karyn was going to make the most of this reprieve while she had the chance, and following his lead was the best option at the moment.

His face settled on a softer, more sympathetic look, and he asked her if she'd like to brush her teeth. She nodded warily, but Bryce didn't untie her. Instead, he prepared the toothbrush, and motioned for her to open her mouth. Karyn complied, parting her lips hesitantly. The feeling of a foreign hand running the bristles against her teeth was unsettling, but not as unsettling as the thought that toothbrush might be jammed down her throat at any moment. He worked the brush gently from one side to the other, inside and out, across the top row and then bottom row of her teeth. The intimacy of this act of personal hygiene being done by another person, let alone one who she swore would never touch her again, made her feel intruded upon and violated, but this was not the time to rebel. She stayed stock still until he completed his task, finishing by bringing the jug of water to her lips again to rinse her mouth. She was sure to turn her head away from him, instead of at him, when she went to spit. Her mouth now cleaned of the residual taste of vomit and dryness, Karyn watched Bryce carefully, but without resistance, and said, "thank you."

No sooner had she spoken, Bryce rushed in and kissed her, taking her face in both his hands. It was such a sudden and unexpected action that she had no time to react negatively. He allowed himself to let the young, undamaged Bryce, the one she had fallen on in the quadrangle, come out for a precious few seconds during the kiss. She suppressed her disgust and the overwhelming urge to pull away; only by imagining it to be William kissing her was she able to continue the ruse until he was done. He stepped back again, the changing emotions swimming across his face, and looked away for a moment. Karyn capitalized on the opportunity. "Bryce…may I go to the bathroom?" she asked, letting her voice sound small. "Please? I really have to."

He considered her request, saying quietly as he undid the knots, "Go into the far corner over there, and don't try my patience. I'll be watching from here." Once untied, she followed his directions to the letter. The pile of trash afforded her just enough privacy for her to relieve herself, although old newspaper was the closest thing to toilet paper she could find. The newspaper was a local one, from the next county over, which meant she might not be as far from home as she thought. The garbage around her offered nothing else useful, and she couldn't risk stalling any longer than necessary to look around. She finished her business and returned obediently to Bryce, who motioned for her to retake her seat on the chair. She prayed he wouldn't bind her as securely, but that wish went ungranted. He resolutely began to redo the ropes around her, but he seemed almost unwilling to do so.

He's conflicted! Maybe some of the original Bryce is still in there…maybe I can talk my way out of this yet…

She paid close attention to his every movement. Any small mood shift or flicker of normalcy might afford her the chance to manipulate his psychology a little in her favor, maybe just enough to figure out what to do next. If his kiss was an indication that some part of the old Bryce was still present, there was hope. Hope was all she had right now.

"Do you…remember…when we first met?" Karyn asked him, the halting words worsening the pain in her cheek.

Bryce's hands paused for a second, then continued tying the knots. His brow furrowed slightly as he went about securing her. "Of course I do," he said in a subdued tone. "I remember it clearly."

Her mind was formulating the next question while the silence hung in the air. She hadn't a reasonable reply ready, and was scrambling to keep the conversational momentum going. She offered up a compliment. "I thought…you looked like one of the painted angels on a church ceiling," she whispered, sneaking a glance at his reaction. Bryce was raised with a strong religious upbringing; she hoped to leverage some part of his past to her advantage. *If I can just keep him in a safe mental place for me…* she thought, and waited to hear his response.

He was not immediately forthcoming. His hands moved more slowly to finish his work, and he didn't look up. Karyn was thankful he was kneeling on the side of her good eye; at least when he did look up, she'd be able to read his face. The silence between them was thick and awkward, and went on forever.

"You were the most beautiful thing I'd ever seen," he finally said. A twinge of shame and sadness colored the end of his sentence, a fact that was not lost on her. His eyes stayed downcast by her feet, almost in avoidance. Gradually, he rose and walked back to his crate; his head still down, but she could see his face was a swirling sea of emotions pulling him back and forth inside. "What did I mean to you?" he asked in an almost pitifully small, child-like voice.

His small question terrified her and her mouth went dry. *How do I answer that and not set him off? What is the right answer?* Their chat suddenly felt more like a game of Russian Roulette. She hoped her answer was the chamber without the bullet.

"You brought me out of a deep depression, and I…I was in a very sad place then." The words felt bitter in her mouth. She acknowledged his value as a decent human being in the past, which was directly contrary to the present; feeling gratitude towards him seemed ludicrous. It was, however, the truth. He had saved her from locking herself away with only her broken heart for company. As much as she hated Bryce for what he became later, he had lifted her up back then.

He shook his head, and she could almost hear the click of the conversation's trigger. She hid her panic.

"You didn't answer the question," he said with a tiny bit of annoyance. "I didn't ask what I did for you. I asked what I meant to you."

Karyn kicked herself for missing a critical verbal cue. More bitter truths would be flowing from her mouth, and she would deliver them in the performance of a lifetime.

"I said you looked like an angel, and…you were. You were my guardian angel. You protected me, and defended me from everything…you made me feel safe, and…and I loved you for it." She quieted the anger in her mind as she finished. "You meant everything to me. I loved you with everything that I had."

*I loved who you **were**. I **hate** who you are,* she said viciously in her head, but her end goal of escape kept her fury in check. She couldn't risk blowing her grand performance when she was gaining ground with him. With a little more bonding between them, he might agree to let her go, or at least take her with him out of this place, where she could make a run for freedom later.

His face lightened at her words, and she breathed a silent sigh of relief. His resolve seemed to be softening; his eyes were a bit unfocused as if he was daydreaming of that better, happier time. "I loved you, too," he said with a low, sparse voice. "I never loved anyone…like I loved you." His daydreaming eyes became very sad and wet.

"Bryce," Karyn began gently, "could we go somewhere else and talk? Maybe we could work this out, and-"

"It's too late for that now, baby," he said, shaking his head with genuine regret. Her insides froze at his statement, and she watched the emotions roll over him again. Anger, fear, love and hatred flashed through his skin like a chameleon on a color wheel, his limp hands clenching up tighter and tighter into balled fists. He lifted them to his temples as if he was in pain. "It's too late for us…too late…to fix it all…" he moaned as his dropped head down between his forearms. Karyn could feel her chance at freedom being ripped away like her skin.

"It's never too late, Bryce," she pleaded, "please, don't give up on-"

"**I never gave up**!" he bellowed as he flung up his head, staring at her with burning, accusing eyes. "You **left** me!"

The blood drained out of Karyn's face at hearing his voice. The voice of her nightmares. The monster's voice, the one that she heard in between the punches and slaps from her past. There would be no denying that Bryce was sliding beyond the reach of reason, but she played her last card in hopes that she could pull him back from the brink of becoming the vile creature she once knew.

"Honey," she began with slow, cautious words, "who was with you when your Momma passed? I was. I was with you when you needed me, right? I was the one who took care of everything for you, remember?" Karyn hoped her gamble would work, but bringing the ghost of Roberta Rutlege into the moment was a reckless gamble. The mere mention of her might blow him sky high, but she bet against that happening. Bryce had already acknowledged his mother was still influencing him, and Karyn hoped the memory of the dead woman would restrain her son from progressing further into violent madness.

Bryce, however, looked unresponsive, staring ahead with teary, unblinking eyes. "Momma…" he mouthed silently, and went quiet again, leaving Karyn panicking in the vacuum of sound.

What now? What the hell do I say now?

She dug through her memories for the next appeasing maneuver while Bryce was subdued. His tears were falling on the floor like sparse raindrops, picking up speed gradually until they sounded like a spring shower in the silence between them. His muffled crying had increased in volume as well, changing from the occasional quick breath and heave of the shoulders, to the deep, gasping, racking sobs that sound like someone drowning. Bryce rocked back and forth with each chorus of pain, his moans escalating into a endless, chilling howl that reminded her of an animal caught in a leg trap. Bryce was now in a guttural wail that rivaled the banshee of myth, the keening resounding off the flat walls and empty space, and the noise prevented her from thinking further; her mind blanked with fear of what was happening.

And then, nothing. Silence.

Bryce was frozen in the same crouch, but without a single noise. The tears had stopped. He was empty-eyed and blank of all expression for a split-second, caught in a moment of catatonia. She watched from her restrained position, unable to do anything, and unsure what to say. She had never seen him like this, and it terrified her.

He shuddered slightly, and his face melted into another round of emotional musical chairs. They swept across his face repeatedly, finally leaving a single deciding persona behind. A slow, cryptic half-smile crept across Bryce's mouth, and his eyes became animated. He raised a hand to his wet cheek, looking truly surprised that he had been crying, and his eyes burned into Karyn as if he held her responsible for what just occurred. Her gamble had failed, and Bryce's face told her that her final hand of cards would be dealt shortly.

"That was an interesting little bit of fun for you, wasn't it?" he asked her as he stood up and wiped his face on his sleeve. "That poor fool really doesn't have a clue about you. You have no conscience, using his love for you against him, making him suffer like that." Bryce stretched his arms above his head and cracked his neck side to side. "You almost had me out of the picture, too." He strode over to Karyn and slapped her face in one smooth motion. The burning sting left by his hand soaked into her cheek. "That won't happen again," he grinned, and pulled the knife from his back pocket.

Bryce cut her left hand loose and pulled it to her right, binding them together before he cut the right one free from the waist ropes. After fashioning a quick loop between her wrists, he moved behind her to remove the rest of her restraints. He was humming happily now, excited at the next thing he had planned for her, and Karyn dreaded what that thing might be.

Yanking her free from the chair, Bryce dragged her past the piles of garbage to the far side of the room where the stairs led down. The dead deer smell intensified as they got closer, and Karyn saw with horror that no animal was the source of the stench. It was a homeless man, tossed onto the backside of the last pile, his face bludgeoned beyond recognition into a pulpy, maroon-black mess. Karyn stumbled and gaped in shock, but he pulled her forward as if she was a distracted dog on a park walk. "He got mouthy with me, even when I was quite pleasant with him," Bryce said brightly, " and wouldn't leave when I asked him to. I was exceptionally gentlemanly, but he insisted this was his flop, so….he can stay as long as he likes now."

The corpse was in the early stages of bloat, slowed by the cool temperatures, but the smell was overpowering. Karyn gagged as she was dragged forward to the top of the steps, her limited vision making her miss the first step down and bump into Bryce's back. She knocked him off balance momentarily, and Karyn hoped he'd fall and break his neck, but he quickly recovered and shoved her down hard against the steps. "Clumsy bitch," he snapped, forcing her to walk ahead of him down the stairs, using her hair now as the leash, muttering, "I swear, you really are the most ungainly creature…" He yanked hard and kept her head pulled backwards to the point where she had to look down her nose to see the next step. The angle allowed her a limited amount of peripheral vision out of her swollen eye, and she scanned the area for further clues as to where she was.

The first floor area resembled more of a barn, with support posts spaced about every fifteen feet. By the time she reached the bottom step she surmised this was probably an older grange-style building, but she didn't know of any in the area; that meant there was a good chance Bryce had driven her far enough beyond her neighborhood into unfamiliar territory, perhaps another county. Her hopes sank further at being found any time soon. Karyn knew she would be next on the corpse pile, unless she could turn the tide of events.

Bryce scuffed his way over to a central post and yanked Karyn's arms above her head, almost pulling her up on tiptoe as he threw the central wrist loop over a spike in the post. She could see the fresh pile of sawdust at her feet; he had placed the hook there in anticipation of this moment, for the express purpose of hanging her there like a side of beef. She struggled to relieve the strain on her shoulders. He enjoyed seeing her uncomfortable and unbalanced, smirking as he pulled up another crate from the corner. "I'm going to stay just out of spittin' distance, if you don't mind," he said with a chuckle when he sat down. "Now, you and I are gonna have a little chat, real friendly like."

"What would you like to talk about?" Karyn said flatly, with no feigned enthusiasm or hope. She made every effort to look submissive again, hoping that Bryce would avoid visiting greater violence on her like he had on the corpse upstairs. Now that she knew he was capable of murder and not just animal cruelty, her fate was becoming darker by the minute. If she could manage to engage him without enraging him, she might buy herself some time. By now, William would have been to the house and called the police.

*Someone **must** be looking for me*, she thought. *They'll see Scraps, the broken window…**someone** will come looking for me. I just have to stay alive until then!*

"Let's talk about family, baby." He stood tall and puffed out his chest a bit, placing a hand to his chest as he spoke. "Family should stick together, right? Momma and I were all there ever was to my family until I met you, and when you came along she embraced you like the daughter she always wanted. That woman was the salt of the earth…" Bryce's voice trailed off and his eyes became a bit glassy and unfocused for a moment, but he quickly regained control of himself again, ending with "…and she knew how family **should** behave - not like **your** family."

Karyn was clueless as to what he meant, and resisted the urge to discount anything he said at this point as the ravings of a mad man. The words of Rumi flashed across her mind as a warning to be attentive; *"I have lived on the lip of insanity, wanting to know reasons, knocking on a door…"* and reminded her that now she needed to be the most aware. There would be no second chances for her from here on out. There was nothing remaining of old Bryce anymore.

23

Mercy

Nurse Meghan Zarnicoff adjusted the IV drip on her patient, and gently checked her charge for any sign of bedsores. For the last two months, that had been of little concern; Karyn Kiplinger had come in with so many injuries that she was practically bandaged from head to toe, but now that most of her soft tissue injuries had healed there were no bandages to run interference between her skin and the hospital bed mattress anymore. In her present state of deep coma, her autonomic nervous system no longer functioned enough to manage the constant small shifts in body position required to prevent pressure ulcers from forming. She was incapable of even breathing on her own; a tower of monitors oversaw her every bodily function, via a snarl of wires, tubes, and sensors. The ventilator kept waltz time with its gasp-thump-thump beat; the only thing she could do was keep her heart beating at a slow, but steady pace.

The nurse saw the worst of the worst in her job, but no gunshot, overdose, or failed suicide victim had ever tugged at her heart like the woman before her. Zarnicoff had been covering a co-worker's shift in the ER when the paramedics brought her in, broken like a china doll thrown from a third floor window. Her body had been savaged almost beyond repair. She had three broken ribs, a collapsed lung, a broken femur, nose and cheekbone, broken wrist, dislocated shoulder, two skull fractures, cerebral swelling, a ruptured spleen, she was covered in bruises and cuts, and had glass in the soles of her feet. The bruises on her body were of different ages, and only a few were from the car accident. She was naked when she came in under the blanket on the stretcher, which meant she was naked when the paramedics got to her; any clothing was always cut off in the ER, not on site. Whatever she was running from when she crashed the car was terrible enough to make her choose escape over modesty in this cold autumn weather. This woman must have been running for her life, and the nurse shuddered when she thought of what might have been chasing her. "It's a sick world out there," she mumbled under her breath as she adjusted the blanket on her bed, "but you're safe now, honey."

As much as her heart was pained by the brutality her patient had endured, it also ached for her survivor, the man who sat by her bedside every day. From the moment visiting hours began to the second they ended, he sat vigil next to her bandaged, motionless form. Sometimes holding her hand, sometimes talking to her, and even playing his guitar quietly for her, he had become such a permanent fixture in her room that the nursing staff often forgot he was there.

Normally, a man of such exceptional good looks would have been fair game for the female staff, if for no other attentions than small talk. His grieving created an impenetrable barrier around him that no woman would dare transgress, lest the nursing staff attack them like angry dobermans. They had become quite protective of William Thalheim during the time his love had been in their care. He represented an unattainable ideal; a man who had set his whole life aside to spend every moment he could by her side. His unflagging faithfulness and dedication set him apart from every visitor in the hospital, and the nurses found that a rare, delicate thing. They were all both envious and terribly sad for the shattered woman in the hospital bed.

While the nurse didn't know the lovers' entire back story, she heard snippets of one-sided conversation as she went about her duties. William would speak quietly into her ear and tell her stories about when he traveled in Europe, or reminisce about things they had done together when they were younger. He recounted how he felt the first time he saw her, when she had a flat tire and no money to fix it, or when they would slip away to the park to make love in the grass. He spoke to her of the places they would visit when she recovered, and the house he wanted to build for her in the mountains, trying to lure her out of her coma with tender words and promises. When his hope seemed to flag, he would slump over his guitar, almost in a trance state, and gently perform the most beautiful compositions, crying silently as the music drifted throughout the hospital floor. Those days were the most bittersweet, and everyone did their best to be as invisible and unintrusive as possible so he might have a space to release his pain in private.

Zarnicoff met William shortly after Karyn was admitted. She observed him sketching out of the corner of her eye, gracefully crisscrossing the paper with a plain pencil, his eyes swollen, red, and immeasurably sad. She was headed to the nurses' station, but doubled back when she saw him leave the room for a moment. It wasn't like her to be nosy, but a burning desire gripped her to see what he was drawing, and she slipped into the room to steal a glimpse of the sketchpad. What she saw took her breath away, and triggered emotions in her she couldn't name.

On the paper was a portrait of a beautiful face. Not a classic beauty in the modern sense, but a face that showed both vulnerability and strength. The face of a woman with intelligence, depth and dignity. The face of the broken woman in the bed.

There was no way to tell it was her, though. At the time, it had been less than a week since she was admitted, and her face was still lumpy, discolored and bandaged. There was no way to know what she had originally looked like before her trauma, until now. Only a small crescent-shaped scar in the corner of her right eye betrayed her identity, which William had reproduced perfectly in his sketch. Zarnicoff had no doubt that this was exactly what Karyn Kiplinger looked like prior to her misfortune; the portrait said this man loved her so much that he wouldn't change or enhance a single detail about her, even her imperfections, and that was what broke her heart for them both.

She readjusted the angle of her bed by a few degrees and pulled up a chair. On quiet nights like this, she'd speak to the unresponsive patients as if they were old friends, hold their hands, and bring them up to date on who visited them that day. Some who were beyond unresponsive, or technically brain dead, were given the okay to move on and leave their pain behind, with the knowledge that there was at least one soul who cared what happened to them. But that wasn't the conversation she needed to have tonight. Zarnicoff was going to call Karyn back, or at least let her know she had a very good reason to do so.

She smoothed the hair from Karyn's forehead, resting her hand on her shoulder. Most of the bruising had faded from her face by now, leaving just a few pale yellow-green traces of the abuse she had endured. Her nose was healing well, and the orthopedic surgeon had done an excellent job of repairing her wrist. Fortunately, the majority of scarring her patient had would be hidden by clothes, although she guessed the invisible scars she bore were far worse. A psychic had once told her that emotional trauma was the reason why some people never came out of comas, even when there was no medical reason for them not to, and she feared that Karyn may be one of them. Her concussion and skull fractures were healed, and multiple catscans had shown no damage, no bleeding, or intra-cranial pressure; in short, there was no physical reason why she wasn't waking up. The nurse guessed that Karyn had no desire or reason to; wherever she was was probably preferable to where she had been. Why should she want to return to a world that had treated her like garbage, she thought.

The dim light in the room made for an almost confessional ambiance, it's solemnity broken only by the occasional beeping of the machinery and the ventilator. Zarnicoff leaned in to speak very matter-of-factly to Karyn. It didn't matter that she was comatose; the ability to hear was the very last sense to leave the body, and although she couldn't acknowledge hearing the words, Karyn would still be able to hear everything the nurse said. At least, Zarnicoff hoped she would. This was going to be a conversation that she rarely had with patients.

Occasionally, the unresponsive patients, the ones whose bodies or minds were irreversibly damaged, would hang on beyond their time. This was familiar behavior in the hospice wing; the terminally ill parent staying their last breath because they felt they needed to remain for their children, while the children's grieving is extended unnecessarily. It was a regular occurrence for people to wait to die until the last of the family gathered, or a specific person arrived to say goodbye, even if their body had quit the fight. Some remained, alone and uncared for, because they had no one to see them off on their journey to the light. In all those situations, the nurses would gently tell the dying or the brain-dead patient that it was okay to leave, that they would be free of their pain and sorrow, and that everything would be fine if they did.

Karyn was a different case, however. She was physically fine, but at the same time absent. Zarnicoff hoped that giving her a small reminder of what she left behind might tip the balance in William's favor, and so she began her one-way discussion with the immobile woman in the bed.

"Karyn," she said, reaching down to hold her hand, "William was here again today. He comes every day. He never misses a day, you know…he's…waiting for you." She gazed at the unresponsive, emotionless face, placid with emptiness. Zarnicoff felt there was very little tethering Karyn to this existence, and measured her words carefully. "I think you're a pretty lucky girl to have a guy like that. He's handsome, and he serenades you with beautiful music…he told me that one piece he always plays, he wrote just for you. That's quite the compliment, dear. Anyone can see…he loves you very much." Her patient was unmoved.

The nurse leaned in closer and confided in her. "I don't mean to be blunt about it, but I think you should know…I see people all the time who have no reason to be here. They're in a far away place like you, but they have no way of coming back, and their families would rather go to the casinos than hold their hand in their last moments here. Sometimes they don't even bother to come in to say goodbye. They don't care the way your William does. He's hoping against hope that you're still in there somewhere, and that you'll come back to him." She pressed her hand a little tighter, and put gentle emphasis into her words. "You can come back if you want to, Karyn; I'm not gonna lie to you, honey…it won't be easy, and it won't be fun, but…you won't be alone. If your parents don't mind waiting a little longer for your company, come back for your man. He's waiting for you, but don't make him wait forever. He doesn't deserve that, and neither do you."

She gave Karyn's hand a small squeeze before rising to continue her rounds. Turning before she reached the door, Zarnicoff looked over her shoulder and whispered with a tiny edge of anger in her voice, "I hope they get the bastard that did this to you. You should be around to see that when it happens." A chill ran through the nurse, and what felt like a light breeze blew past her as she walked away, missing the tiny tears forming in the corner of Karyn's eyes. They slid down her face, unseen, unnoticed, and disappeared into her pillow.

24
William

The ceiling needed painting. The same two nail pops stared at him impassively, along with the cracking drywall tape edge that ran the length of the bedroom. The moonlight enhanced the defects, which hadn't changed in the seemingly endless hours William had been staring at it, unable to sleep.

"We have to wait and see, Will," the doctor had said. *"There's a lot of damage, and I'm afraid we don't know the half of it right now."* Although his words cut deeply into William's soul and crushed his hopes, he hadn't been wrong. Given the laundry list of trauma done to Karyn's body, there should have been a funeral for her by now, and not the waiting game of near impossible recovery, but, she was recovering. Every day he went to the hospital expecting to find her hospital bed empty and waiting for the next patient, but that hadn't happened. Her bones slowly mended, the angry reddish purple bruises calmed down and faded, the scars settled into almost normal flesh again, and the Karyn he had longed for rose to the surface of her skin…but that was only her outside. Her inside was a different story.

Her comatose mind was elsewhere. Blunt force trauma, concussions, and intracranial pressure had taken their toll on her brain. Although she had physically healed from each neurological challenge, her brain function had not returned to normal. Her EEGs showed the deep silence of coma and her hippocampic functions were nil; 'persistent vegetative state' was the phrase her neurologist used, but what he meant was she was a hair's breadth from being classified as brain dead. Karyn had survived a horrific situation, only to be caught between worlds where she was not quite dead, and yet not totally alive.

He refused to accept that she wasn't mentally present, even before he heard her voice that day. She didn't feel like an empty shell to him at all. There were signs of conscious life that gave him hope for her return; an eye flutter here, a hand movement there, and other small hints that the medical staff wrote off as "involuntary vegetative movement", but Will embraced as a glimpse of her eventual return. He tried his best to cultivate and nurture them until she came around, and his day was structured around her care. He played music by her bedside, held her hands and massaged her feet, quietly told her stories until visiting hours were over, but Karyn showed no interest, no interaction beyond the rhythmic pulse of the respirator. When her voice came out of thin air, it was as if he went deaf to everything else in the world.

It materialized between the notes of the sonata he was playing at the moment, ethereal and invisible, and floated into his ear. The dusky resonance of it, the unique vocalization of those few words, were unmistakable. At the time, all he could do was shake uncontrollably from shock, but there was no doubt; it was **her** voice filling his ears, even though the woman in the hospital bed next to him was silent.

Since then, William's sleep had been spare and inconsistent, and he was obsessed with the event. Occasionally drifting off for a few hours was the best he could do; the sound of her voice had consumed his every waking moment, forcing him to replay the incident in his mind, hoping that there would have been more words. Those few sentences rocked his reality, then…nothing. Silence again. Deafening, empty silence.

At first he thought he was losing his mind. Karyn was three feet from him, unconscious, intubated, unable to converse, yet he heard her voice clearly. Positive that he wasn't hallucinating it all and desperate for an explanation, he contacted Nils Forsythe, an old friend from his early studio set days. Nils was a sound engineer on the very first studio gig William ever played, and the two quickly became brothers in music. When Nils wasn't busy in the recording studio control room, the British ex-pat was a shaman, doing spiritualist clearings and house blessings; not exactly the field of expertise that William thought he needed, but Nils turned out to be the perfect man to explain what the hell was going on, and what might happen from that moment forward. He hopped the first plane he could and William picked him up from the airport.

"So, let me get this straight, Will," Nils said as he clicked in his seatbelt, "this is the girl you constantly spoke about every waking moment when we worked together?"

"Yes." William's face was ashen and drawn, and Nils could almost feel how exhausted he was. "There is no other."

He rubbed his forehead and looked out the window at the rain. "Man...that's tough. How long has she been...absent?"

"I don't know if I get what you mean. She's been unconscious since the day they brought her in from the accident. She's not even breathing on her own right now."

*Nils shook his head. "That's not the kind of unconsciousness I'm talking about, Will. I mean, I **am** talking about consciousness...but not in the way you're used to thinking about consciousness." He sat sideways in his seat to face William. "I'm talking about her soul being present."*

"She's in a coma, Nils - she's not dead. Doesn't your soul only leave the body when you die?" Will had a rudimentary grasp of shamanic concepts, nothing at the level of Nils's training, but he knew he'd be getting educated fast. Karyn's life depended on it.

"Not always. You can lose pieces of your soul due to trauma. For example, if a person is molested as a child, part of the child's soul may try to escape the body to avoid the pain and suffering of the abuse; it's a way of the soul protecting itself from complete loss by not keeping all its eggs in one basket."

Will was digesting the information while navigating them ever closer to the hospital. The sheeting rain made it hard to see, and he had a mind full of questions.

"Where do these pieces of the soul go?" he asked.

"They normally seek other realms that are invisible to us, the 'Otherworld'," Nils said.

"Otherworld? Sounds like something out of Harry Potter," Will said with a scoffing tone. Nils let it slide, and explained.

"The Otherworld is a plane, a realm, actually, of fond memories, fantasy, and magical places where the soul feels safe and in control. It even includes the Underworld, the plane of the deceased. Kids have spent less time in this realm, so the boundary is more easily accessed by them, and they're often quite keen to get back there. That piece of their soul is like Peter Pan, stuck forever at the age the trauma occurred and tucked safely away from harm."

"Karyn's a grown woman, not some abused kid. What exactly makes you think she's in this Otherworld?"

"Not much, not having seen her yet, but enough to believe it's as good a possibility as any - and age is not necessarily a factor. The severity of the trauma and the sensitivity of the individual are decisive factors in whether their soul becomes broken. When you heard her voice, where did it come from? Was it from inside your head?" he asked.

"No, it was definitely from outside of me. I was sitting down and she sounded like she was a little above and in front of me." Will shook his head vigorously in agitation. "I'm not crazy. I'm telling you, Nils - I didn't imagine it!"

The Brit gently laid a hand on his arm, and said reassuringly, "I know. I believe you, mate. I'm just fact-checking to make sure, that's all. Did she call you by name?"

"No," Will said with a tinge of sadness, slumping a bit in his seat. "It sounded like she didn't know it was me."

"Was anyone else in the room at the time?"

"Not then. One of the neurologists had just been in discussing her case with me, but he left before I heard her."

"So there was nobody other than you who might have heard the voice."

"It was **her** voice!" William protested.

Nils spoke quietly, in a way that one would to calm an angry child. "No, it **may** have been her voice, or it may have been something else entirely. All you've told me is that you heard a voice that sounded **like** Karyn, but that doesn't mean it **was** Karyn. There are a host of things it could have been."

"Like what?" William demanded.

*Nils sighed and struggled for the best way to explain.
"Look, Will, the things we shamans deal with do not fit in the
world of modern science. They aren't easy to accept, but they
do exist. I need you to put aside any preconceived notions you
have about what's real and what's fantasy, because that won't
help you at all, and it surely won't help Karyn." William
clenched his jaw and focused on the road; Nils searched for a
way to better explain his concerns without exacerbating Will's
anxiety. "The Otherworld, the Underworld, the
Middleworld...all these fantastic-sounding places exist, outside
our understanding of time and space," he stated. "My biggest
concern is the status of Karyn's soul, and where the soul
shards have gone if she has become fractured from her
trauma."*

*"What happens to the rest of the soul, uh, or the person,
once that happens?" Will asked quietly.*

*"They become poorly functioning human beings. They
develop addictions, mental illness, depression,
aggression...with a chunk of the soul now missing, any number
of demons can insert themselves into that open space and make
it their home."*

*Will stole a surprised look at him. "Do you mean real
demons? Is that what you think her voice was?"*

*Nils laughed lightly. "Not necessarily, and I don't
mean demons with bat wings and forked tails, but negative
energies that become entrenched in the broken person and
twist the psyche, like...like a possession. It's the reason why
people don't heal, why they get worse, and why some never are
'right' again." He glanced out the window again with a
distant, concerned look. "You'd be shocked if you knew how
many fragmented, broken-souled people are out there,
man...it's scary."*

*"I have a pretty good idea. The music industry thrives
on damaged, talented people," he replied without emotion.*

*Nils smiled. "Why yes...yes it does, William." He
looked back out the window at the wet city lights and asked him
softly, "How long have you been clean now, man?"*

"I don't count time anymore. I just am," he said stoically.

"You haven't slipped since we last talked, have you?"

"Not once. That life has long passed."

He reached over and squeezed William's shoulder. "That's fucking fantastic, Will. I knew you could do it." He let out a sigh that spoke volumes between them. "You're going to need all your reserves for what's coming. I'm not psychic, but I can guess the condition your girl is in, and I'm going to assume the worst."

"How bad are we talking, Nils? She's in a coma, for Christ's sake; how much worse can it be?"

Nils took a deep breath and measured his words carefully. "Sometimes, Will, a person's entire soul can leave the body depending on how bad the trauma is. And based on what you told me that poor girl has been through, I'd be surprised if she has a single piece of her soul left in her body."

Too exhausted to move from the bed, yet not exhausted enough to sleep, Will hovered in a twilight space of non-existence. The past two months had eaten into his reserves, preventing him from doing anything other than wait for her to return. All of his basic needs were shelved and his life held in stasis, poised for the moment when he could look into her eyes and hold her again in his arms. He had lost so much weight that the nurses began bringing him food on the sly, placing the meal orders under Karyn's name. "The kitchen won't know she's not eating it, and nobody will be the wiser - but you need to keep up your strength," one of the nurses had said when she slipped him the food tray and pulled the curtain around so he could eat in privacy, "so don't disappoint her."

Don't disappoint her. That phrase stung him.

If only he hadn't left for Europe…if only he hadn't lost touch with her…if only he hadn't lost himself…if only he had arrived earlier that weekend…

He could still see the front door wide open in his headlights when he pulled into her driveway. Karyn's car was gone, the foyer was covered with leaves blown in from the yard, and he was awash in a hot, sickening unease, the kind you get when you know something is instinctively wrong. He walked into the doorway, calling her name, becoming more unsettled as he moved further into the house. Seeing the broken window and the dog's carcass pushed him into a full-blown panic; by the time the police arrived, it was all he could do to not scream at them to find her. The condition of the house and the dead dog inspired them to put out an alert, but William was still considered a suspect, until Karyn magically appeared in Mercy Hospital's ER, as a crushed, destroyed version of the woman he loved.

No longer able to lay there, he threw his legs over to the bed's edge and wearily pushed himself up into a slouch. The suppressed grief hit him with such force upon sitting up that he burst into tears, smothering his sobbing in the palms of his hands. He let the stress flow out of his lungs and eyes until he felt empty, and there was nothing left. The pain in his soul was so intense, so constant, that he wanted to vomit. *I don't know how much longer I can take not knowing*, briefly passed in his thoughts. *Where is she right now? What is she doing? What did she decide?* He forced himself out into the kitchen and put the coffee on. The counter tops gleamed in the moonlight pouring through the window, and Will didn't turn on the light. The darkness was oddly comforting.

Karyn's house was spotless in her absence. After the police were done documenting the scene, he'd spent endless, sleepless hours cleaning and tidying her home so it would be perfect for her return. There was no evidence of violence to be found anywhere now; he had buried the dog, scrubbed away the blood, cleaned up the glass and repaired the window. William had even asked Nils to purge the house of any residual negative energies just to be safe. All that was missing now was Karyn, and he had no idea if she was coming back.

He took it upon himself to manage Karyn's affairs for her in her absence, like some well-heeled butler from Edwardian England. Far from being a squatter on the premises, William carried the expenses and costs for all the repairs and improvements he did; money was the one thing he was not short of, having built a solid professional career that afforded him anything he could desire. He paid her bills, covered her mortgage, and handled all the house maintenance and upkeep. Those activities distracted him from the crippling impotence he felt when hospital visiting hours were over. At Karyn's bedside, he could be supportive, but upon leaving the hospital, his usefulness disappeared. Being busy and constructive gave William just enough control to make it to the next day, until he could be by her side again. This house could have easily been a place that Karyn and he might have lived in together, had he not taken the dark choices his profession offered him long ago. The furnishings, the colors, and even the mug he poured his coffee into was scented with her personality, her style, and her sense of taste. Living in her house, sleeping in her bed, and surrounding himself with her trappings was a paltry substitute for Karyn in the flesh, but they kept him from madness and self-medication; two things he never wished to experience again.

Fortunately, his subconscious mind knew the best medicine, and he dreamed of her. The dreams had helped ease his misery slightly. The few nights when his exhaustion had finally crashed the barricades of sleep, he was blessed with beautiful memories of what had been, many years ago. They were a much needed balm to his wounded soul, and he reveled in those illusory moments where he could be with her again, when they were both young and shared a promising future as a couple. The nocturnal reveries soothed his spirit, gifting him with the one thing he couldn't have in his waking life, until the night his dreams took an unseen turn when Karyn stepped out from behind a living room chair. Waking from that dream left a deep unease in his gut, and with no one else to consult, he called Nils again that morning, hoping he might have an answer to what it all meant.

*"I don't know what to make of any of it, Nils…it was **her**. I **know** it was her, the **real** Karyn, the Karyn I see every day in the hospital."*

The silence on the other end of the phone was thick, but not dismissive, but it still aggravated William. He knew he sounded like a crazy man, however, Nils was the only person he could approach with such an experience. Will endured the prolonged quiet without complaint.

"When I told you to pay attention to your dreams, I didn't expect something like this, Will. Soul contact rarely happens, and when it does, it's normally because at least one of the people involved has exceptional spiritual abilities or training. What you described isn't lucid dreaming; it's dream travel, and that's a skill that only a few shamans and medicine men have."

"I don't give a shit about any of that. She was there, and she was very different than the Karyn in the beginning of my dream. She was her current age, and she looked as surprised to be there as I was to see her."

"What makes you think it was her spirit, instead of part of the dream?" Nils asked. He could hear William take a deep breath before replying.

"She seemed like she was out of sorts, like she stepped off a bus at the wrong stop and wasn't sure where she was."

"That's hardly reason enough to think it was her. Dreams are illogical places of fantasy; your own mind could have created that scenario. Think about it…it would ease the lack of power you feel in the rest of your life if you could rescue her in your dreams, Will."

"Maybe, but I doubt my mind would script a dream like that. Her presence there felt out of place to me. She wasn't supposed to be there."

"Don't you think that's because the younger version of her was already there, upstairs? Your rational mind would see that as incongruent," Nils countered.

"No, I don't think that had anything to do with it," William contested. "It had to do with her behavior. Her reactions were…different. What I experience in my dreams is always a replay of memories from our past. Nothing new or different ever happens in them; they're totally predictable, but how she reacted to seeing me and being there was completely unscripted."

"You're basing this purely on the fact that your dreams followed a pattern? You're not convincing me, Will."

"It's more than that, Nils...she was **aware** that she was in a dream."

"What do you mean she was 'aware'?" Nils asked. His voice was edged with curiosity, and he could hear William shift in his seat on the other end of the phone.

"She told me as much. She wasn't sure whose dream it was, but it was obvious she wasn't any creation of my imagination. Her manner was cautious and unsure, and she was watching my reactions like a hawk. You could almost see her processing our conversation and her surroundings, and the whole time I could hear you in my head, from when we left the airport, and suddenly it all made sense to me; she was in between worlds, just like you said she might be."

Nils hesitated a moment before asking another question. William knew what he wanted to ask, and let him. "Did you tell her anything about her current situation?"

"No."

"Why not?"

"She seemed really fragile...and I wasn't sure at the time if all of it was part of the dream. She got pretty upset when I tried to touch her, and after everything you told me about these other realities it didn't seem like a good idea. I don't know exactly why I didn't tell her...that was just my gut feeling."

Nils breathed a sigh of relief. "I'm **very** glad you didn't, mate. Doing so might have set some things in motion that we don't want, and we don't have enough information just yet to go tinkering."

"Like what?" William pushed. "Just what are you going on about, Nils?"

"Because we don't have real proof that what you experienced was really Karyn's soul reaching out to you and not a dream, we have to err on the side of caution. If it **was** her soul that spoke to you, there's a risk that any interaction with her could influence her decisions."

"What decisions? What decision can a comatose woman make?" he asked, confused.

"I've told you before, Will - the Otherworlds are entirely different realities than our physical world," he said *with slight irritation, trying to impress that fact upon him. "Karyn's soul, or some part of it, is able to travel **anywhere** now that it's been ripped away from her body. If she knew what condition her physical body was in, she might decide to completely abandon it and never come back. Conversely, she could also decide to stay just connected enough to linger forever in the coma until her physical self expires. Wherever she is, those decisions have to be left to her alone; her consciousness must figure out her future without outside influence. As badly as you want her out of that coma, Will, you can't push her. It's her life, and she has the sole right to make that choice, not you."*

William carefully weighed the significance of his words, and immediately noted what Nils left out. "You didn't mention anything about her recovering, Nils."

*"You're right, I did not," he sighed, "and that's because I don't want to get your hopes up. This is **bad**, Will. I can't impress upon you enough about **how** bad it is. When I saw her physical self, she had so little connection, so little soul left in it that I expected her to pass that very hour. The fact that she hasn't means she's strong, but she's broken, mate. She's gone somewhere where we can't get to her, and she's got to work out what she wants to do on her own, in her own time, and time in the Otherworld is not linear, like here. There's nothing you or I can do, and I doubt there's a shaman alive who could."*

"You're wrong. I know in my heart that you're dead wrong," Will said with absolute conviction. "If she came out to me in a dream, then she's reachable. I just have to be there for when she does."

*"And do what? Spend your life sleeping in the hope that she travels again?" Nils said with slight sarcasm. "You could die of old age in the meantime because it's **not** that simple. Her body is a shell without consciousness right now. I couldn't sense enough prana in her to anchor what few soul fragments might remain, and without knowing where the rest of them have gone, her soul can't be made whole. You have to reunite the fragments with the rest of the soul in order for the person to truly heal and...I'm afraid she's beyond reach."*

"And what if she isn't? What if she's out there and trying to find a way back?" he argued.

"That's highly unlikely. She's not a shaman, and that could have been a dark spirit capitalizing on your pain."

"Just work with me here, Nils - what if I see her again? What should I do? Tell me!" he pleaded.

*He sighed again into the phone, and indulged William's scenario. "Okay, mate…if you two **do** cross paths again, and it is really her soul you're dealing with…you must not, under **any** circumstances, divulge what you know of her in **this** reality. To do so would affect the natural course of her existence in the Otherworld. You cannot influence her soul with what **you** want; there are karmic restrictions that you transgress if you do. Do you understand the gravity of what I'm telling you?"*

"I do, and I promise I won't tell her anything. I swear." William agreed. He had never heard Nils so dire, so incredibly serious before.

*"It won't be easy to do if that happens. **If** her soul is really traveling across planes, it's because she is seeking something, probably an answer to where she is. She may even be drawn to fragments of her own soul that are out there in the aether. The Otherworld does not behave by set rules of reality, so she may be confused by her surroundings, or in conflict with where she is and where she wants to be. That confusion will drive her to find someone she has history with, someone that she trusts. If you're that person to her, Karyn will press you for answers; a lost soul like that can be angry and aggressive, like a wounded animal, so no matter what she says or does, do **not** tell her anything."*

"Okay, but, you make it sound like she'd be a demon."

*"Lost souls can **become** demons, Will!" Nils yelled. "Stop thinking this is the woman you knew! This is a soul that has been ripped from it's mortal coil and its native plane of existence, and has nothing to anchor it, ground it, or contain its evolution in the Otherworld, and without that tether, they can become corrupted into the basest forms of emotion; there is no guarantee that Karyn's soul hasn't already changed into something else!"*

Will was taken aback by the outburst from his normally easygoing, genial friend. "Easy, Nils! I get it, I get it! I'll be careful!"

*Nils drew an exhausted breath and apologized. "I'm sorry...look, mate...I didn't mean to blow up on you. It's just that all this is some crazy shite that I'm not skilled enough to really help with. This is high level holy man type stuff, like the stories I heard when I was a novice in training. I don't know if my teacher would be able to help if he was alive, and...I'm just trying to be flat out straight with you. The unseen world is nothing to be tinkered with, and the chance that your girl is out there actively trying to find you is almost beyond even **my** belief. There's always a chance, but the odds are incredibly slim." His pause revealed he was calculating what to say, and how to say it without crushing his friend's one remaining hope. William knew Nils understood, and relieved him of further explanation.*

"I'm sorry, Nils...I just refuse to believe otherwise. She's beaten the odds so far, and I can't give up on her now. I need to keep hoping. It's...all I have left." The energy drained out of Will's voice as he pleaded his case. Nils silently nodded his head on the other end of the line, and warned him with the tenderness of one who knew the pain of deep loss.

"I know, Will. Just be aware that you might get your heart broken, and lose a piece of your soul, too."

The coffee maker announced the finished brew with a trio of beeps, and jarred William from the memory in his head. He poured the rich, aromatic liquid into a hand-thrown stoneware mug and stared out the window. *Did I say too much?* he wondered. *Did I blow it, like Nils warned me not to? Did I condemn her future because I was weak?* He rubbed his face with regret, reviewing their last meeting in his mind and comparing it against everything Nils had told him might happen.

He had not been prepared for how aggressive she was; the Karyn he knew was never that vitriolic. Was that aggression just intense frustration from her, or had she already changed into some rage-filled entity? William had done his best to not influence her by warning her off her line of questioning, but she was like an attack dog. The anger he saw in her face was frightening, and he almost doubted that it was Karyn.

His instinct told him it **was** her, though. The smell of her hair and the taste of her lips convinced him. That was the Karyn he remembered, and he was sure it was really her in the brief seconds they embraced in the dream. Will prayed that he had done the right thing in that moment, but his cell phone interrupted that thought. The hospital was calling him in.

25

Crucible

"**Y**our parents got what they deserved."

Karyn lifted her head up and blinked her one good eye in disbelief. "What did you just say?" she asked. She had been tuning out Bryce's rant about family values, the proper role of women, and the blessed sanctity of his dead mother when he spit out that last sentence. It made a sound in Karyn's consciousness like a brick through a plate glass window.

"You heard me," he repeated with a light dusting of venom. "I said they got what they fucking deserved, for interfering in our lives."

Her parents had been nothing but generous and gracious to Bryce every time they had visited. She had no idea what he was talking about, and her face told Bryce she was clueless as to what he was going on about. He looked surprised she didn't know, and laughed.

"I guess you never knew about the little 'conversation' your Father and I had. He said he wouldn't mention it to you; turns out old Ethan **was** a man of his word, after all," he said wryly. Karyn still looked confused. "Well, since you obviously are in the dark about what I'm talking about, let me clear the air about your dear parents. Remember when we had that little tiff about you teaching night classes?" he sneered.

She remembered that fight as if it was yesterday; it was the first time he had raised his hand to her, after months of psychological abuse. It took weeks for her shoulder to heal, and she lied to her parents about how it happened, hoping that the event was a fluke, that he would realize what he had done and get some help for his anger and depression. He hadn't, of course, and shortly afterward her life took a sharp drop off into oblivion and misery. That was the point of no return in her past life, the point where she could have changed everything, if she had only been smarter.

"Your Daddy seemed to think that I had something to do with your dislocated shoulder, and we went for a little walk outside after dinner while you and your Momma cleaned up." Bryce tapped out another cigarette on the pack lid. "He was real sociable - real sneaky, more like - asking me the same question in twelve different ways, over and over again. 'How exactly did Karyn fall? What did she land on when she fell? What was she doing just before the accident?' Blah, blah, blah, over and over again, hopin' to catch me in some lie when we both know it was your fault, right?" he asked her for confirmation. Karyn just stared blankly while he talked. Bryce enjoyed having the spotlight, and rambled on.

"Just before we went back inside, he hinted very indelicately that I wasn't being honest with him. He so much as flat out said he'd take me to the woodshed if anything else unusual happened to his baby girl."

"He would never say something like that. I don't believe you," she spoke up. Her dismissal of his statement made a crooked smile spread over Bryce's face.

"Oh, but he did!" he corrected her. "He used fancier words, and carefully crafted turns of phrase, but he basically made it clear that he thought I was a liar."

*You **are** a liar, you deranged fuck*, she yelled in her head.

"I felt that was rather insulting," he continued, strutting around in front of her, "especially since I thought I was doing such a fine job of caring for you and correcting you on your shortcomings. I took serious offense to that, girl. He did me a great disservice by saying those things and questioning me like a common criminal. In the old days, I would have demanded satisfaction in a duel, the way gentleman ought to settle differences…but I never thought your father to be a gentleman anyway, so I found another way to regain my honor." He was smiling that self-satisfied smile again; the same one he had plastered on his face when he boasted about Scraps' murder. Her stomach churned with the intuitive knowledge that he had

done something terrible, but she held her tongue. She would
not give him the satisfaction of asking any questions, or walk
the path he wanted.

Instead, Karyn focused on rubbing the edge of her wrist
against the corner of the post. Her fingertips had found a rough
spot on the beam when he first hooked her there; every
moment he was faced away from her, she ground away a few
fibrous strands of the rope. Her calves were aching from
constantly being on tiptoe, and she sacrificed her shoulder
joints to rest them by hanging briefly. She guessed she had the
rope halfway through by now, and with any luck, the
combination of rubbing and stretching the hemp would break
her free in time, hopefully at the most opportune time for her to
get away somehow.

Bryce lit another cigarette, and she changed the subject.
"When did you start smoking?" she asked.

He looked up at her with surprise. "Are you concerned
for my health, darlin'," he said with a raised eyebrow, "or are
you just making light conversation?" He flicked an ash off the
end, and waited for her reply.

"You always said -" she began, and quickly cut off her
statement. Her memory worked against her by remembering
too well.

"- that smoking is a filthy habit of the uncultured?" he
finished for her. "Yes, I did say that, didn't I? Are you saying
I'm uncultured, Karyn?" His tone was teasing, but malevolent.
This was a bad rabbit hole to fall into, she thought.

"No…I'm just surprised at…how much you've
changed," she mumbled.

"Changed how?" he pressed her, still bemused.

"Changed…so much…from…who you were." She let
the words out slowly, trying to prolong the moment before he
snapped again.

He sidled up beside her and whispered in her ear, "Who
was I, then, Karyn?"

His breath was hot against her lobe, and Karyn felt the
chill from his closeness down to her toes. She had to give an
answer now, and part of her no longer cared to play this game.
She was tired of indulging him and his sickness. The urge to

enlighten him was dangerously tempting, and she wanted to push that forbidden button so badly, if for no other reason than to finally speak her mind.

"You were…beautiful, once."

Her words hung in the air between them; Bryce looked even more amused, but there was no levity in his eyes as he moved around to face her. They were cold and dark like the abyss. "And now, what am I?" he asked with cold curiosity.

"You are not Bryce."

The words fell out of her mouth onto the floor with a flat thud. She looked at him directly when she said it. There was no fear in her eyes, only condemnation and disgust. Her demeanor slapped Bryce full in the face, and her eyes peered deep into his soul, seeing him for what he was: a damaged, pitiful creature. She looked down at him, icily, pitilessly, and the revulsion emanated from her in waves. He instantly felt exposed and lessened; the power, the control drained from him with four words and a stare. It was more than he could handle, and he exploded with rage.

"How dare you look at me like that, bitch!" he shouted as he swung a fist into her ribcage. The wind was crushed from her lungs, and she hung limply from the hook, gasping. "You have no right to judge me! You had everything given to you - and I lost **everything**!" Another punch to the stomach came in from the opposite side, leaving her wheezing between her teeth. Unable to answer, Karyn shook her head mutely and corrected him when her lungs refilled.

"You…lost…**nothing**." she said hoarsely, with the same defiant eyes.

He railed at her. "I did lose everything! I wasn't raised with a silver spoon, like you - you, with two indulgent parents to spoil your princess ass while Momma and I struggled!" he hissed. "Every **day** of my life was hard, and when Momma passed…I had nothing left!" He spun around and stomped in a circle, and his face was wrinkled and red with emotion. "You don't know anything about me, about what I've been through!"

His tirade flipped a switch somewhere in Karyn's head. The absurdity of her abuser claiming to be a victim while he was using her as a punching bag was sickly funny to her, and the laugh rose up from her bruised gut and poured from her mouth. It started slow and rough, like an old car engine, and increased in speed and volume until her raspy laughter reverberated through the trash-filled room, mocking his pain.

"I know **everything** about you," she croaked, seeing through him with her one good eye. "I know all about that sad little bastard son of a Bible-selling drifter, and how much he wanted to be a prestigious, honorable southern gentleman…but all I see is a filthy, uncultured, piece of white trash who ruined his **own** life all by himself." She smiled crookedly, and spat at him, "Your own mother wouldn't recognize you now."

The shock on his face was gradually being replaced with black rage at her words, but Karyn didn't care anymore; when it was clear that there would be no reasoning with the madman, she lashed him with the truth she had held back for so long. She mentally prepared herself for what was to come next, because there was no doubt it was coming. Karyn spoke the verboten truth, and she would pay for it.

Bryce stormed her, crushing her against the post with his forearm across her windpipe. He was hell bent on caving in the cartilage in her throat, and she bulled the muscles in her neck against his increasing pressure. With as much force as she could muster, Karyn yanked down on her rope, pulling both her knees up into his balls hard. The unfrayed part of the rope gave way with the strain and she hit the floor awkwardly on her hip. Bryce crumpled backwards over the crate, clutching his groin in pain.

Karyn lay gasping from the choke hold and her shoulders felt like they'd been pierced with hot pokers, but she wasted no time feeling pain; her primary goal was to get out of there before Bryce recovered from his bruised balls. Pulling herself up into a crouch, she got to her feet, and searched for an exit. The layout of the room gave no clue as to where the door was, and in a panic she ran towards a wall of piled up furniture. As Karyn turned the corner of an upended sofa, her feet were pulled from under her and she slammed face first onto the floor. Bryce had her by the ankles, and was slowly, deliberately dragging her back to the center of the room.

It took a second for her to realize what had happened, but the moment she did, she kicked him with all her might. Her shoes went flying from the effort to wrench herself free, but Bryce's fingers just dug deeper into her flesh the more she struggled. Karyn could see his grinning face over her shoulder, eyes blazing with a mixture of fury and delight, set in a face that clearly had no sanity attached to it.

"This is gonna be so much fun, little girl," he growled as he pulled her up by her wrists, with her twisting against his grip. Once she was on her feet, Bryce cocked his arm back and released the full force of his fist into her jaw. Karyn's body was lifted off her toes into the air with a resounding crack and catapulted into the nearest trash pile. Bryce followed the arc of her trajectory to continue his attack and leaped on her, overjoyed at having her at his mercy as he stomped her.

From Karyn's perspective, time had slowed from the moment her rope gave way and she fell to the floor; halfway through that fall, the world rapidly decelerated, and she felt as though all life was winding down. Everything was moving a frame at a time, this brutal scene progressing in slow-motion, her visuals blurred by her bruised brain and the sound dialed down to the white noise of shocked eardrums.

How interesting that it comes to this, she thought, while she slipped away. *I should feel something...I should care...I don't mind it so much anymore...none of it matters now anyway...* Her body was no longer a physical place to her. There was no attachment, no need to be connected to her pain. Karyn disengaged from her flesh while her mind was slowing, floating out of her self and the desire to escape fading away like a bad memory. She watched Bryce above her with idle attention, thrashing her without sound and smiling with so much delight. The seductiveness of the soft, deaf quiet was so lovely, so far removed from where she had been only moments before, that she embraced it, allowed it to envelop her, and closed her eyes.

26

Failing

By the time William arrived at the hospital, he could barely breathe. His heart was chugging uncontrollably in his chest like a runaway train, and his mouth was bone dry from fear of what the doctors would tell him when he got there. *This can't be good news*, he thought, and his anxiety was justified. Anything about Karyn's case before had always been discussed during visiting hours, and never in the middle of the night. Something was seriously wrong, and his assumption was confirmed when all eyes turned to him as he practically ran into Karyn's room.

Rick Waterstone, the neurologist, was the first to approach him and place the classic calming hand on his shoulder. He could see the fear in Will's eyes, and sought to bring down his level of panic with a few soft words. "Easy, William…take a breath and slow down; Karyn's still with us, but there's been a change in her behavior."

"Meaning what?" Will asked with a cracked voice. "She doesn't **have** any behaviors; she's in a coma, so what the hell are you talking about, Rick?"

Waterstone paused, and it was apparent to Will that whatever the doctor was going to say did not sit comfortably with him. "She's become…convulsive."

"Convulsive?" Will parroted, unsure of exactly what that meant.

"It started about an hour ago. It's only happened twice so far, but it's like nothing we've ever seen in a vegetative patient before." He grabbed Karyn's chart from the foot of her bed and flipped through the pages. "And we have no idea why it's happening. All her blood work is fine; calcium, sodium, magnesium…all her electrolytes are just fine," he said while he reviewed the reports, and set the chart back on its hook with a sigh. "But that's not the biggest mystery, which is," he said, waving a hand towards the electroencephalogram, "why her EEG shows no abnormal electrical brain activity when she seizes. If it was trauma-induced epilepsy, she'd have brain activity even when she was unconscious, but the EEG barely registers any brain activity at all, and those needles should be practically leaping off the paper given the level of myoclonic seizure we've witnessed." Waterstone dropped his forehead into the palm of his hand and rubbed his face thoroughly in frustration, and looked apologetically at William. "I'm sorry, Will. I'm stumped on this. Up until now she's been classified as persistent vegetative and-"

"Stop calling her that!" Will snapped, and immediately apologized for his outburst. "I'm sorry," he said weakly, looking a bit ashamed. "I didn't mean to bite your head off."

Waterstone smiled gently at him, and touched Will on the shoulder. "It's okay. You've been through a lot, and weird shit like this doesn't make any of us feel any better about her condition," he said. "I'm just glad I was still in house when she had the first episode. I just finished an emergency head trauma and was halfway to the parking garage when they called me."

He's been here almost twenty hours so far, William noted; the clock read 2:35 a.m., and Waterstone's shift began early yesterday morning. *We're lucky to have someone so dedicated, even if he doesn't know what's wrong with her.*

Rick looked exhausted, but didn't stop his analysis. "She's shifted through several states already, from vegetative to standard coma and back again, and we still can't figure out what the hell is going on. I'd be concerned about seizure-induced brain damage in her condition if she had borderline brain function, but all indications have been to the contrary. There is **no** good reason why she's still comatose at this point, Will, and if this happens again-"

His commentary was cut short by the quickening pace of Karyn's heart monitor. The screen blips were coming fast and close together, and her blood pressure was on the rise, all while the EEG showed nothing. "She's seizing again," cried one of the nurses, and moved quickly to keep Karyn's lines from being ripped out as her body jerked up and down in the bed uncontrollably. William, shocked by the vision of his immobile, silent love thrashing about like she touched a live wire, pushed his way to her side and covered her body with his own.

Her chest thumped against his in violent spasms, while he cradled her head protectively in his one arm. "Easy, baby, easy, easy, easy…" he whispered to her in a strained lover's coo, knowing full well that she was beyond reach of his voice. As Karyn rose and fell under him, he thought of everything that brought them to this point; everything Nils had said, his dreams of her, and his part in it all. *Is she suffering now? Did I influence her when we met?* Will wondered how much responsibility he bore as she bucked beneath his body. He pressed her down to prevent disrupting her IVs and intubation, riding her until the seizure slowed, embracing her until she stilled again and the heart monitor resumed its usual tempo.

Had it been a different time, a different place, their bodies together might have been a passionate, beautiful event, but the setting and situation was a cruel mockery of the moment, and lying upon her had opened his eyes to a cold truth. Karyn was dying. There was barely more life force in her than that of a doll, and although her body was still alive, her soul was missing. Will didn't have to be a shaman to feel that the inner energetic warmth, the radiance that one felt in the presence of another living being, was absent from her. Her body was slightly more real than a mannequin; it wasn't until he was in direct contact with her whole body that Nils' education on the soul hit home. Karyn's body was healed, but her soul was shattered. Faced with that knowledge shoved right in his face, William couldn't deny that he would lose her soon. It was just a matter of time before they were separated again forever. His tears fell on her shoulder, and he buried his face in her neck.

He could hear Waterstone calling for another blood draw and the footsteps of nurses hastily scampering around, but that was all background noise to Karyn's heartbeat in his ear.

It was slow and steady again, as if nothing had happened, as if nothing had changed. The perfume of her skin was untouched by the acridness of hospital disinfectant, filling his nose; he breathed her in deeply to suffocate the fear in his own heart. "I will never leave you, darling," he mouthed in her ear, "please come back…please come back...please come back." He pleaded once more, and promised to stay with her for what little time was left between them. The room was respectfully silent when he stood up and walked over to Waterstone, now angrily poring over Karyn's chart again in an effort to catch any missed information.

"Rick," he said, gently taking hold of her chart in his hand and placing it back at the foot of her bed. "Give it a rest. You won't find any answers in there. You've done everything you can." William's eyes were soft and sadly serious. "Karyn has to decide what she wants to do now. It's not up to any of us."

Waterstone was struck dumb by his statement. "What the hell are you talking about?" Rick snapped, "This is **my** patient, and I'm going to find out what-"

"-you won't, Rick," Will somberly interrupted. "You won't find out a thing. Modern medicine has no cure for what's wrong with her. I have an idea why, but you won't like what I have to say."

He rubbed his forehead in annoyance, confused by the abrupt about face Will had made. "Well," he said with resignation, "if you're gonna tell me shit I don't like, let's go to my office so I can be pissed off in private." Waterstone turned on his heels and stomped out of the room. William followed the exhausted physician, noting that even the ICU nurses were touched by Karyn's predicament. Their eyes were moist as they went about their business.

"Shut the door behind you, and have a seat," Rick grumped, plunking himself behind his desk. "If I wasn't so damn tired, I'd be very intrigued at what you said out there. So forgive me if I'm not so very intrigued at why my patient is both responsive and unresponsive in all the wrong ways, and I don't have a fucking clue what to do next," he grumbled. Will nodded respectfully, and slipped into the chair across from him. Waterstone was wrung out; what he really needed was a full day of sleep and a shower, but his brief outburst helped to relieve the pressure he was under, and Will knew it.

"I didn't mean to upset you, Rick," he began. "I just didn't want you banging your head against the wall. You really have done everything you could for her."

Rick lifted his head from his palm and stared at him. "Are you giving up now, after she's come this far? Do you remember her initial physical condition? I thought you **loved** this woman."

"I **do** love that woman. I love her more than I've ever loved anyone or anything in my life," Will assured him, "but there's a time when you can't force things, and this is one of them. You can't fix this. Karyn is outside the realm of medicine now." A deep sadness flashed over his face. "That became painfully evident to me when I was holding her down just now."

"Really," he said with heavy sarcasm, "so tell me what **you** know that a twenty year career in neurological pathology forgot to teach me." *He's so frustrated*, Will thought. *I doubt he'll be receptive to anything I say right now.* He took a deep breath and hoped he didn't offend Waterstone further.

"First, please understand that I am extremely grateful for the care Karyn has received here. Your people have saved her life, several times. By all rights, she should have never survived all that trauma, and it was only because of your skills that she is lying in that bed and not buried six feet underground. But…" he paused and framed his sentence carefully, "a person is comprised of more than just a body. A body can be healed. A soul is a different story." He paused to get a read on Waterstone's face, which was tired, agitated, and now a bit confused.

He groaned out loud. "Why don't I think I'm going to like where you're going with this?"

"Because you're not. And if I were a brilliant man who dedicated his life to the study, practice, and research of western medicine, I wouldn't either, but hear me out." He slumped back in his chair and nodded for Will to continue. "There are things we never knew existed until we had the scientific tools to study them, right? Gravity, X-rays, radiation…all these things were invisible, magical things until our sciences had the math to measure and document them as real forces. What if the human soul is one of those things, Rick? What if the real definition of a complete human being includes a body **and** a soul?"

Waterstone shook his head. "Christ almighty…you think I haven't heard this crap before? I hear it every time this hospital toys with the idea of bringing in Reiki and Rife generators. It's metaphysical mumbo-jumbo and not science-based medicine. Doctors deal in facts, not fantasy." He looked slightly disgusted now.

"Facts like why Karyn's EEG is almost flat when she's seizing?" he countered. Waterstone's face reddened, and Will backed off. "Look, Rick, I'm not trying to pick a fight. I just want you to open yourself up to the possibility that there's a key piece of information that we're not privy to that could explain what's going on." He slouched back in his chair. "Let's just assume, for one moment, that the human soul **is** real and is an integral part of a human being. Pretend it's an energetic part of the body; bioelectrical activity is a real thing, so that shouldn't be too hard. Now, assume that the soul can be damaged, just like the body can be damaged, but by emotional trauma. And every time the soul sustains an injury, a piece of it is chipped away. At some point, so much trauma chips away too much soul, and there isn't enough left to sustain the whole human being. Just like blood loss - you can only lose so much of it until you can't maintain blood pressure and the body crashes, except, when the soul has run out, the body can still function at a bare minimum. Like in the case of vegetative coma."

Waterstone didn't look convinced, but he didn't look angry either. Will could almost see the wheels turning in his head, fighting his deep discomfort with the theory. He took a sip from his coffee cup and got up for a refill. He gestured to Will, while reaching for the pot on the bookshelf. It was almost as black as the night outside, but Will gladly accepted his offer; it created a bit of breathing space between them.

They sat quietly, each sorting out their own thoughts as the caffeine pushed aside their fatigue. Rick broke the silence with a sigh, returned to their discussion.

"So now that I've assumed that the soul and the body are two halves of a whole human, tell me how this applies to Karyn."

Will sat up in his seat and leaned on the edge of the desk to explain. "When she was brought in, her physical condition was terrible. God only knows what happened to her before the car accident, but it's safe to say she suffered something devastating. You said some of her injuries predated the crash, correct?"

"Yes," Rick said, "she had definitely been beaten repeatedly, and stomped. She had heel marks on her torso, remember?"

"I remember," he winced slightly. "I think that experience may have been traumatic enough to do the kind of damage to her soul I was theorizing about, leaving her with just enough soul to stay in a coma, but not enough to come out of it."

"You still haven't sold me," Waterstone stated. "Lots of people get the shit beat out of them and experience horrific things. Why are they all not in a coma, eh?"

"I don't know about them, but I do know about Karyn. She shared with me a little of what her life had been like before she moved here. It wasn't pretty, and I'm sure she didn't tell me half of what really happened, but there was a lot of abuse in her past; I just know it. Maybe the coma is the cumulative result of all that trauma, and this last event was the final straw for her. She's smart, but she's also sensitive…" he said wistfully, "maybe it was all just too much."

Rick's face showed no acceptance. William sighed. There was no way he was going to ruin his case by divulging any of what he and Nils had discussed, because his theory would be summarily dismissed in a split second. He decided to stick with the medical angle to support his argument instead.

"You said there was no physical reason why she was still comatose," he began. "Her last CT scan showed no hemorrhage, no stroke, and no brain damage."

"I'm not sure if that's still the case," Rick cautioned. "Those three seizures were significant enough to scramble some ganglia, even if the EEG doesn't show it."

"Noted, but let's add to our list of assumptions that Karyn's brain is not damaged enough to warrant her current condition anyway. If you have nothing else to explain this neurologic…phenomena, wouldn't my theory be plausible? Even a tiny bit?" Will coaxed. "If that key piece of unmeasureable energy or function is missing, wouldn't that explain her current condition?"

"But her body is almost completely healed," he argued.

"This isn't about her body," Will reminded him. "Remember, the assumption is that the body is only half of the person; her body could be pristine and untouched, but if her experiences were too much for her to handle emotionally, then-"

"-the other half of her, her 'soul' or whatever, would be damaged and gone. Okay, okay…I sorta get it." He sipped some more coffee as the wheels continued to turn behind his eyes. "So this is what you meant when you said medicine couldn't help her now? What makes you think nothing can be done for her?"

"She's unreachable."

"What the hell does that mean?" Waterstone questioned.

"It means you've only been able to treat **half** your patient, and the half you've treated has done very well. The other half needs a specialist we don't have."

Rick shook his head down right into his chest. "Jesus…we've got some of the best medical staff in the country here; cardiologists, neurologists, and now you tell me we need a…soul-ologist? Where do you find one of those?" He look defeated, closing his bloodshot eyes. "That still doesn't explain the seizures, Will."

"I have a theory about that, too."

"Will I like that theory?"

"Probably not." He drank the last of his coffee and set the cup down, running his finger along the edge of the rim.

Waterstone pushed his chair back, sighed again, and looked out the window. "You might as well tell me then. No sense in breaking your streak now."

Will rested his head on the back of the chair and stared at the white blankness of the ceiling. Nils' coaching didn't cover this part of the journey, and his gut told him things that he could never share with the neurologist; Karyn's spirit was detaching from her body, and the seizures happened each time it pulled further away. He closed his eyes and thought of better times while he spoke dark words.

"She's dying, Rick. And we have to sit and watch."

27

Remembering

The sun felt heavenly. It basted Karyn's flesh, melting through her skin and dispelling the chill from her bones. Its blazing radiance glowed through her closed eyelids, leaving her feeling deliciously languid like a cat in a sunny window. She had no desire to go anywhere or do anything as long as the sun shone upon her.

Her ears did all the work while she soaked in the early summer sun, and reported on the activities taking place around her. Squawking seagulls were passing overhead. Sounds of dog feet padding across the sand, and someone's hand slapping against the water were to Karyn's left. Squealing children at play were several yards away, and the endless, repeated sound of waves gently washing along the beach lulled her into a light trance.

"Are you hungry yet, baby?" William asked her softly, in case she was truly asleep. She stretched out and shielded her eyes from the sun before squinting at him.

"Mmmmm...not really," she yawned, adjusting to the brightness above. He leaned over her to shadow the glare, and the backlighting graced him with a halo of gold. He could have passed for a classic bodhisattva, down to the gilded bronzed skin and radiant look of compassion on his face. She reached up and ran her hand across his cheek stubble, feeling the sandpaper of his beard and the velvet of the skin underneath. "Didn't you just shave this morning?" she laughed lightly.

"I surely did," he sighed, and moved the umbrella to shade them both. "I'm getting five o'clock shadow now at half

183

past two. At this rate, I'll resemble a grizzly bear more than a human soon."

Karyn gave him a broad smile and pinched his cheek. "Teddy, perhaps," she said, "but definitely not grizzly." Her eyes looked past his shoulder to the children running down the beach, chasing each other with smiles and laughter. They were so light on their feet, bouncing effortlessly across the sand like summer sprites, and for one moment she envied their innocence and lack of care. She was absorbed in their beauty and the way they radiated joy in the simplest of actions. A small smile crossed her lips as they cavorted further down the beach.

"Penny for your thoughts?" Will asked, reaching into the basket for an iced wine cooler. He popped off the top and took a swig while watching her out of the corner of his eye.

"I was just wondering if I had ever been that carefree," Karyn replied, still entranced by the kids. She looked back at him with soft eyes and added, "Hard to believe we were ever that young, you know?"

He chuckled out loud. "I don't know about that...at least once a day you tell me I'm behaving like a child; when I last checked, by the way, we weren't senior citizens." He dug around in the bag for a sandwich, glancing over to her sideways while he unwrapped his lunch. "What's going on in that beautiful brain of yours, baby?" he asked. His eyes twinkled with curiosity while she was contemplating his question, but then she gave her full attention back to him, and the sandwich poised at his mouth. She snatched it from his hand and stole a huge bite, politely placing it back in his fingers as if nothing had happened. A wide smile broke across William's face as he noted the neat row of teeth marks across the pumpernickel bread. "I thought you weren't hungry?" he chastised her.

"I wasn't," she mumbled through the unladylike mouthful, "but I am now."

"Guess it doesn't matter if I look like a bear when my woman was raised by wolves," he smirked as he relinquished the shark-bitten sandwich to her and acquired a new one. The ocean breeze blew light and fresh, pushing the few clouds in

the sky out to sea. She cherished this unhurried time between them, when there were no distractions, and no interruptions.

William didn't pursue his earlier question, and threw an old name into the conversation ring instead. "Miriam Holtz came into the shop today," he said, rather casually.

Karyn's eyebrow lifted. "Oh, really? For what, pray tell?"

"She needed a tuneup...for her Camaro," he teased.

Karyn feigned a pout. "Tuneup, my ass..." she teased back. "That woman tears the clothes off of you with her eyes every time you cross paths."

"Now, how can you say that? You're rarely with me when we've 'crossed paths'...so how do you know she views me in a state of undress, eh?" he challenged. "Got spies I don't know about?"

She shook her head and finished chewing. "I don't need spies, darling - she was undressing you when we ran into her at the concert last month. If she's shameless enough to imagine you naked while I'm standing right there, she's definitely doing it when you're by yourself and I'm nowhere around. Ugh," she muttered into her napkin.

"My, my, my...I never realized how much you feared for my honor, baby. Maybe I should share some history with you as to why your fears are unfounded."

Karyn shot him a look. "Don't tell me you slept with her; I hope you got a rabies shot if you did," she chided.

Will looked falsely shocked at her comment. "There is no vaccine for Miriam, however...I may have discovered the closest thing to a vaccine, completely by accident. Wanna hear the story, or would you rather maintain your illusion of my visual defilement by Miriam's eyeballs?"

"Go for it," she mumbled through her sandwich, "but it better not spoil my appetite."

*"I can't guarantee that, but I will do my best." He shifted on the blanket and gave her the look of a boy who just put a toad in his sister's underwear drawer. "I told you she'd never ask me out again," he said, "but did I ever tell you **why** she'll never ask me out again?" His devilish grin telegraphed that this was going to be interesting.*

"Did you tell her you're gay, or some similar rot?" she said in a mock accusing tone.

Will feigned a pout now. "I would never lie, even to save my own skin from that she-devil. No, the gods spared me." He put his food down and shifted around behind Karyn, so she could lean on him while he spun his tale. The salt air mixed with his natural muskiness to create an intoxicating cologne that was perceptible only to her, and she settled against his chest, munching away. "Well," he began, "about a year before I met you, ol' Miriam and I crossed paths at Kenny's when she had a flat tire, and a few days later she came back and asked me out to dinner and a movie."

"Oh yeah...the Goodyear Dating Service," she snarked, remembering how they had first met.

"Shush! I'm trying to spin a tale here!" emphasizing the seriousness with a wagging finger. "Anyway, I get the Javelin washed and waxed, get myself cleaned up, and swing by to pick up Miriam. When she answers the door, she looks past me and says, 'Where's your car?' I point to the Javelin and her face gets all wrinkly, like she smelled a skunk. Turns out she thought the yellow Corvette I was test driving that day for Kenny was mine, and not the brake job I had just finished. That should have been my sign to get out while the gettin' was good, but I had promised her a night out, so I was gonna see this through.

"She gets into my car with her wrinkly, disdainful face, and starts talking. And talks...and talks...and talks all the way to the restaurant, and all through dinner. The entire time she didn't shut up once. To make matters worse, she went on and on about how much money her father had, how nice their house was, how much she spends on her clothes, her makeup, her hair, and how her Daddy gave her anything she wanted, whenever she wanted. It never once occurred to her that perhaps I might like to join her in conversation at some point; that's how self-absorbed she was."

Karyn whistled in amazement. "She never heard of Emily Post, eh?"

"Nope."

"How'd you survive the evening? You hadn't even made it to the movies yet! I would have driven her right back home and tapped out."

"I told you - I was rescued by the gods," he laughed. "On the way to the movies I was praying that the movie theater would catch fire and shorten the evening, hopefully with me in it, but as we got closer to the theater, I knew I was doomed. And then...the gods intervened!"

"This, I've got to hear," Karyn said, pulling a wine cooler from the basket.

"The road was dark - both metaphorically and in reality - when the gods placed a rabbit in the path of my tires. I couldn't stop in time, and the bunny was left flopping around in the road." Karyn gasped. "So I backed up, with Miriam still flapping her gums a mile a minute, got out of the car with my tire iron and-"

"-You didn't!" she said, with wide eyed shock.

"I most certainly did. I couldn't let that poor rabbit suffer, so I gave it a merciful whack and sent it packing to bunbun heaven," he said, "and when I got back into the car, well, you should have seen the look on Miriam's face. She was pale, and she had stopped talking. It was like she thought I was a serial killer or something. So I seized the opportunity and said, 'You don't look well at all, Miriam; I think I should take you home.' She didn't disagree, and she practically ran into the house when I pulled up. And that, my darling, is why you need never fear the likes of Miriam Holtz taking advantage of your true love."

Karyn almost laughed wine cooler out her nose. "The gods would never sacrifice even an animal life for someone who knowingly decided to go out with Miriam Holtz. You must have been pretty pitiful in their eyes."

William dismissed her comment with a wave of his hand. "Well, I like to think that I'm some deity's favorite, so I'm sticking with divine intervention," he said with bravado, kissing her on the top of her head.

"There are some parts of you that are divine," she giggled, "when you're not being a child," and twisted around to steal another kiss, then settled back against his chest with a sigh of contentment. They watched the waves lap at the beach in silence.

"Are you happy, Karyn?" he asked her gently, nuzzling her ear.

"Why do you ask?" she said, still looking out at the ocean.

"Because you had that far away look in your eyes before...like you were contemplating something deep." He traced his finger along the edge of her shoulder, lingering at the slight depression above her collarbone, planting an occasional small kiss along the way. An elderly couple was making their way down the beach towards them, holding hands and smiling. Karyn couldn't see their faces, but she could tell they were happy.

"I was just thinking how different my life would have been without you," Karyn mused quietly, and glanced down the beach at the children again, who were now building a sand castle at the water's edge. She reached for his hand and gave it a small squeeze. "I never thought I could be this happy, Will; I always thought I'd be alone, and now," she said, nuzzling him back. "I know life can be so much richer, so much more...all because you're in my life now." She relaxed completely in the cradle of his body, and he brushed a windblown lock of hair from the side of her face. The older couple was keeping a slow pace, talking to each other affectionately. Something about them seemed familiar to her. They probably had a beach house close by, or maybe they had passed them before.

Will held her a little closer as he confessed into the warmth of her neck. "When I first saw you at Kenny's, I never imagined we'd be here right now. I knew you were different...I just knew it, like I knew my own name...but if you'd told me how fixing some broke girl's tire would bring me to this moment...I would have laughed. I would have said it was impossible. And yet, nothing seems impossible now...not as long as you love me."

Karyn let his words wash over her, their meaning infusing her with the happiness that had eluded her for years. Being with Will erased every bad relationship and every sad *moment from her existence. He had healed her wounds with his optimism, and lifted her spirits with his humor. His presence was more than a catalyst for change for her; he was an essential piece, a necessary part of her being that Karyn doubted she could live without. As she dreamily watched the older couple, she imagined the two of them in the couple's place, years from now, walking hand in hand on the beach with a lifetime of love and memories between them.*

She could almost see the couple's faces clearly now, but they had stopped their stroll. They were familiar in a way she couldn't define, but she knew them. They were smiling at her. A part of her wanted to go to them, to talk to them, and she found herself drawn away from William and walking up the beach. Will didn't question her actions, but remained in place, as if nothing unusual was happening. The ocean breeze surrounded her with his scent as she walked, the smiling couple's hands were outstretched, inviting her over, and a thick mist from the ocean was rolling in around her. The sound of the surf and seagulls almost covered William's voice, but she heard him, his voice as quiet and clear as it had been on the blanket, swearing to her, "I will never leave you, darling...please come back...please come back...please come back."

28

Broken

*P*lease come back...please come back...please come back...

The words were clear in her head, but she heard nothing; her ears were stuffed with cotton. The crazed mumblings of Bryce were blissfully muffled while he was moving about, and the comfortable numbness that encased her began to fade away, allowing her nerves to interface again with the outside world. Slowly, the cotton was being teased away, tuft by tuft, from her ears and her hearing returned. The ripping of fabric was what she heard first, coupled with the coldness of metal against her body, and then frigid air over her skin. The crisp breeze forced her attention, and she opened her eyes to see Bryce's blurry shape looming over her. Two of him were mouthing words in unison, the volume gradually increasing until his voice created a painful thumping inside her head.

At first, Karyn couldn't make out what he was saying clearly; her head was awash in pain, which made focusing a challenge through the incessant pounding in her temples. She was still seeing double, and the twin images danced in and out of the frame of her vision, but even though her sight was compromised her other senses were becoming sharper. Bryce had cut away her clothes while she was unconscious, leaving her naked, bruised skin exposed to the November air. She shivered uncontrollably in an effort to stay warm, but the motions racked her body with pain. Her mouth was bloody, probably from the last time Bryce punched her, and the smallest breath informed her she had broken ribs. Her body temperature was dropping from shock, and the realization that she was going to die on a trash heap, probably gutted like her beloved dog, finally sunk in. Karyn's awareness faded in and out, opting for the comfort of unconsciousness again to escape from her agony. A sharp slap in the face brought her quickly back to reality.

"Pay attention, princess," he said with a sickening sweetness, holding her cell phone up to her face with his one hand and his favorite knife in the other. "You need…know what I'm…do to you, and why, darling…know what you've been planning…unfaithful…that fella, the one you were shacked up with before me…" Bryce's voice faded in and out, but she could still piece together what he was saying, and it kicked her adrenals into high gear. The adrenaline boost enhanced her hearing; Bryce was now broadcasting crystal clear, thanks to the incredible fear gripping her.

But it wasn't fear for herself, oddly enough. She feared for William, with all her heart.

"…you were gonna meet up, right? Well, when I'm done with you here, I'm going to pay him a little visit. Maybe I'll bring him back here and show him just how much I loved you…see what he thinks of that. We can have a little heart to heart chat over your body, real civilized like." He was grinning like the Cheshire Cat now, wild eyed and pompous, and it infuriated her to the core despite her terror.

The anger bubbled up from deep beneath her fear and pain. It pushed through the ripped fibers of torn muscle and broken bone and gained momentum as it left her bloodied lips. "Don't…you…dare…touch him," she hissed with what little strength she had left, and tried to rise up on one elbow. The pain in her ribs worsened with the effort, but she had to try to warn him off William, even if the attempt was a feeble one.

Bryce's face instantly darkened at her warning, and he shoved the cell phone in her in face again. "Oh, no, Karyn…that was the **wrong** thing to say, because I **am** going to touch him - because he was going to touch **you**, and **you** were going to **let** him, weren't you?" He thumbed through her text messages to emphasize his point. "There's a whole lot of conversing in here about how much you missed each other, how you couldn't wait to see each other…and not a single mention of you ever missing me." He pointed at her accusingly. "Did you know that, darling? You never once spoke of me. Not **once**."

With that, he backhanded her with the phone so hard that it flew out of his hand and bounced across the floor. "Not ONCE!" he shouted, picking her up by the shoulders and throwing her across the room. She crashed against the piled furniture, bouncing off and onto the floor like a rag doll. "**You never once mentioned MY NAME!**" he bellowed as he followed through and punted her further into the garbage.

Karyn lay face down, still, and moaning quietly. Time was slowing again for her; the connection to her physical body was becoming more distant as the seconds ticked away, but she could still feel things around her. Both her arms were elbow deep in rubbish and the back of her right hand rested against a piece of wood. It had weight to it. Instinctively, her fingers closed around it as her mind became hazy.

She could still hear Bryce talking, and his scuffing walk on the floorboards. He was half-singing his intentions as he closed on her broken form. "Oh yeah…I'm gonna fix this. I'm gonna fix your man, just like I fixed your parents. Just like I fixed your mutt. Just like I'm gonna fix you…right now," he said, digging his fingers into her bare left shoulder. "**Look** at me when I'm talking to you, girl!" he growled, clicking the blade of his knife in place. "I want you paying attention for this!"

He flipped Karyn onto her back, exposing the soft, unprotected front of her, and straddled her waist on his knees. Smiling a dark, manic smile, he slapped her face repeatedly, waiting until she came to again; he idled away a few seconds by drawing the blade of his knife across her skin lightly, carving a line along her collarbone. Bryce was humming, delighting in seeing the droplets of blood well up from her wound. The fresh pain brought her around, and she grabbed at the thread of consciousness to stay focused.

William…must keep him from William… was all her concussed brain could process. The swelling in her skull made coherent thought fleeting, and only the most important things were allowed through, with survival being number one. She could no longer feel her right arm, but she knew her hand still held an opportunity, if she could only stay conscious long enough to use it. Turning towards the pain, towards every cut, bruised and broken part of her, she channeled that pain into the acute awareness she needed. Her nervous system met her halfway there and funneled the input from a million raw neurons back into her mind, giving it the energy to think clearly. As she lifted her head, time slowed again; her vision refocused from doubled to high definition, giving her a panoramic view of the room beyond Bryce above her. What she saw in the background almost stopped her heart.

It was Roberta Rutlege.

Standing just to the right of Bryce and a few feet behind was his mother, and she looked directly at Karyn, with soft, sad eyes. The crisp print dress and the classic white apron were unmistakable. The elderly woman's hair and makeup were immaculate, and she easily could have removed her apron and been on her way to evening church services. A silent sentence, meant only for Karyn, crossed her lips and she gazed at her son, who was unaware of what Karyn was witnessing.

"Roberta," she mumbled through split lips, causing Bryce to look up from his carving. He could see her looking beyond him, and a fleeting glimpse of confusion crossed his face. Roberta only smiled apologetically, and nodded to her in acceptance. An understanding passed between them, a knowledge of what was to come, and could not be avoided. The gesture tugged at the deepest bits of Karyn's soul. "Roberta…I'm so sorry," she rasped. His mother closed her eyes, dropped her head, and faded from her sight.

The mention of his mother's name and the shocked stare on Karyn's face instinctively forced Bryce to look over his right shoulder. In slow motion, he turned to see what was behind him, and in that moment, she struck him with her whole being.

The arc of her arm rose from the refuse, with plastic bags and papers falling away, leaving a series of ghostly images behind as it passed through the air on its trip to Bryce's skull. Only then did she see what her hand gripped, hidden from her vision for an eternity; an ancient brick hammer, repeatedly repaired and patched by its long-dead owner. Karyn watched impassively, from a distance, while the hammer connected to Bryce's head with such force that she could see the shockwave ripple across his face. The head of the hammer gave way during the blow, and flew off gracefully sideways, free of its cobbled shaft. She heard it thump and roll across the floor seconds later, in time with Bryce's body falling sideways and her own collapse back onto the trash pile.

The exertion was a monumental effort, and the urge to lay motionless and just sleep romanced her. It whispered in her ear that she was safe, that she could rest, but Karyn knew it was lying. She thought she was safe all these years, only to be where she was now, battered and bloody in a filthy building. Safety was an illusion, and she wanted hard proof. The hard proof she wanted was lying on the floor a few feet away, bleeding from his ear and temple. A trickle of clear fluid ran from his nose. She rolled over on her cracked ribs and slowly got to her knees. Time was of the essence; her focus was fading as the adrenaline washed out of her bloodstream. Karyn moved as fast as she could to crawl to his body and make sure he was down for the count.

His eyelids were half open. Before she hit him, Bryce had turned his head just enough to meet her eyes on impact. He was completely surprised that she dared to assault him in his moment of glory, and Karyn made sure he saw her true self, full of defiance, refusing him. That energy was draining away now, making her vision poorer by the moment. She clumsily patted him down for his car keys, disgusted at the thought of touching him while she dug in his pockets. Bolts of pain shot down her left shoulder and arm when she forced them to move; the pain kept her aware and bought her precious time, however, and held the coming shock at bay. *Embrace the pain*, she chanted, and pulled the sacred keys from his front pants pocket.

Finding her clothes and shoes was more difficult. Her vision was becoming blurrier by the minute, and her clothes were lost among the sea of trash surrounding them. She crawled to where Bryce had cut them from her but found nothing recognizable or usable. Her best option was the most repulsive one; take Bryce's clothes, or stay naked. Painfully making her way back to him, she pulled at his shirt with her one good arm, but didn't have enough strength to roll him over to remove it.

Bryce moaned, and Karyn leapt back from him like a scared cat. Her heart pounded in her chest as he tried to rouse himself, and she went into full survival mode to find an exit. The corner where Bryce had first tackled her had sunlight coming in behind the piled furniture. *That must be where the door is*, she rationalized, and limped her way towards it. She could hear him moaning louder behind her, and the ungainly noises of him trying to get to his feet, but her body was betraying her; she couldn't breathe, she could move fast, and his beatings had taken a severe toll on her. Even with undamaged legs, the most she could manage was a stumbling walk.

"KAAARYNN!" came the howl from behind her. Her blood pressure skyrocketed and propelled her forward across the floorboards like a gusting wind. Her feet moved on their own, crunching across the debris and broken bottles without feeling, until she got to the source of those shining rays of sunlight. The barn-style door was askew on two hinges, wedged in place with a short length of fence post; Karyn kicked at it frantically until it fell aside and almost landed on her. She slid past it to the grassy outdoors and bolted for Bryce's truck.

Her fine motor skills were almost nonexistent, and the sun had dropped behind the tree line, making it hard to see the door lock. She prayed the truck would be open when she pulled at the handle. Her one ear was trained behind her, and she could hear the door of the building scraping as Bryce pushed it free. The door mercifully opened and gave her access just as Bryce burst from the grange.

"KAAARYNN!"

He was screaming now, dragging himself in a loping run towards the truck. His voice pushed her again, launching her into the truck seat, and then frantically digging at the ignition with the key. *Please, please, please…*she prayed silently as the tip of the key found its mark and engaged the engine. With only a few yards left between her and Bryce, Karyn threw the truck into gear and spun through the gravel and grass. Her last view of Bryce was shrinking in the rear view mirror, as he stumbled and fell to the ground.

By the first quarter mile, the overgrown road from the grange's clearing began to look more used, and by the first half mile, Karyn knew she was close to a paved highway. She still didn't know where she was, but she knew she had to get to a hospital as soon as possible. Her lung was collapsing, and she was gasping for air; each breath was more and more shallow, and her strength waned as her mileage increased. Her heart beat was finally slowing from its triphammer pace to a more manageable one, but Karyn's system was wrung out. She was out of adrenalin, and rapidly riding the road to shock.

I've got to get to a main road where there are houses, she told herself, but the multiple images distorted her vision again, and with the daylight almost gone it was harder to see the road. She braced the steering wheel against her knee to free her right arm and fumbled for the headlights, and completely missed the intersection stop sign. The Ford F250 never had time to stop, and plowed into Bryce's puny Nissan at fifty miles an hour.

Karyn spun and skidded across the intersection as if the ground was iced, rolling over twice before landing in a lilac hedge. The branches reached through the broken glass into the battered shell of the truck, and dried clusters of the once fragrant flowers decorated the cab around her. The darkness almost obscured them, but a residual trace of their perfume wafted past her nose. *I love lilacs*, she mused with her failing faculties. *William used to bring me lilacs…William…*

The cold night air draped over her nude skin like a numbing blanket. There were voices in the distance, and the sound of a siren very far away. Gasoline permeated the ground from the cracked gas tank, replacing her floral memories with its acrid aroma. The crumpled metal of the door pushed against her broken thigh, but her pain was fading away again as the delicious coolness of shock seeped in. A few final concerns passed through her consciousness before it, too, wanted to rest.

It's okay. It's all okay now. I can leave this all behind. I tried...I really tried my best, but I'm so tired. So very tired...of...everything...

The whispering seduction began again, and this time Karyn didn't fight it. With no reserves left to give and her body and spirit broken, her soul relinquished its delicate hold in her flesh. The small, glittering fragments of light moved out into the near dark sky, and she noticed how amazingly delicate and beautiful they were as they passed by her eyes. *They look like snowflakes*...she thought briefly. *I love the snow*...and she closed her eyes to the world.

29

Knowing

She heard the steady beep and hum of equipment before she saw anything. The mechanical whirrings created a rhythm and pace that was occasionally punctuated by the clink of a metal something in a metal bowl. Karyn had heard that sound once before, when she had large splinter of wood removed from her foot as a child. She had run outside barefoot, stepping on a broken branch hidden in the grass, and the noise it made when the ER tech dropped the hemostat into the kidney pan was identical.

"What's the spleen look like?" said a voice.

"Ruptured. Clamp that off," said another voice.

There was a palpable tension in the air, which was cool but stuffy at the same time. The space gradually filled in around her, granulating in pixel by pixel, revealing an operating theater full of masks and gowns, all concentrated around the woman on the table in the center of the room. Few words were spoken, save for the surgeon requesting the next tool of use. Karyn knew who the patient was, but her curiosity still moved her to see with her own eyes, herself. Sliding between the medical staff, Karyn peeked over the shoulder of the anesthesiologist and was shocked.

Her face was purplish green in places, swollen and disfigured to the point where she was almost unrecognizable. The carved marks along her collarbone confirmed that it was her body, but Karyn felt nothing for the woman before her. She felt none of the pain physically, and none of the emotional pain that had wracked her being, either. She was an isolated in a bubble of disconnection that surrounded her, as she strolled around the room.

Insulation from her physical self was somberly liberating. It allowed her to inspect the suturing skills of the staff that just set the compound fracture in her femur, and watching the surgeon unceremoniously drop her torn spleen in a bowl didn't upset her in the least. She silently admired the professionalism of the staff, each group working to repair a separate, damaged part of her body, speaking quietly over the even quieter classical music on the theater speakers. They were working diligently to fix a body that Karyn didn't care about, or need, anymore. Even the intern picking glass from the soles of Karyn's feet had the focus of a brain surgeon.

Having had enough of observing her repair crew, she wandered out the operating room doors and down the hospital corridor, taking in the scenery like a ghostly tourist. The conversations of nurses hanging about at their station filtered through the general hustle-bustle hallway noise, leaving small impressions in her memory. The snippets of daily working hospital life wafted around her like scent.

"Did you see that guy with the full back tattoo in 314? That must have cost him a fortune."

"Grab me two slices of pizza before hematology eats it all!"

"Can someone cover my shift on Friday?"

"Are we out of Foleys already? What the hell?"

"Where are the labs on 622?"

The chatter faded out as Karyn, noiseless and invisible, meandered along the hallway unhurried. She felt exceptionally light; her feet barely touched the tile floor, and her mind was bathed in crystal clarity, as if it had been stripped of the constant, niggling thoughts of consciousness. None of the usual monkey mind chatter was present, and she was content to observe from her unique, detached perspective.

A few delicate, musical notes permeated the membrane of her insulated bubble, and floated into her ear. She recognized the guitar style, feeling nothing, but her attention shifted immediately, and she followed the sonata dreamily down the corridor to the dimly lit room from where it emanated. As she entered the room, Karyn noted the bandaged figure in the bed and William, slumped over his guitar with tear-stained cheeks, resting his head on the bed's edge. He held her hand gently as he slept, covering it completely with his own, as if protecting the only undefiled part of her against further evil. He was sleeping fitfully, and woke the moment the nurse entered the room.

"Mr. Thalheim, you really need to go home and get some rest," the nurse said as she adjusted the light and checked Karyn's IV. "I promise you we'll take good care of her," she assured him, but he dismissed her suggestion.

"I'm sorry…I can't. I promised her I would never leave her again," he said apologetically, looking at the still woman.

"I'm afraid you'll have to, sir," she said. "Visiting hours will be over soon. You can't stay. It's hospital policy." He nodded slowly that he understood, allowing the nurse to fulfill her responsibilities without further interference. He packed up his guitar as slowly as possible, trying to stretch their time together, and leaned over her to whisper in Karyn's unbandaged ear.

"You're going to be alright, baby. The doctors did a great job, and you're so strong…" The tears were falling again, but his voice never wavered. He didn't want to risk her hearing the weakness in him, so he kept his voice steady as he assured her he would be back in a few hours. He kissed her hand, and dragged himself past the observing Karyn and out the door, all in smooth slow motion.

The slowness allowed her a close look at every detail of his face as he moved by her. She could see every pain he carried, right there just beneath his skin, and the aching darkness in his eyes. His laugh lines were wet from channeling away his sorrow. The silver gray at his temples reflected the bright hallway fluorescence. She felt a tugging from inside of her core as they almost touched sides in passing; he felt…less substantial to her, as if he, too, was somewhat absent in his body. And then, time sped up the moment he left.

The activity level in the room increased with the fast-forwarding of time. The clock hands spun as hours passed in minutes and seconds, while Karyn watched the flurry of nurses and doctors come and go from Karyn's bedside, checking over her, changing bandages, shifting her pillows, removing stitches. William returned and left repeatedly in high speed, consulting with the physicians, serenading her, sketching, talking to the nurses, and massaging parts of her as they healed in an endless loop of attention. She witnessed her recovery like a time lapse nature film, her body transformed and emerging from the chrysalis of bandages and damage to unwrapped and almost normal. The angry red of her scars faded in record time, the casts removed from her thigh and wrist, and the color of her face rose up beneath the bruises and replaced the purplish green from before. When the last bruise had almost faded completely, the fast-forward button was released, the natural progression of time promptly returned, and the tugging inside her began to pulse.

The energy of the nurse that entered behind her surprised her. She gave off a vibration that tingled as it rippled through Karyn's ethereal self, ignoring her insulating barrier. She moved efficiently throughout the room, scrutinizing the various areas on Karyn's body that had been the most injured, checking the respirator and monitors, and adjusting her drips. "It's a sick world out there, but you're safe now, honey," she mumbled under her breath as she adjusted the blanket on Karyn's bed. When all seemed in order, she settled down in the chair next to her, and began to talk.

Karyn was hit with a massive blast of déjà vu, knowing almost what the nurse would say as she said it, and with every word she whispered to Karyn, the stronger the pulsing inside of her became. As the conversation continued, the pulsing from inside became a pulling from outside of her. Like a wave, it washed her a little farther away like a riptide current from the scene she was watching, washing her gradually out of the room, and washing the room gradually away into misty grayness, until the nurse could no longer be heard.

30

Limbo

The misty, tidal pull carried Karyn gently away and deposited her in a fog bank. The whitish fog limited her distance vision, but she didn't let that slow her pace. Her feet felt like they were on solid ground, and although the mist hung in a thick blanket around her ankles, it parted just enough for her to see ten or so feet in front of her. Hazy wisps of fluffy whiteness floated about, some hanging in midair, and some guided by an individual, unseen hand. The pulsing was subsumed into the rhythm of her own heartbeat; the first time she had noticed it since her transition, in fact. The insulated bubble that protected her from connecting with her life began dissolving the moment the nurse confided to her physical self; since then the emotions, thoughts, and cognizance of her life had been seeping back into her consciousness.

She was less than pleased. That blessed detachment was bliss, and the loss of it only made her crave more. The last thing Karyn wanted to think about was the disaster that was her life, an almost never ending tale of loss, disappointment, shame, fear, and pain. Those moments she spent just watching the world as it spun around her, without its acknowledgment, without her engagement, were so peaceful. She was done with being an active participant. The rising well of her senses and the memories they carried with them were not welcome. She kicked at the mist like a grumpy grade schooler.

"But this is what you wanted, Toots. What's the problem now?" said a woman's voice behind her.

Her feet stopped in place. *Toots*. Nobody called her 'Toots' except...*Aunt Josie!*

Karyn hoped to see the face that matched the voice of her favorite Aunt when she turned around, and she wasn't disappointed. Aunt Josie stood there in her classic Birkenstocks, broomstick skirt and tank top; her arms crossed over her chest expectantly. She was the picture of health, robust and tanned, and exactly as Karyn preferred to remember her, before the cancer had taken her away. She flipped her braids over her shoulders and raised an eyebrow. "You look like you've seen a ghost, kiddo. Did I get the visual wrong?" she joked, waving a hand from top to bottom. Her smile was as bright and wide as ever.

Karyn ran to embrace her but stopped short, afraid that Aunt Jo would dissolve into nothing, but Josie dismissed her concern. "There's no problem touching here; the aethers are like a touchy-feely Italian family, as long you and I are close to the same plane," she said, "and we practically are, now that you're here," she added, "but hold your jubilation for a moment, darling." She held Karyn at bay for a moment longer with a raised a hand and shook her head dismissively at their surroundings. "We need better scenery than this for a family reunion." She waved her hand and the fog withdrew to reveal an intimately familiar location. Josie's organic farmstead at its prime, rampant with animals and a cacophony of barnyard noises, manifested through the mist around them. The grass rose up underfoot cool and soft, and the breeze was sweet. Karyn almost bowled her over with enthusiasm as she buried herself in her arms.

"I've missed you so much, Aunt Jo," she cried. "So much…I can't even begin to tell you." Josie stroked her hair while she sobbed out her grief, standing like two embracing statues in the pasture. The lowing of cows could be heard in the distance. "How did you find me?" she sniffled.

"It wasn't hard. I've been watching, from a distance," she said.

Karyn pulled back and looked at her. "The whole time?" Josie nodded. "But why-"

"-didn't I come and save you?" Josie finished with a parental tone. "I think you know why. For the same reason William couldn't tell you what he knew; it was not our place to meddle in your life." She brushed a piece of hair behind Karyn's ear. "I didn't meddle then, and I certainly won't now."

Karyn looked her up and down with big eyes. "You look...great," she said with childlike wonder, which made Josie chuckle.

"Toots, I only look like this because this is what you want me to look like. In truth, I don't **look** like anything now; my consciousness doesn't need a container, so I don't bother creating one. It's like when you have no neighbors and live alone - you don't bother to get dressed, you just walk around naked all day."

Karyn burst out laughing. "I think...that's just you who did that, Aunt Jo."

Josie winked at her. "Perhaps...but everyone is naked sometimes," she said mischievously, taking her hand. They walked together across the field and had a seat under the barn overhang. The mustiness of old hay, leaves, and chicken feathers tickled her nose, and the rough wood of the handcrafted bench was reassuring.

"This is amazing..." Karyn said wistfully, remembering the favorite moments of her childhood here. Aunt Josie's farm was a real treat growing up; her hippie sensibilities and her lack of regard for societal norms were a refreshing take on the world. She'd been longing to go back, but the farm had been sold and the land developed when she died. This might be the only time Karyn could immerse herself in those cherished memories. "You've recreated every detail."

Josie declined the credit. "This is no witchcraft of mine. Anyone on this side can do it, and you already know that, because you've done it yourself, haven't you," she said, with a raised eyebrow and a smirk.

Karyn suddenly felt like a child who got caught playing with matches. "I was just testing some theories, and...I really didn't think it would work, really. It was almost...accidental."

"Don't give me that crap; more like intentionally accidental," she laughed, wagging a finger at her, and then gazing out over the pasture. "The power of human consciousness is unlimited. The only thing restricting us from really cutting loose is our own self-limiting beliefs. Well, that and a severe lack of understanding about quantum physics," she sighed. "We're so backwards, as a species."

She leaned up against Josie and closed her eyes. "I could stay here forever."

"Ohhhh no, no, no, no. Absolutely not," Josie disagreed, pushing her up with a tiny shove. "You've been avoiding too much already. No more of that on my watch, no, no."

Karyn was hurt. "Why not? Why can't I stay? This is heaven!"

Josie shot her an unusually stern look at the mention of heaven, and scolded her. "This is **not** heaven, Toots, not by a long shot. This is a plane of existence that responds to the commands of your consciousness, not some fluffy cloud covered Michaelangelo fresco. And you're not dead - which is a problem here."

"How so?" she asked timidly. Aunt Jo was not to be trifled with when she was annoyed in real life, and Karyn doubted she was anything less now.

Josie put her arm around Karyn and leaned back against the barn. "You're not supposed to be here, at least not in your current format. And you're not in any condition to be here for very long. You don't have any defenses." She had a look of concern that baffled Karyn. It suddenly darkened their conversation, and weighed it down.

"Like what? Why do I need...defenses, Aunt Jo?"

She turned to her and said bluntly, "Because it's not all rainbows and unicorn breath here; there's some nasty shit lurking around in these planes." Josie flipped her braids back over her shoulder and tried to explain. "Remember I said the aethers are touchy-feely? That's because the name of the game in the non-physical world is permeability. Without the restrictions of a corporeal form, there's nothing to ground you, and grounding biology is the first line of protection against things in other planes. It's a great, although mortally limited, line of defense. The soul or spirit, whatever you want to call it, is the incorporeal part of that, and you...well...you're a hot mess all over, Toots."

"I don't know if I should be flattered or insulted," Karyn said.

"Be a little of both; your situation is unique, even in this space. You have a foot in both planes right now, and with an incomplete soul, you're extremely permeable. Anything can touch you here. Things can attach themselves to you all too easily, especially if your mood invites them." She looked confused, so Josie elaborated. "At any moment during your time out here, did you ever find yourself becoming aggressive and not know why?" Karyn thought back to how she had verbally assaulted William in an effort to get information, and nodded. "Bingo," she said. "Something was trying to squeeze itself into your soul holes, Toots. Every time you cracked off a piece of your spirit, you left a chink in yourself for something else to take it's place, and nature abhors a vacuum, right? If you were in your physical body, you might take up an addiction like gambling or heroin to fill the void; but since you're enjoying an out-of-body vacation right now, you're at risk of getting soul-jacked instead."

"By what, exactly?" she demanded.

"You needn't worry about what; you're not going to be here long enough to find out. Just trust your crazy dead Aunt on this one."

She pouted and pushed for more details. "Why is it such a big deal? You're just fine here, so I'll be fine, too!"

Josie spoke with choice emphasis in her words. "I am fine for a good number of reasons, child - the biggest one being that I made peace with my soul before I landed here. I had the experimental 70s, years of psychotherapy, and months of cancer to teach me how to gather my broken bits of spirit and glue them back together. You haven't done any of that. You haven't made peace with your soul - you've made pieces out of it," she reprimanded her. Her statement stung Karyn like a slap in the face. Josie knew she had been a bit harsh, but it was necessary to get her point across. She softened a bit, but a quiet sadness permeated her demeanor. Karyn wondered what she was thinking about in that moment.

Josie caressed her cheek as an apology. "Honey, you chose to walk away from an exceedingly nasty, dirty room in your House of Life. I realize it was a room filled with pain, cruelty and desperate sadness," she said, "but you just closed the door. You didn't clean out the room and put it back in order. That sets the stage for the **worst** psychological outcome possible…and now you're sort of here, sort of there, and your soul is almost nowhere."

"But I want to be here," she whined. "I want to stay with you, in this place!"

"You can't, at least not until you commit to the decision you made…or have you forgotten about that already? Remember? You made a decision to walk through that apartment door and accept what was beyond. You even actively sought it out, so there's no backpedaling now." Josie stood up and began to walk away, and Karyn ran after her.

"Wait, Aunt Jo! I didn't mean to make you angry!" she shouted, and grabbed her hand.

Josie turned around with a gentle smile and said, "I'm not angry, Toots. I just want you to think very carefully about what I've said. This wonderland will still be here, waiting for you at the right time, when you are ready. But if you haven't cleaned your House of Life, you are not ready. **Own** your life, Karyn, and then you can own your death. And don't haunt those who care about you by sitting on the fence."

She kissed Karyn's cheek, and sauntered away slowly, becoming more transparent with each step. Karyn knew not to follow, but her heart ached for more time, more of her presence. As she faded out, another form coalesced from the fog, taking shape as it walked towards her. The walk of the person was very familiar, and as the form filled in with color and clothing, her heart leaped in her chest and she ran to meet him.

"Dad!" she squealed, throwing herself at him at a full gallop. Ethan Kiplinger had materialized just enough at that point to keep his daughter from falling through him, and caught her up in his arms.

"Hey there, kitten," he said, squeezing her close. "It's been a while, hasn't it?" Karyn was crying again, burying her face in his chest while he stroked her hair. "Don't waste your time here crying, Karyn," he said, lifting her face up and wiping away her tears with his thumbs. "We have a lot to talk about, and little time to do it."

"Why, Dad? Why so little time? I thought time didn't matter here!" she whimpered.

"Time doesn't matter for us, but it does matter for you," he said, leading her back to the barn bench to sit down. He patted the seat beside him.

"I don't understand what you mean," she sniffed as she wiped her eyes, "and why isn't Mom here?"

He sighed. "I'll get to that in a minute, but right now, the most important thing to me is you. You're running out of time, honey," he said tenderly. "Your body is languishing in the physical world. You left it with so little spirit that it's barely hanging on. You're in Limbo, kitten, and there's precious little time left to change that."

Karyn looked down and rubbed her foot against a clump of grass. "I don't see what the big deal is…"

"You don't, eh?" Ethan asked his daughter with mild disbelief. "Keep in mind that I was privy to everything you and your Aunt just discussed, even if you couldn't see me. She made it pretty clear what the big deal is." Karyn avoided his gaze, and his voice dripped parental sternness. "When you petitioned your subconscious for access to your blocked memories, that knowledge came with a price. You agreed to pay that price, and now you're reneging on the deal. You can't cheat yourself, Karyn; your own consciousness will take you to the woodshed if you don't follow through."

Her face was impassive. "I've already been there," she replied icily.

"No, you haven't," Ethan replied with equally chilly severity. "But you will, and what awaits you is far worse than anything you can imagine."

Karyn snapped back at him. "How so, Dad? How can it possibly be worse than what I've already been through? I spent the last handful of years running and hiding, finally get myself safe and on track, just to have life fuck me over again. What was the point of it all? Why should I give a single shit as to what happens in the real world when I have the ultimate freedom here to do as I please, live the fantasies I create, and

I'm unrestrained…I'm finally free of all restrictions!" she shouted, with her hands raised up to the sky. Her eyes were slightly wild and distant.

"Because this is **not** real, and you are **not** whole!" he shouted. His words resonated inside her head; they were her own words, the ones she had used to convince the Gatekeepers to let her pass. Her father saw her eyes refocus and chased her attention. "That's right, this is **not** the reality, the real life, that you begged for. And just because your real life is in a hospital bed with a heart full of regrets doesn't mean you avoid it. It means you see your actions through to the end - not try to have your cake and eat it while you play at being Schrödinger's cat!"

He got up from the bench and gently took her by the shoulders. Ethan hoped he had inspired some thought in her; she was vibrating internally, but her exterior said nothing of what she was thinking. There was an emptiness in the pit of her stomach that made her insides feel hollow.

"You have to make a decision, kitten. You can't have a foot each in both worlds. Not only are you an incomplete soul at risk of being shanghaied, you're causing the people caring for your body serious grief. Nothing you do exists in a vacuum, honey," he said softly. "Even something as simple as being kind to the kid who pours your latte has an impact, and that pebble of action casts rings outward everywhere. Your actions are dominoes in an endless chain of dominoes that run throughout other humans' lives." He reached down and held her hands in his. "You have a responsibility to them. People like William; that man has connected himself to you so deeply that he can't move forward until you make a decision. He has stopped the progression of his life to wait for you, and your choice will directly influence his life. How you live your life, and how you choose to leave your life, affects others," he said.

"That person abandoned me," she said in a raw and bitter, low tone. Ethan carefully studied his daughter's face, and he could see the seething anger simmering just underneath the surface.

"It's not your place to judge. We all have a responsibility to care for each other, Karyn," he countered. The hollowness inside Karyn quickly filled with heat at his concern of the 'others', and the deep, smoldering aggression that had gripped her with William boiled over, expanding into every empty space she had. She yanked herself from her father's hands.

"Why?" she erupted. "Why should I care what happens to any of them? Did they ever think about how **their** actions would affect **me**? Did William consider that when he forgot about me in Europe? Did Bryce think about that when he was beating me every night? Did any one of them ever once think about me?" Karyn's voice had become an infuriated shriek, and her face was mottled with rage.

Ethan was taken aback. This was not his child, and he could sense she was being taken over by the very energies Josie had warned her of. Her countenance crawled around her face while she spouted the litany of injustices that life had committed against her, the hatred building in her every second. In a desperate effort to pull her back in, he summoned his innermost reserves, and focused it directly into the center of his daughter's torso as he bellowed her name.

"KARYN!"

The sound of her moniker transmitted a shock wave of etheric force that displaced the raging entity inside her. Karyn felt the oppressive presence crushed from her anterior, and blown out the back of her being. Heavy black tendrils of fury rose from her spine and were sucked away by the residual drag of Ethan's verbal blast. Her face blanked as her legs buckled; Ethan caught her and carried her to the bench. She was dazed, and it took a few moments for her to think clearly again.

"What just happened?" she asked in a small, frightened voice. Her eyes reminded him of when she was little, and awoken from a nightmare.

"Something just tried to take you for a ride, kitten." He smoothed her hair back from her forehead while she was cradled against his shoulder. "What do you remember?"

Karyn shuddered and burrowed deeper. "I remember feeling empty inside, and your voice sounded very far away, and then…I felt this sickening, hateful…vile thickness all around me. And I was saying awful things, but it wasn't me that was saying them." She rubbed her temples and shuddered again. "It felt horrible, like it was devouring me from the inside out. I couldn't do anything to stop it or control it."

Ethan was silent in his gratitude; his gut instinct had chosen the right action, fortunately. The last thing he wanted to witness was his daughter become corrupted by her unresolved pain with him unable to stop it, but it was the perfect example to use and drive his point home. "I want you to think about something, while this experience is fresh in your mind, Karyn," her father delicately suggested. "Imagine spending all of eternity like that, consumed by that hatred and anger, unable to control your actions and eventually being consumed by that evil." Karyn trembled at the thought. "**That** is what your Aunt and I were warning you about," he said somberly.

Aunt Josie's words suddenly had a whole new meaning to Karyn, and she hung her head, embarrassed at her ignorance. A part of her could still feel the residual filth of the invader clinging to her, vaporous and offensive, like the smell of an open sewer, or a funeral pyre. She wanted it out of herself completely; physically shrugging herself down to dislodge the memory of it helped, but the event was meant to stay with her. It was a lesson she needed to learn, albeit the hard way. "I never do learn things the easy way, do I, Dad?" she asked, turning slightly to look at him. Ethan smiled, but that didn't hide the wet corners of his eyes. He hugged her closer.

"I'd say you specialize in experiential learning, honey. It's a talent." The cows idly watched them, endlessly chewing a single mouthful of meadow grass.

After a brief pause, Karyn spoke up. "I know I can't be in two places at once, and I have to make a decision, but…do I still have some time to ask you a few things?" Her father smiled and gave her a knowing nod. She shivered again, thinking back to all she had witnessed in reviewing her life, but still asked him, "Why was it necessary to take me all the way back and make me relive all the pain, Dad? If I'd already been there, why revisit it?"

"You had to. For one, you demanded to be shown your real life. But more importantly, you had forgotten it by locking yourself inside a time capsule in your head. Our consciousness processes and stores memories in many different locations, both physically and psychically, so your mind created opportunities to reintroduce small things that would lead you back, like a trail of breadcrumbs."

"So that's why I went from feeling nothing to-"

"-feeling everything? In short, yes. But your subconscious would only give you as many crumbs as it thought you could handle. It still wanted to keep you safe, but also appease the part of you that was searching for answers. Not having answers creates stress and unease in our psychological system, so your subconscious did its best to balance the two as you journeyed, until you argued to be allowed beyond that last, most formidable blockade. At that point, your emotional homeostasis was not a concern; your conscious self had decided to learn the truth." He shifted his position on the bench. "Which brings us back to reason number two: the experiential learner thing. You must have made an exceptional case to the Gatekeepers for them to open the floodgates like they did; they believed you needed to relive it in order to make the correct decision about your future, otherwise you wouldn't have experienced it in such…excruciating detail." She could feel him wince as he finished. Karyn hoped he had more advice.

"Do you know how to repair a broken soul, Dad?"

Her father shook his head. "I was always better with bikes and skateboards," he smiled and winked, "but if I were to hazard a guess, I'd say it requires forgiveness, compassion, and acceptance - for yourself, and those who've wronged you. Grudges and bitterness never hurt the other person; they only hurt ourselves. The irony is that when we remove the parts of our souls that hurt so we can't feel the pain associated with them, it's the loss of that soul that really damages us in the end. Without the ability to feel the bad things, we limit our ability to feel anything at all," he said, stroking her hair again. She listened carefully to his every word, and enjoyed the lazy comfort of being with him.

"Why isn't Mom here with us?" Karyn finally asked. Her question caught her father off guard; the flow of his energy hiccuped like an unexpected speed bump.

"Karyn," he began with an apologetic voice, "your mother would be here, except she's dealing with problems of her own right now."

Karyn sat up, alarmed. "What kind of problems? Is she okay?" she asked, rapid fire.

"Your mother has…bound herself and refuses to move forward. She won't release the anger she carries for Bryce, and the regret for leaving you, even though that was beyond her control. She blames herself for not intervening." A heavy look of sadness colored his face. "The emotional turmoil from her life is holding her hostage. It won't release her, and there's nothing Josie or I can do. We can only watch. She has to work this out on her own, and I'm not sure she will."

"My god, Dad, she's…like I was?" Karyn asked, shocked to learn of her mother's predicament.

"Like you could be again, Karyn," Ethan reminded her, "but slightly different. You have a physical connection in the tangible world, and I think that may have saved you just then. Your mother doesn't have that anchor, and she's so…angry…" his voice trailed off.

"Is it true, what Bryce said? That he killed you both?" The question was oddly unemotional, given its nature, but Karyn was only looking for facts. She didn't know if she'd have another chance to learn the truth.

"Yes. Bryce tinkered with the Acura's brakes, and it had the end result he wanted. Our last discussion didn't agree with him, apparently." Karyn didn't flinch with the information, and Ethan was surprised, but the light in his eyes showed he was pleased. "You're a fast learner, kiddo - I didn't expect you to be so composed."

She smiled and kissed her father. "I'm here with you now, and nothing can be done to change what's already happened. If I don't want to invite more of those…things into whatever I am now, I need to take responsibility for my actions. Accept what I can't control, and change what I can." She scratched her head and stood up to face him. "I think I'm beginning to get the point of all this, Dad."

Ethan stood up as well, and embraced his child with a warmth that filled them both with a glow. He held her face with both hands and gazed at her. "Kitten, whatever you choose to do, know that I love you, and that you are never alone," he said. "You are a part of me for all eternity." His hands slid from her cheeks, and he turned to face the pasture again. She watched his familiar gait cross the grass, becoming fainter the further he was. Just before he faded from sight, Karyn asked him a final question.

"Were Tesla and Lanza right?" she shouted to him, as he walked across the meadow.

Ethan Kiplinger paused in his stroll, shouting back to her over his shoulder, "You'll have to find out for yourself!"

31
Choice

The room felt dishearteningly dismal. William slept with his upper body laying on the foot of Karyn's bed, undisturbed even though visiting hours were over. The dark circles under his eyes were worse than ever, Zarnicoff noted as she checked Karyn's vitals. His face was far from the restful, dreamy expression she wished for him, and he looked as if he'd aged a decade in the short time he'd been watching over Karyn. The recent turn of events did not bode well for her patient, not at all.

Several nurses had been chattering away at the station about the latest bizarre behavior of Waterstone's coma patient when Nurse Zarnicoff rolled through on her way to Karyn's room. She shot them a disapproving look and snapped, "Don't you all have something to do?" making them scatter to their duties like roaches when the lights come on. "Stop your cackling and do your jobs - or you won't have a job when the next round of Press Ganey comes out!" Zarnicoff had precious little patience for this latest batch of nurses, who always had their noses in their phones. "And they wonder why patient satisfaction is at an all time low," she grumbled quietly to herself as she scanned Karyn's chart.

"Thank you," Will said, giving Zarnicoff a start.

"Oh! I'm sorry, Mr. Thalheim…I didn't mean to wake you. Sometimes I forget myself while I'm working," she whispered. William gave her a tired, understanding half-smile and brushed the hair from his eyes.

"It's fine. I'll get some rest soon enough. Everything will be resolved…soon, I think," he sighed, giving a glance to Karyn and resting his head on his one hand. The exhaustion coated him like a blanket, and Zarnicoff suddenly felt the urge to console him.

"I hope so," she said, "for both your sakes. You've both been through so much." She bent over Karyn and fussed with her pillow, smoothing her hair to one side. Just as she righted herself to leave, William came around the bed and touched her on the shoulder.

"I know we've never really talked this whole time she's been here," he began awkwardly, "but I feel you're…different than the other nurses. You know where the patients…are." He struggled to find the right words, but his lack of sleep made it difficult. "You seem to have a sense of where they are in their recovery. I see how you relate to them - it's a gift you have. So, I hope you don't misunderstand me when I ask you if…" he paused, fighting to control his emotions, "…if you could promise to not resuscitate her if she codes." His eyes begged her to agree.

"I can't promise I will be here if that happens, Mr. Thalheim, but I will make your wishes known to the appropriate staff," she assured him. Zarnicoff found it difficult to not cry herself, given the nature of his request and the poignancy of the situation. Being the silent observer meant you saw beyond the casual glimpses of a patient's day to day; you often witnessed more than you wanted to. Months of watching this man sit vigil over Karyn were coming to a close, and nobody knew that better than Zarnicoff.

William seemed relieved that she wasn't offended. "I knew you'd understand," he said, and took his seat next to the bed again, "and I can't thank you enough for everything you've done for us." The redness of his eyes conveyed a gratitude that couldn't be spoken. He took Karyn's hand between his own, and was lost in his thoughts once more. Zarnicoff nodded, and left them in respectful silence to check on her next patient.

Further down the hallway, two interns were taking bets on which hockey team would win the Stanley Cup, and an orderly whistled off-key as he rolled a gurney along. While the rest of the world was fast asleep and only the night owl staff kept watch, the hospital settled into the late night quiet of the witching hour.

Why did I leave? What made me think that was the right choice? Will thought. Repeatedly reviewing his life was the worst way to spend his time by Karyn's side; the more he examined and re-examined his path, the less he believed he had made the right decisions. *Are you paying the price now for my weakness then, love? Can you ever forgive me?* He watched her impassive expression as if she might absolve him of his guilt, but she didn't oblige him. Her silence was a painful reminder that there was no changing the past.

*I thought about you every day, baby. Every day I was away, every day I missed your face, I missed your smile; but no matter where I was, I could always **feel** you with me until one day...I couldn't. I couldn't feel your presence anymore, and then there was a giant hole in my life. I lied to myself and just worked harder so I could come back sooner, but that didn't fill the hole either. Music didn't fill it...then drink didn't fill it, or drugs...and so much time had passed...I was so ashamed at how pathetic I had become, at **what** I had become, and I thought you hated me for disappearing...and I hated myself. So many times I woke up after trying my best to put myself out of my misery...and now, you're the one who's not waking...*

The chill in Karyn's hands interrupted his thoughts; they were becoming cool. He lifted the sheets from the foot of the bed, only to confirm his worst suspicions. The skin on her feet were mottled, and they were cold as well. Karyn's body had begun to shut down. She was finally dying.

Will squeezed his eyes shut, but that did little to stop the flow of tears. He tucked the covers around her feet with the tenderest of care, and returned to his seat, and her hand. There were things he needed to say now, before it was too late and her hearing failed. He brought her hand to rest against his cheek while he spoke his soul.

"Baby, I don't know what you've been going through where you are, but I'm sure it's been hard for you," he began, keeping his voice steady. "I want you to know how proud I am of you for enduring all of this. You've proved to me that you're even tougher than you are beautiful, and I've always thought you were the most beautiful woman in the world. Soon," he swallowed hard, "you'll be able to take it easy and relax, and not worry about anything…and I want you to know that, even when we were apart, there wasn't a single day that I didn't think of you, and love you. I have always loved you, and I always will, Karyn."

William's cheek was almost as cold as the back of Karyn's hand now. The pale translucency of her skin gradually took on a slight bluish tinge at the fingertips, and he braced himself for the moment when there would be no whirring, no beeping, no mechanical sounds disturbing his love's rest. Her face still divulged nothing. Will would never know if she heard a single word he said these last months, and the sadness that she might leave feeling unloved tore at him as he filled his eyes with her. It was only when he leaned down to kiss her cheek that he saw it; the smallest tear, sliding from beneath the fringe of her lashes, follow the curve of her crescent-shaped scar, and drop to the pillow. Her hand spastically contracted in his palm, and the heart monitor began to race.

He had no time to call the nurse. Karyn's body lurched upwards from the bed just as he covered her with his own. The force almost knocked the wind from his lungs, leaving him gasping for breath as he struggled to hold her down. She thrashed as if possessed, lifting and pushing erratically from every limb. Will clung to her desperately, whispering, "baby, don't fight it, let it go, just let go," while she convulsed. Trickles of blood seeped from Karyn's clenched fists where her fingernails pierced them.

The monitor's rapid pace increased, matching the sound of running footsteps as Zarnicoff raced back into the room. "She's tachycardic!" she shouted, and threw herself over Karyn's legs. Her pulse rate was not slowing, and the nurse feared it would be more than Karyn's heart could take. No sooner had the thought crossed her mind, Karyn dropped flat on the bed, and the monitor traded its individual beeps for a single, long tone.

Zarnicoff rose from the bed and stepped back, gesturing for the other staff to leave the room. They backed out, unsure of why the crash cart wasn't there until the nurse mouthed

"DNR" to them; Meghan hadn't had time to share William's wishes as she had promised, but she was determined to respect them, even though the moment had taken them by surprise. She turned around to find William sobbing quietly, with Karyn propped against his chest in his arms. He was inconsolable, rocking her tenderly while he buried his face in her neck. Zarnicoff wiped her eyes, and turned away from heartbreaking scene of a crushed man and his placid, motionless love. Her private wish for a happy ending for them had not been granted.

William tried his best to memorize everything about her while he could. He inhaled her, filling his lungs with her essence, cementing her place in his senses so he'd never be without her in his memories. The warmth of her against him would be fleeting, but at least he could feel her next to him one last time, he thought, before he had to leave. The heart monitor's continuous tone was briefly interrupted by a single beep.

The single beep made him lift his head and look at the monitor. Another beep, and then another, and another, until the beeping rhythm continued and settled into a stable pace.

Zarnicoff had just passed through the door threshold when she heard the unmistakable sound, and spun on her heels to face the couple.

They both stared at the monitor incredulously, not comprehending what they were seeing initially, and William was searching the nurse's face for an explanation when he felt the muscles in Karyn back and stomach flex slightly, and then flex again. Her movement was pained, like that of one fighting their way out of a bad dream. Karyn's forehead wrinkled and she slumped forward. The discoloration was already fading from her hands as she weakly raised them to her mouth and scrabbled at the tape securing her ventilator tube. Her bloody fingers wrapped around the mouthpiece, heaving as she pulled it free of her throat and tossed it aside to the floor. The clatter of the plastic was followed by the sound of several deep, ragged, sputtering breaths as she collapsed back against William's chest.

Time stood still while Zarnicoff and William were immobile and silent, until Karyn tilted her head back and opened her eyes to see his shocked, tear stained face and croaked, "Aunt Josie says…you have a great ass."

32

Here

"**Y**ou've got physical therapy this afternoon; do you want to eat before or after," Zarnicoff asked her. "I'll do my best to jog it up here before it gets cold," she assured her.

"But I ordered egg salad, Meghan. It's supposed to be cold, isn't it?" Karyn questioned her innocently, knowing full well that the nurse was joking.

"Just testing your cognitive skills, dear," Zarnicoff said with a wink while giving a disapproving look to William, sitting in his usual spot by her bed, and in the process of stuffing the last of a sugary palmier in his mouth. "Shall I bring some real sustenance for you as well, sir? Or would you prefer a side order of Metformin to go with that pastry?" He did his best to chew the ungainly mouthful up before answering the nurse, but spoke anyway.

"Does Metformin taste like pastry?" he asked in the voice of an 8 year old, teasing her as he wiped the last crumbs from his lips.

"Ummmm…no. It does not."

"Then I'll pass," he said cheerily, and leaned into Karyn's shoulder.

"You should," Meghan said, wagging a finger, "because you have plenty of calorie-free sweetness right there." She directed her attention back to Karyn and flashed a broad smile. "I'll bring lunch up after; you'll need your blood to be in your muscles for PT instead of your stomach. I want you to be in your best form for your rehab." Zarnicoff waved as she cruised out of the room. Karyn watched the little spring in her step with amusement.

"Are the staff here always so happy?" she asked him. He pretended not to hear her as he rifled around in the bakery bag for another palmier. "William!" Karyn said, smacking him half heartedly on the arm. The nail marks in her palms had almost completely healed by now.

"Ouch!" Will winced, feigning a pain and rubbing his arm with B-movie acting skill. "I don't hear a peep out of you for months, and now you're all bossy, demanding and whatnot. Can't a man eat bad food in peace?" The expression on his face was so ridiculous that the laugh escaped her mouth despite her best efforts to be serious. They both giggled like children, and the sound peppered the room with joy that was almost visible.

He dropped the bag on the side table and slid onto the bed next to her. She shimmied over to make space, leaving a gap for him to slip his shoulder behind her. "To answer your question, before you so casually cracked me on the arm," Will said as he settled in, "the staff have a really good reason to be happy now. Patients that don't get well and recover is hard on them. You were a particular challenge, especially at the end." He nuzzled behind her ear. She looked out the window, and admired the warm beams of sunshine pouring in.

"It feels…odd, to be here. I mean, it feels more real every day, but for the longest time, I didn't know what was real," she said, her eyes drifting beyond the window. She felt him nod in agreement against her neck.

"Nils would tell you it was all real," he stated as he raised his head, stroking her hair over the ear he just nuzzled.

"When will I meet him, Will? I have so many questions to ask him about what happened."

"You'll meet soon enough, baby. To be honest, it will be a relief to stick the two of you in a room together for a few hours so I can get some work done. My callouses will suffer if I don't play more often," he chided her, "and he's been pestering the crap outta me since you woke up. He wants to interview you for some spiritual conclave that's happening in the fall." She yawned and sunk further into his shoulder.
"Why don't you catch some sleep before PT, Karyn? Maybe if you rest before, you won't be as exhausted afterward." He got

out of the bed and rearranged her pillows so she could lie down.

"But I feel like I've slept a hundred years already," she protested, yawning again. "Will you stay with me until I go to PT?" She looked at him with a slight insecurity. He kissed her deeply, savoring the softness of her lips after a lifetime of being denied them.

"Of course I will. I'll be here the entire time, baby."

He drew the curtains and she settled into the pillows. Her regular breathing announced that she was down, just as Waterstone peeked his head in the door. William tiptoed over and met him in the hall, closing the door enough to still see Karyn from where he stood.

"Ever watchful as always, I see. I think you can take a vacation from your guard dog duties, don't you?" Rick commented. "She's out of the woods now; you have nothing to worry about, Will. Her scans are perfectly normal." He waved the reports in front of him.

"Sorry, it's a habit I've developed out of necessity," Will said, with one eye trained on her bed. "You said her CT was normal? Nothing out of the ordinary at all?"

Waterstone shook his head back and forth with a grin. "No evidence of neurological trauma whatsoever. I'd be unbelievably frustrated if I wasn't so happy, but I've got all the documentation to prove it really happened. I'm sure it will come in handy at some point," he shrugged, "should I ever see something as bizarre as her case again."

"I hope to god you don't," he said sincerely. "I'd hate to think this could happen to anyone else. I'm still trying to remove the memory of the first night I saw her after she was admitted here. When she detailed the whole thing to the detectives, it made me so violently ill that I had to leave the room to vomit; and then I wanted to hunt down that bastard and make him pay." He physically shook off the thought, and muttered "son of a bitch" under his breath.

Rick gave his shoulder a reassuring squeeze. "Don't worry, man, they'll get this guy. He'll show up sooner or later and try the same thing. These type of nutjobs always do." William had not disclosed all the facts of Karyn's case to anyone outside of the police; Waterstone might have spoken differently had he known her assailant was all too familiar to Karyn. Fortunately, Rick was fascinated with Karyn's brain, and not so much the consciousness within it. Still, William was fairly sure that Rick gave more consideration to his theory than he admitted. There was a secret glint in his eye that probably meant he was working on a conference paper, and Karyn's case would be the topic, but until that was confirmed, Will wouldn't bring up the theory again. He wanted the last few months as far behind them as possible so they could have the life they had both missed the first time around.

Rick glanced at the clock and apologized. "Gotta check in on my other patients, or I'll have somebody on my ass. I'll catch up with you after my shift, okay?"

"Sure thing," Will replied, his eyes now focused over Rick's shoulder and down the hallway at the detective headed towards them. Waterstone trotted off without a look back, and fifteen seconds later Detective Robert Campagna stood in his place.

His sharp eyes missed nothing. In the casual stroll down the hallway, Campagna had already mentally noted every face he saw. It was a skill that served him well in his seventeen years on the force, and coupled with an eidetic memory, there was little he had to write down that wasn't already stored in his data banks.

"That her neurologist?" Campagna asked, already knowing the answer while he shook Will's hand.

"Yeah, and he's one of the best," he said with deep respect.

"He looks like an interesting guy; you never really get a feel from reading a medical report what the doctor who wrote it is like," he mused. "There's always so much medical jargon that I usually get the coroner to translate for me." He smiled and scratched his chin. "Fortunately for Ms. Kiplinger, she didn't get to meet the coroner." He snuck a peek into her room. "How's she doing, Will?"

"Grabbing a nap before her physical therapy later. She still gets exhausted really easily, but I guess that's to be expected after months of being bedridden. Every day she gains a bit more stamina, though. The attending said she could probably be released as early as next week, provided that the remaining tests they want to do come back clear." He gazed at Karyn's resting form, curled up against the pillow.

"No nightmares? Flashbacks?" the detective asked.

"Believe it or not…none. She seems like she's okay," he said, turning back to the detective. His eyes were pleading as he asked him, "Please tell me you're close to finding him, Rob. I don't want Karyn thinking that he's still out there, waiting for her."

"Not yet, we're not," Campagna said stonily, observing the other end of the hallway traffic. "But, we have discovered other things that are a tad disturbing. For one, the truck Karyn crashed was not Bryce's; it was stolen. The fella that it belonged to was found dead in a South Carolina quarry from blunt force trauma; his girlfriend's body was found three counties away in an abandoned house, and..." Campagna paused as he locked eyes with Will and said, "she looked a helluva lot like Karyn."

William's stomach collapsed like he had been punched. The detective immediately reassured him. "Don't go there just yet, Will. If what your girl told us is accurate, she did some serious damage to him. He could be rotting in the woods right now as we speak. We've checked every hospital and urgent care facility in a hundred mile radius from that grange house, and nobody fitting Bryce's description passed through any of them." He loosened his tie a bit. "He's probably dead."

"I hope you're right, I really do…but Karyn survived her trauma, so who's to say Bryce didn't as well?" He stared at the sleeping woman in her hospital bed, completely relaxed down to the tiny smile on her dozing lips. "I won't sleep like that until I know he's dead or locked away." He flexed his jaw muscles in constrained anger, and Campagna didn't doubt him.

"I wouldn't either, if I were you," Rob agreed. "Trust me, Will - I want the same thing you do. If he's alive, we'll get him, and you'll be the first one I call to tell you so."
Campagna smiled as he took a last look in Karyn's room, and gave him a pat on the back. "I'll be in touch. Now, get back to work keeping an eye on her." The detective sauntered back

down the bustling hallway, disappearing among the white coats and scrubs, no doubt having memorized every face along the way.

Karyn sighed and shifted her position, commanding Will's attention away from Campagna's exit. Her face was soft and dreamy, and revealed nothing of the journey she had completed. She was timeless and classic, as she had always been in his memory. And she was real, whole, and they were no longer apart. He whispered to himself, in the lowest of voices, the promise he held in his heart, and closed the hospital door.

J. Lauryl Jennings (or Jenn, to her friends) loves to do book club appearances, store signings, literary discussions, interviews, reviews of other authors and any other activities that get her out and about. Contact her at jlauryljennings@gmail.com

or

P.O. Box 482
Waterford Works, NJ 08089

www.ingramcontent.com/pod-product-compliance
Lightning Source LLC
Chambersburg PA
CBHW070449120726

47910CB00003B/992